Silver Moon

Over 100
Great Novels
OF
Erotic Domination

If you like one you will probably like the rest

New Titles Every Month

All titles in print are now available from:

www.adultbookshops.com

If you want to be on our confidential mailing list for our Readers' Club Magazine (with extracts from past and forthcoming titles) write to:

SILVER MOON READER SERVICES

Shadowline Publishing Ltd
No 2 Granary House
Ropery Road
Gainsborough
DN21 2NS
United Kingdom

telephone: 01427 611697
Fax: 01427 611776

NEW AUTHORS WELCOME

Please send submissions to
Silver Moon Books
PO Box 5663
Nottingham
NG3 6PJ

Silver Moon is an imprint of Shadowline Publishing Ltd
First published 2007 Silver Moon Books
ISBN 9781-903687-96-3
© 2007 Syra Bond

Trojan Whores

By

Syra Bond

Also by Syra Bond
The Roman Slavegirl
Trojan Slaves

All characters in this book are fictitious, and any resemblance to real persons, living or dead, is purely coincidental.

This is fiction - In real life always practise safe sex!

Preface

After the tragic death of Professor Harrington, I stayed in Austin, Texas with one of his colleagues, a senior lecturer in the Archeology Department, Dr Werner Harris. Dr Harris, for that is what he always insists I call him (and then only when he gives me permission), not only worked with Professor Harrington professionally, but also shared his interest in sexual experimentation and depravity. Before his untimely death, Professor Harrington had been thinking of handing responsibility for me over to Dr Harris. With this in mind, he had already passed instructions on how I should be dealt with, together with notes on how he had kept me since we met. He had also informed Dr Harris that, at times when he judged fit, I should be allowed to continue my work on the manuscript which he had translated, and from which I worked to produce Trojan Slaves. This manuscript, written in Attic Greek, had been recovered from the library of the Villa of the Papyri in Herculaneum, Italy, where it had been buried since the eruption of Vesuvius in AD 79. It dates from an era much earlier — the era of Homer — and gives an insight into the lives of the Ancient Greeks as they fought a terrible war against the powerful city of Troy.

Immediately after Professor Harrington's funeral, I went willingly to Dr Harris' house seventy miles or so north of Austin. I have remained there since that day.

Mostly, Dr Harris keeps me shut up in a heavy wooden wardrobe. I have to sit naked with my knees up and my hands folded around them. Sometimes, he gags me with a leather strap, but not always. Most nights, if he leaves me there, he pulls a black hood over my head. It gets hot. My breath warms the skin around my mouth, and my cheeks flush with the moist heat. When I inhale through my nose,

I can feel the hotness around the edges of my nostrils. When I am like this, in the middle of the night, I take my hands from around my knees and push them between my legs. I lay my fingers against my flesh — it is always wet and warm. I do not have to push my fingers in, I simply have to touch the soft flesh, or sometimes perhaps just the tip of my clitoris. That is enough. I have to be careful then, not to make any noise, not to gasp too loudly, or cry out. Once, when I did, he came to me, took me out and bent me over his knee. He held me down with one of his hands while he thrashed me with a thin cane. I squirmed and cried out but he only stopped when he was satisfied I had been sufficiently punished. I had to stand in the corner of the room for the rest of the night and, when it was light, he thrashed me again in the same way, before he would allow me to sit.

At other times, he keeps me in a cage. It is hardly big enough for me. Sometimes the cage is suspended from the ceiling of the cellar beneath the house, sometimes he pushes it into the corner and drops a heavy cloth over it. He brings me food in a bowl, and I have to eat it without using my hands. He brings me milk in the same way, and I have to lap it up with my tongue. Sometimes he calls me his 'puppy'.

When he releases me, I am allowed to work on the manuscript. It is hard, not knowing how long I will have until he takes me again and puts me into captivity. It has taken me nearly a year to complete this latest work. And there is still more to do. The Museum of Antiquities in Rome has sent Dr Harris the transcription of a further papyrus which records the events of the terrible return journey of the Greeks from Troy. There is still so much to be completed. I only hope I will be allowed the opportunity to do it.

This then, is the second part of my interpretation of the

original manuscript. It covers the latter period of the Greeks' war on Troy. A war invoked by Paris' abduction of the beautiful Spartan princess Helen, wife of King Agamemnon's brother Menelaus. A war fated to lead only to destruction and death — the ruination of Troy, the loss of the Greeks' greatest warrior and, ultimately, the decimation of the whole Greek force.

Syra Bond
Waco, Texas, January 2007

Chapter 1

Sappho and Chryseis — priestesses of Apollo

Sappho stood back as the naked young girl knelt and offered up her wrists for binding. She looked up at the young man who stood above her — her dark eyes wide with anticipation, her body shivering with apprehension. She waited for the wet leather thong to be brought forward. Sappho could see it was the girl's only wish — to be enslaved, tied, bound. It was as if she had waited all her life for this moment, and now, at last, it was here. The girl's chest rose and fell with her heavy, excited breathing. Her full lips trembled. The small pink nipples on her modest breasts hardened with every moment of expectation. Her slim body, shaven of all hair, glistened in the light of the torches which surrounded the sunken altar. She tipped her head back further. She kept her eyes fixed on the young man's face. She sighed helplessly and dropped her mouth open.

Sappho swallowed hard. She squeezed Chryseis' hand. Each of them stood decked in ceremonial robes and plumed headdresses, in front of the massive marble altar. She could hardly believe what was happening. She could hardly believe that she was to be crowned as a priestess of Apollo. She could never have dreamt that, one day, she would stand with Chryseis at the temple altar. She could never have thought that there would be a time when the followers of Apollo would see her as next only to the god Apollo himself. She shivered with excitement at the thought, and squeezed harder onto Chryseis' hand.

Torches set on massive columns surrounded the huge glistening altar, itself raised up several steps for prominence, yet set on the lowest part of the floor at the heart of the temple. Naked young girls, their shaven heads crowned with yellow and white flowers surrounded it. They scattered flower petals from silver baskets, throwing them out in multicoloured showers. Their bodies had been oiled, and they glistened as they moved. The tight slit fronts of their naked cracks revealed the promising dark cleft which ran down to their succulent cunts. Some of the fluttering petals stuck to their gleaming skin.

Surrounding the steps to the raised altar, more tiered steps rose to the columns like a theatre. On these, worshippers were packed, some naked, some wearing ceremonial clothing, some standing with hands together, some kneeling, some lying prostrate. At the uppermost tier, a row of columns formed a towering square and between them stood statues of the gods Apollo, Hera, Zeus and Aphrodite.

Chryseis turned to Sappho and smiled. Her beaded headdress hung in heavy strands against her smooth cheeks. When she moved, it swayed heavily against her tender skin. In her free hand she held a massive staff. It bore the emblem of her authority — a ram's head with huge in-curling horns. A golden robe draped from her shoulders. It parted at the front, revealing her well-shaped breasts, her firm flat stomach, and the tight slit at the front of her closely shaven cunt.

'Sappho, we can do anything we wish now. No one will dare defy either of us. See, they treat us like gods. All our desires can be fulfilled. Never again will we have to serve as slaves to the wishes of others.'

She turned and held her hands out, blessing the grateful followers. Those that stood, dropped to their knees immediately, clasping their hands together and praying as if their lives depended upon their obedience.

Chryseis smiled with pleasure.

'Look at all those men. They worship us, but their faces betray their desires. They have only one appetite. They are hungry for the bodies of young women — desperate to penetrate them, to abuse them, to treat them as their slaves. Look how they ogle the young girls. How they leer at the shaven clefts between their tight buttocks as they bend in unquestioning submission to their priestesses. See how they lick their lips at the thought of bringing a smacking hand down on them, or a cane, or a cracking whip. Sappho, my flesh moistens at the thought.'

Sappho nodded, barely able to contain her excitement — the ceremony, becoming a priestess, all the men, the description of their desires. She licked her lips and trembled at the thought of it all.

Heavy perfume hung thickly in the air. The naked girl kneeling at the altar, urged her wrists forward. The young man, dipped his hands in a bowl and drew out a dripping leather thong. He held it up and looked towards Chryseis for approval. Its wet, shiny surface sparkled with yellow flashes in the torch light. Chryseis nodded slowly. The man turned to Sappho. Sappho's stomach filled with nervous excitement. She did not know what to do. Suddenly she realised what was expected of her. He was waiting for her permission, and he would not act without it. She could hardly believe it. She bit her lips. All eyes were on her. Everyone was waiting for her approval. She flushed. She nodded. The man nodded back respectfully, and stepped a pace forward. The worshippers murmured with excitement.

Tears welled up in the young girl's eyes as the man held out the soaking leather thong. At last, it was her time of sacrifice, of submission. She only had a few moments of freedom left. Once she was bound, she would no longer be under her own control. She would be a slave of the temple, a chattel of the priestesses, an object of pleasure, an acolyte, a plaything. Once bound, she would have no mind of her own, no will; her subjugation would be total, her life would be prescribed by the will of others.

Sappho imagined the girl's fate, bound by the leather thongs, led by her new master, no will of her own, dedicated only to pleasure, to submission, to the bidding of another. It excited her, the thought of being in another's power, of being controlled. Her lips dried as she imagined herself being tied up like the young girl. She felt her throat tightening at the idea of being controlled in every way, in everything she did. Her heart quickened its pace — she felt it pounding in her chest. She sensed the tension of her hardening nipples — pulling stiffly at her breasts, aching, pulsating, heating with the fire of her growing expectation.

The young man draped the wet thong over the girl's wrists. Sappho licked her lips — her tongue was dry. The man pulled the thong around in a binding. The slimy, wet leather slipped around the girl's skin, sticking to it, enveloping it. Water dripped onto the ground. Sappho imagined that it was the girl's blood draining away, running around her feet as her will was drained and her life with it.

The girl held her breath. It was as if the wet confines of the wrapping leather were smothering her. The man pulled on them tightly. He folded the ends into the beginning of a knot. The girl winced, tightened her buttocks and rose up on her knees. She dropped her head, but, all the time, she kept her doe-like gaze on the young man. She pushed her wrists forward more. She needed to show him she did not mean to react against him, that she was completely willing, that she wanted the binding as tight as he could make it.

'She will soon feel the pain of the tightening leather,' said Chryseis to Sappho. 'When it begins to dry, she will know for certain that she has been enslaved. There is no other pain like it. It creeps over the body like a slowly burning fire. It increases all the time. It never eases.'

'Have you felt its pain?' asked Sappho, still unable to take her eyes off the girl.

'Yes. When I was brought into the priesthood. I had to suffer the pain of the shrinking leather.' She held up her wrists. 'And I still bear the scars. They are reminders of my suffering, my penance, my obligation.'

The young man bound the leather tightly around the girl's wrists. She got up, her head bowed, and waited for his instruction. He reached forward and took hold of each of her nipples. She tightened her shoulders and bent slightly as he increased the pressure. He squeezed harder. Sappho watched the girl biting her lips, trying to hold back the pain. The man rolled the girl's nipples between his thumbs and fingers, squeezing them, pinching them hard. The girl bent forward, unable to stand still as the pain in her breasts intensified. He did not let go. She let her shoulders drop forward, trying to soak up the pain, trying to absorb the fiery tongues that were now penetrating every part of her.

Sappho was suddenly seized by her own passion. She let go of Chryseis' hand. Her hand felt hot. She pulled the front of her robe aside, exposing fully her breasts, her hard nipples, her flat stomach, her shaved slit. She looked around. All eyes were on her. She was not embarrassed. The worshippers' stares only filled her with excitement. She drew her right hand across her hip and let her fingers rest near the base of her stomach. She trembled. The feeling of everyone watching was setting her senses on fire. She moved her fingers down onto the inside of her thigh. Shivers of joy ran through her.

She watched the man leading the girl by her nipples, drawing her back down onto her knees, guiding her, commanding her with pain. She followed his command unerringly. She could not escape, and did not want to escape, the control he now had over her was her only desire.

Sappho reached her fingers up and touched their trembling tips against the edge of her swollen flesh. She felt its heat, its throbbing, its expectation. She pressed her fingers further, into the silky crack, into the moist valley that lay between the two fleshy edges of her delectable cunt. She glanced at the eyes of the worshippers — fixed on her, watching her every move. She inhaled deeply and bit hard onto her lips.

The young man pulled on the girl's nipples, making her bend forward. She reached out her bound wrists in utter submission, and laid her elbows on the ground. The man released her. She stayed there, silently waiting for her next command or, if there was not one, for eternity.

Sappho looked at the form of the beautiful girl, oiled and glistening in the torch light. She was so slender. She described a perfect shape, bent over, her back straight, her buttocks rounded and taut and held high. Sappho looked at the girl's slit, squeezed between her firm buttocks, a succulent oval, split by the crevice of her cunt which glistened with beads of shiny moisture. The girl stretched more, reaching her bound wrists as far forward as she could. When she could stretch no further, she inclined her face gently down towards the ground, stopping when her nose and chin touched it.

Sappho pressed her finger into the crack of her cunt. The fleshy sides opened easily at her touch, welcoming, peeling apart, inviting entry. She touched the tip of her clitoris, throbbing, heated, swelling, hardening with every second. Thrills of excitement shot through her. They filled her stomach, her chest. They tightened her throat. She struggled to breathe. Her eyes rolled upwards.

Two naked men stepped forward from behind the altar. A heavy sheep's fleece hung in their hands. The young man who had bound the girl's wrists motioned for them to approach. They stood either side of the girl, holding the fleece over her back. The girl remained still. Another signal and the two men lowered the fleece slowly over the girl. They let it down onto her back, draping her with it, only leaving exposed her upturned buttocks and the delectable slit of her cunt that was squeezed between them.

Sappho pressed her clitoris at the tip. It was on fire. She took it between her thumb and forefinger and squeezed. She imagined the young girl's nipples in the man's grip. She imagined herself being led by him, his fingers pinching her clitoris, forcing her wherever he wanted, taking her under his control. She pictured herself bending before him, like the girl, submitting to his will, his control. She saw herself on her knees before him, bound and enslaved, waiting for him to demand whatever he wanted. She imagined the feel of the sheep's fleece on her back, heavy and warm, pressing her down, accentuating the exposure of her upturned buttocks. In her mind, she felt the glare of the worshippers on her cunt, peering at it, squeezed and tight, moist at its centre, waiting to be used.

She worked her fingers around her clitoris, squeezing it, poking it, tantalising it, inflaming it. She breathed in deeply, aware of the joy that was spreading between her hips. She felt a dribble of spit at the corner of her mouth. She licked it back. The warm moistness of it sent a wave of pleasure through her tongue and down her throat. She gasped. She let out a short cry. She did not stop.

'Look,' whispered Chryseis. 'They are coming. They have the scent. Look, Sappho!'

Sappho kept her fingers between the soft, swollen flesh of her cunt. She still touched her clitoris, but did not dare to squeeze it for fear of losing control. She breathed heavily.

At first, she saw some movement between the crowds of worshippers near the top of the tiered steps, in front of the statue of Apollo. It was a man covered in a ram's fleece. A ram's head shrouded his face. Its curled horns shone in the torchlight. His muscular arms strained as he worked his way down the steps on all fours. He looked from side to side, seeking out his victim. Then another, descending from behind the statue of Zeus — the father of all gods. Another worked his way around the effigy of Aphrodite — the goddess of passion. Then a last, emerging from the back of the statue of Hera — the ox-eyed goddess. The worshippers stepped aside as slowly all the fleece-covered men worked their way down the steps.

Sappho again pressed hard against the tip of her pulsating clitoris. She could not hold back. It was impossible. She held it between her thumb and forefinger and pressed her other fingers deep into the open flesh of her wet cunt. They slid inside, penetrating her as deeply as she could get them. She squeezed as hard as she could on her clitoris. She panted in short gasps. She felt the fire of delight blazing out of control through her burning body.

The four men gathered around the girl by the altar. Still, she had not moved. They sniffed around her, in turn. They pressed the noses of the ram's heads between her buttocks. They inhaled her scent. They licked along the slit between the soft, youthful oval of flesh on either side of her succulent crack.

Sappho imagined how the girl must feel. Waiting, anticipating and yet unsure what would befall her. Holding still, not daring to move because her master had not instructed her otherwise. Keeping her nose and chin against the ground, opening her mouth, licking her tongue out, filled with fear. Feeling the cold noses against her slit, wondering what would happen. Gasping as her heart beat loudly in her chest.

Sappho groaned loudly and dropped to her knees. She stretched her arms out like the girl, reaching them forward as she bowed down and raised her buttocks as high as she could. She wanted her wrists tied in the same way as the girl. She wanted to feel the drying leather thongs tightening. She wanted to experience the pain of captivity, of submission. She gasped as she felt a wave of pleasure running through her. Just to hold her buttocks up for everyone to see, just to be ready for one of the men to take her, was enough. She did not need to feel their bodies against hers. She did not need to be penetrated, or smacked, or thrashed with a cane, or whipped. She shuddered and trembled as her joy coursed through her. She shouted out again. This time louder. This time, a scream.

She heard it in her head — shrill, piercing, a shriek. It was all she could do. Her head was full of it. Shouts and screams, howling, voices. She dropped forward gasping. But she could still hear the voice above her own frantic breathing. She felt a moment of panic. What was happening? Everything was out of control. The world was in turmoil.

The voice boomed out.

'Now! Now! Take hold of the imposters. Stop them now before they corrupt our ceremonies to Apollo. Stop them now, before they bring his anger down on us for blasphemy and irreverence.'

She heard stamping feet and noisy clatter. She turned and saw Priam's cruel son, Prince Polydorus, standing next to the statue of Apollo.

'Take them!' he shouted, pointing down at Chryseis and Sappho. A large ruby set in a massive golden ring flashed on his forefinger. 'Take them!'

He marched down the steps towards the altar. The men threw off the fleeces on their backs and took hold of Chryseis and Sappho. Sappho was dragged to her feet. She looked around wide eyed and confused.

'And any of their followers! Take them too! Are there any here who see these pretenders as the true priests of Apollo? Are there any who think the great god of prophesy, Apollo, could be served by such as these? If there are, speak now.'

All the worshippers shrunk back. Polydorus' reputation

for cruelty and quickness of action were well known. No one dared stand against him or his ways. Many shook their heads, many shouted his name, none proclaimed allegiance to Chryscis and Sappho.

'Then that is settled,' he roared triumphantly. 'I will take over as the priest of Apollo. My act will finish the reign of the priest Pelador and his faithless daughter. Bind these two with the wet thongs they had prepared for others. Let them feel the pain of the drying leather as they come to terms with being in the thrall of Polydorus.'

Sappho and Chryseis were dragged outside. Polydorus marched behind them in victory. The worshippers crowded around the door of the temple, afraid to speak against Polydorus, fearful for their own lives. Sappho blinked in the bright sunlight. Her robe was ripped from her and, naked, she was flung to her knees.

Polydorus climbed up into a small trap pulled by two tall women with large feathered headdresses. They were both naked except for tight leather thongs pulled up between their legs. These were secured at their waists onto shiny leather belts with elegantly worked silver buckles. They had metal bits in their mouths which led from rings at the ends into shiny leather reins. The reins were drawn through small silver hoops on the front of the brightly painted trap.

Polydorus pulled the reins into his hands and tugged at them. The two women's heads were pulled back. They bit hard onto the reins. Their eyes opened wide with expectation. They both snorted as they fought with the frustration of waiting for their orders to move.

'Take these pretenders away,' he shouted. 'They will serve me, and anyone who cares to pay. I will use them as entertainment for anyone who can afford it. That will be a fitting occupation for the "priestesses" of Apollo — the slaves of Polydorus, the Trojan whores. Take them away!'

He snapped at the reins and the women, relieved to move, pulled him away on the ornate trap.

A cage was brought on the back of a cart and Sappho and Chryseis were forced into it through an opening in the side. The door was slammed shut and locked. There was barely enough room inside the cage for the two of them, and they were squashed together and unable to move as the cart was pulled away.

Sappho could already feel the wet thongs shrinking. Her wrists were already tight together but now they were being drawn against each other with agonising pressure. She could not move, but with her eyes, she drew Chryseis' attention to them, showing her that she too, shared her friend's suffering. But now it was not a recognition of sharing the pain required as an entrant to the priesthood. Now it was an acknowledgement of sharing the suffering of being plunged into servitude and slavery. Her bonds were testaments to a future which promised only fear and the unknown.

Chapter 2

Torture in the Greek camp

It had been ten years since the Greek army had arrived at Troy. Their beached ships, dark and forbidding against the turquoise sea, were dried out, their planks shrunk. Armour, piled in heaps outside the now ragged tents, was more dented, less bright than when it had first been carried enthusiastically onto the Trojan sand. Swords, stained with blood and entrails from defeated adversaries, and speared into the ground like massive crowns, had duller edges and were more chipped. Achilles, though still angry at Agamemnon over his theft of Sappho, no longer withheld his support. His friend and lover, Patroclus had been killed. Achilles had revenged him with the merciless killing of Priam's brave son, and the best warrior of Troy, Hector. Defying the convention of respect to those fallen in war, Achilles had contemptuously trailed Hector's dead body behind his chariot, beneath the walls of Troy. For two days he continued his deathly parade, defiling the once perfect body, bringing terror and anger and dishonouring the inhabitants of the great besieged city.

Achilles, the greatest warrior Greece had ever known, his long black hair streaming behind him, and reinvigorated by his conquest of Hector, again led his ferocious Myrmidons into battle. But for all the killing, all the sacrifice, there was no gain. Troy was too strong to be entered — its walls too high and thick, its army too brave and determined to protect its sovereign right. And so, still the war saw no victory. The two armies opposed each other across the great plain of Troy in entrenched stalemate. There was no going forward, and there was no going back. The beautiful Helen was still within the Trojan walls. Helen, lover and ally of Priam's handsome son Paris. Helen, the object of Agamemnon's mission to gain the return of his brother's wayward wife. Helen, the cause of this dreadful conflict.

During this time, the alliance of Praxis, the blind slave master, and Calliope, the former slave, had firmed. Now, Calliope was never out of the company of Praxis, never excluded from his confidence, always in his favour. She shared in his plans, his hatred of Ajax, and his desire to gain increasing power. With her strengthened influence and standing, she had become more beautiful. She kept her dark hair cropped short. It contrasted with her pale, smooth skin, itself aglow with the satiny gloss of youth. Her head was perfectly formed, smooth and oiled. She stood erect, her body always held to its full height, her square shoulders pressed back, her long arms trailing loosely at her sides. Her breasts were firm and her dark nipples always erect. She had a noble bearing and usually went naked. If she did wear clothing, it was only a silk scarf around her waist, or a leather belt slung diagonally across her chest. Her pubic hair was carefully shaved and the front of her crack was tight and pink against her pale skin. By day, the faceted gold ring in her clitoris glittered in the bright sunlight, by night it reflected the light of shimmering torches or flickering lamps. As she walked, confidently thrusting each hip forward in turn, the crease at the base of her buttocks deepened slightly and directed the eye into the dark crevice that lay beyond. Sometimes, as she strode forward, the valley of her crack could be seen — a beautiful silhouette outlining the perfection of the moist flesh of her cunt. Her naked, statuesque form, was at once, alluring, divine and bewitching. The blind Praxis called her his "angel". She stood before him when he requested, so that he could run his hands up and down her body.

Master Wang still attended Praxis, and led him everywhere but now, he was not his master's only aid, for

Calliope was always clinging to Praxis' muscular arm.

The longer the deadlock with Troy continued, the more the bored soldiers sought entertainment and distraction. Praxis made it his business to supply their needs. He had several large tents set up between the beached ships. Each was joined by a covered walkway. Banners and flags fluttered from poles near the entrances to the tents. Multicoloured bunting hung from the centre poles on ribbons pegged to the ground.

At the end of the largest tent were two massive, claw-footed chairs. Calliope sat naked in one, Praxis, resplendent in burnished armour, in the other. Calliope sat with her knees slightly apart. The golden ring in her clitoris gleamed in the lamplight. When the flaps of the tent were drawn aside to allow customers to enter or leave, the facets of the ring caught the rays of the evening sun and flashed with multicoloured beams of light. No one who entered could avoid the captivating lustre of golden brilliance.

Eva was dragged in through the entrance. Since being abandoned to the beggars and vagrants at the gate of Troy by Sappho and Calliope, she had been enslaved to Praxis. He had brought her back to the Greek encampment as part of his booty, and had humiliated her with torture and suffering every day of her captivity. But, no matter what depravity she was subjected to, she managed to assert her pride as a northern princess of noble birth. Her defiance was indomitable — her resistance to suffering inexhaustible.

Eva spat dust and sand from her mouth and bit onto her full, broad lips. She had been agonisingly bound. Her arms were pulled behind her back, her legs were bent backwards and her ankles and wrists were bound together. She was dirty and dishevelled. A torn cotton smock hung loosely around her shoulders. Her long red hair was knotted and tangled in a mass of dishevelled curls. Her skin was pale and covered in reddened scratches and smudges of caked mud. Her elbows and knees were bruised and dirty. But, when she looked from side to side, her bright blue eyes still shone out piercingly.

She glared at Praxis, fixing his unseeing eyes with a defiant stare.

'Is it my dear Eva?' asked Praxis holding his hands out in front of him.

'Yes, my lord. She has been brought for her daily torture. What have you planned for her?'

Eva flashed her eyes at Calliope. She stared hard at the beautiful woman. Calliope stared back, returning the haughty resentment that Eva displayed. Eva spat again. She let it dribble on her bottom lip, bubbling it purposefully with her urgent, gasping breaths. Her shoulders ached and pains between her shoulder blades travelled down her arms and into her tight bound ankles. She closed her eyes for a moment, as if to compose herself for what lay ahead.

'Something special, my angel. Let me show you.'

Calliope smiled and rested back on the claw-footed chair. She allowed her knees drift apart. The golden ring in her clitoris twinkled in the light from the oil lamps fixed to the poles of the huge tent. Its golden reflection played in spangled shards on the insides of her thighs.

Eva looked at her tormentors. She despised Calliope's beauty, her clean, oiled skin, her ease of manner, her lack of fear, her freedom. She had suffered so much, she could no longer imagine what it would be like to be free, to be bathed and oiled, to be ennobled and admired. She bit harder onto her lips and craned her head backwards to try and ease the pain in her shoulders. But there was no relief. She rolled onto her side and felt the spit on her lips running down the side of her mud-covered cheek. A wave of shame flooded over her. She felt desperate and humiliated.

'Master Wang!' shouted Praxis.

Master Wang scuttled out from the shadows cast by heavily folded curtains drawn between the tent poles.

'Master?' he fawned, running up and dropping to his knees in front of the blind Praxis. He touched his red pillbox hat with his fingers. He looked like a spider, his spindly arms sticking out from the huge sleeves in his shiny silk robe.

'Take her to the oars. Have her hauled up high.'

Master Wang did not hesitate. He motioned to two soldiers who stood guard. They pushed one spear underneath Eva's arms, high up beneath her armpits. The other they thrust painfully underneath the bend of her knees. They lifted her sharply.

Eva gasped for breath as her weight was taken on her upper arms and legs. The pain was intense. She could not keep her mouth closed. She panted in time with the shocks of pain as they jolted her roughly outside and over to one of the black planked ships. Her mouth filled with sand as they dropped her unceremoniously to the ground.

Two ends of a rope were lowered from one of the oars which poked out horizontally from the side of the ship. The soldiers secured one end to the spear that jutted out from Eva's left side and the other to the end that jutted out from the right. Another rope was dangled from the next oar and this was attached in the same way to the spear that was wedged behind Eva's knees. They hoisted her up several feet from the ground, just above head height. She did not spin on the ropes, but swayed giddily from side to side. Each time she reached the bottom of the swing the pressure caused by her weight increased and the pain built accordingly. She held her breath at the bottom of the swing and gasped in air when some of the pressure was released at the top.

Praxis was led out by Master Wang. Calliope held onto his other arm. She walked proudly alongside him, smiling at the soldiers who had gathered for the entertainment. If she caught their eye, they looked down, fearful of her wrath, or the wrath of her protector.

'Is she tied like a filthy wild hog?' asked Praxis.

'Yes, master. Yes.'

'Good! Now, we will make her squeal like a hog!'

Master Wang waved to soldiers leaning over the side of the ship. One emptied a bucket of water over the side. Eva did not see it. She did not know what to expect. The water fell through the air, starting in a barely fragmented mass before quickly breaking into a myriad shower of droplets.

They landed with great force, striking her across the back of her head. She gulped in shock, for a moment, not knowing what was happening. The water ran around her face and dripped from her chin. She watched it splash to the ground below her and soak straight away into the hot sand.

Another bucketful was thrown down. It struck her between the shoulder blades. It was cold and shocked her. The jolt made her rear back as much as she could against her bonds. She tightened her body. The water ran between the cleft of her buttocks and between her legs. She tightened her buttocks and the insides of her thighs as it ran coolly along the taut crack of her cunt. She shivered. Another dousing bucketful fell. This one also struck her in her back, but slightly higher than the other. It ran around her chest and dripped from the tips of her hard, aching nipples.

There was a pause. Eva choked as she tried to blow her wet tangled hair away from her face. It stuck to her cheeks in strands and caught in the corners of her mouth. Calliope walked beneath her. Eva stared down, drenched, shocked and helpless.

'She certainly needs a wash, my lord. It's hard to tell the colour of her skin beneath the grime. I think she needs more.'

'As you wish, my angel. I only want to hear her screams. She has been silent too long today. I am growing impatient for the sound of suffering. Wang!'

Master Wang waved up to the men on the deck of the ship. A hose of leather was dangled over the side. It ran from a massive water butt set in the centre of the ship's deck. Eva heard the gurgling above her as a huge force of water erupted from the end of the hose. She listened to the torrent as it spewed down towards her. She felt the shock of it as it struck her fully across the buttocks. It was an enormous flow — heavy, powerful, painful. It drenched her like a storm. It reddened her skin and glazed its surface with a cold sheen. A silver mist arose around her in a cloud. It rained back onto her like a sudden storm. It streamed around her body and flowed to the ground.

The cold water ran back along her arms and into the straining nape of her neck. It rushed over her head. It soaked her hair, pulling it down forcibly across her face. It tugged heavily at its ends before cascading to the hot dry sand beneath her. It ran from her bound ankles, down the back of her legs and into the crease of her buttocks. She tried to tighten herself against it, as if tension in her body would somehow stop the drenching onslaught. It was hopeless, the force was too great and, as it ran along the crack of her cunt, it opened it. She felt the folds of her flesh bisected and bruised by its power. She sensed the edges prised apart, but the dull tingle that she felt on the surface of her flesh turned to excruciating pain as it entered her and penetrated her body. The rush of cold water into her cunt made her shiver. It was like a torrent of ice inside her.

She gasped, struggling to get her breath back against the shock. As the torrent continued, her gasps turned to cries, her cries turned to screams.

She swung from side to side on the ropes, surrounded by a fog of spray, drenched by the waterfall, rent with pain from the cold shock of the water's penetration into her body. She heard Praxis' cruel laughter and, amidst the deluge of water that flowed around her, she saw Calliope prowling beneath like a stalking panther.

Eva shivered with cold. The heat of the sun was burning her skin, but she was filled with the coldness of the water as it flowed deeper inside her cunt. She ached inside – drenched with an icy flow from the very centre of her being. She felt her eyes rolling upwards. She tried to keep her focus on Calliope, but it was impossible. She felt dizzy and disorientated. She screamed louder. She could barely hear Praxis' exclamations of pleasure. Her face was covered with the heavy wet strands of her soaking red hair. Her body was engulfed with pain.

She stopped yelling and bit onto her lips. She fought to keep herself conscious, fearing the dreadful abyss of darkness which unerringly beckoned. Her hips ached. Her whole body strained against the constricting bonds that held her body captive, and the pain which emanated from within it.

Calliope stood beneath with her mouth wide open. Eva watched her taking the overflowing water between her wide stretched lips. She let her mouth fill then overflow down her body. Eva watched the pool of bubbling water glistening inside Calliope's mouth. She sensed Calliope's excitement — allowing her mouth to fill to the brim, feeling the force of the water as it ran down her cheeks, onto her breasts, down her stomach, into her crack and onto her feet.

Eva realised the water Calliope was drinking in so eagerly had run across her own body, had picked up the grime from her own skin, was a drain of her own brutal suffering. She felt a burst of excitement. She arched her back, trying to encourage more water from the still running hose, trying to bring down a greater torrent so that it could pass over her and nourish further the thirsty Calliope below.

Eva watched Calliope running her hands across her breasts, teasing out her erect nipples, pinching them, squeezing them hard. She watched her choke as, when she gasped for breath, the water ran down her throat. She watched her delving her hands between her thighs feverishly seeking out her aching slit. She saw her pulling her fingers between the wet crack of flesh that yearned for attention. She saw her open its edges — exposing it to her view and to the sluicing torrent of dirty water that rained down on her.

Eva fixed on Calliope's stare. She looked deep into her eyes. She saw the yeaning, the desire that they held. The iciness between her hips warmed. It crept across her skin. She felt the throb of her clitoris hardening against the water, responding to the icy saturation with its own heat, its own burning desire. Then she felt a warmth against her flesh. A sudden burst of heat. It was not the warm moisture of her cunt, it was the warmth of her urine. She could not hold it back. It poured from her. It splattered its heat and mixed with the cascade from the pouring hose. It ran quickly from the crack of her cunt and flowed down into Calliope's eager, gaping mouth.

Eva let it flow. It relieved the aching in her hips. She saw it mixing with the water that flowed down — its golden hue tinting the torrent that filled Calliope's mouth. And she saw Calliope taste it. She saw the moment she recognised its salty tang. She saw Calliope's eagerness increase as she knew that she was filling her mouth with Eva's fluid. Eva watched Calliope drinking deeply, swallowing as much as she could. She watched her rise up on her toes as, when her urine flowed along Calliope's arms, her hands and into her cunt, she lifted herself in a sudden, gasping, and uncontrollable orgasm.

Eva reared back further. With no more urine to flow, she was seized with a sudden, gripping tension of pleasure.

Her eyes went bleary. The fog of spray around her enveloped her. She bit hard onto her lips, but it was impossible to keep her mouth closed. She watched Calliope. She fixed the image of Calliope's gaping mouth in her mind. She saw nothing else. She let her own orgasm flow.

It mingled with the torrential storm that ran around her, and she felt as if she too was draining down into Calliope's mouth. Calliope stared up, her face letting go of tension as she was relieved by her jolting orgasm. Eva could see that they were sharing their pleasure. Their joy was happening at the same time. They were in tune — in sympathy with each other's ecstasy.

The water stopped. Eva let spit run from her mouth. It trailed down in a long sticky strand. Calliope let it fall into her own still waiting mouth. She sucked it all in and swallowed it eagerly.

Eva was lowered from the ropes and dropped onto the ground.

Calliope sprawled forwards across Praxis's knees. Her taut buttocks held high and exposed. Praxis ran his hands across the two delightfully curved symmetrical lines of smooth skin. They bent out from the dip in the small of her back and returned to tight creases which folded sharply at the top of her smooth thighs. He pressed down on them. They sprang back when he withdrew the pressure. Calliope drew her face close to his ear. She whispered to him — as a lover would. He smiled and nodded.

Eva watched them, Calliope licking the shiny bronze armour that adorned Praxis' torso, Praxis smoothing his large hands across the tight rise of Calliope's buttocks. She watched as Calliope responded to Praxis' touch, raising and lowering her buttocks, opening her legs, displaying the split oval of flesh that lay between them. She saw the glistening ring emerging from the fleshy surrounds, and the glistening moisture that ran in the slit of softness at its centre. Eva wanted to take Calliope's place. She wanted to lie across Praxis' knees. She wanted to feel his massive hands against her skin. She wanted to feel the weight of them — their potential. She wanted to taste the metallic tang on her tongue as she licked the hot armour. She wanted to seek out his cock, to feel its hardness in her hand. She wanted to grip its massive throbbing length, its lusting thickness. And she wanted him to bring her relief. She wanted him to bring his hand down on her buttocks in heavy punishing smacks. She wanted him to thrash her hard. She wanted to take his cock between her lips and, as she tightened with every blow of his heavy hand, she wanted to suck on it until his semen filled her mouth.

Eva rolled on the floor. Sand and dust stuck to her body, her face, her hair. She smelled it in her flared nostrils. She rolled the other way, exhilarated, afraid, still in need. She smelled her own urine and again felt the warmth of its flow between her legs. She forced her knees to open more and felt the gaze of the soldiers on her open, wet cunt.

Calliope bent down to Eva. She grabbed her long red hair in a wet bundle. Eva bared her teeth and spat.

'I think poor Eva has been our victim long enough. Perhaps it is time to show her some mercy, my lord.'

Praxis settled back in his chair and smiled.

'You are so merciful, my angel,' he said. 'How could I possibly resist any request my angel makes?'

'Then I would like Eva to become my attendant. She could help bathe me and oil my body. She would be free, of course, and no longer under threat of torture and humiliation.' She let go of Eva's hair and bent on one knee beside her. 'Would you like that, Eva? Could you be my friend? Would you like to bathe me? Would you like to oil my body? Would you like to shave my cunt?'

Eva licked spit from her lips. She thought it was a trick.

She looked from side to side suspiciously. She had still not forgotten how she had been deceived by Sappho and Chryseis — their tormenting jeers still rang in her ears. She did not know what to do.

'Mistress?' she said, as if someone else was speaking for her.

'Yes?' said Calliope. Raising Eva to her feet and linking her arm into Eva's.

'Is this true? Can it possibly be true?'

'Yes, my dear Eva. You have suffered enough. It is true. Come, we have things to do.'

Chapter 3

The "shrinking man"

Eva was taken to Calliope's tent, a high roofed octagonal structure made from heavy drapes of white and pink. Young girls attended her. Some had been taken from the Temple of Apollo in raids on Troy, some had been brought from Persia, some from Thebes in Egypt, and some from further south in Africa. Some belonged to Praxis, some had come as gifts, some had been left temporarily by guests, and some tended as payment for debt. All had their heads shorn, their pubic hair shaved, and all were forbidden to wear any clothing. Their young bodies were slim and oiled. They were trained in suppleness and athletics each day. Some wore crowns of flowers, some garlands of leaves around their necks. They fussed around Eva inquisitively. They touched her tangled red hair, and ran their hands across her pale northern skin.

They led her to a massive bath, shaped from bronze and set in the centre of the tent. Garlands of white flowers draped its sides, aromatic steam rose from its surface. The giggling girls removed her dirty smock, took her hands and encouraged her up small steps set at the side of the bath. As she entered the warm mist, her head was filled with the delightful aroma of oils and fragrances — cedarwood, bergamot, tolu, frankincense and nutmeg. She could hardly believe what was happening.

One of the girls stood in the bath and took both of Eva's hands.

'I am Weena, mistress' she said. 'Come, I will bathe you.'

She drew Eva into the warm water. It rose over her body, soft and gentle, cleansing and caressing. She sank into it.

Weena entwined her arms around Eva. She pressed her own slim body closely against Eva's. She drew her legs up, and moved her thighs against Eva's hips.

'I will cleanse you with my body,' said Weena. 'I have been trained to please.'

Eva lay back in the water. Weena rubbed her all over with her own body. She coiled around her like a snake. She pressed her stomach against Eva's. She urged her shoulders beneath Eva's armpits. She opened her legs and massaged Eva's breasts with her delightful slit. She raised her buttocks, drew Eva's face between them, and rubbed them against Eva's cheeks. She opened her legs more, bringing Eva's lips against her anus, allowing her to kiss it, lick it, insert her tongue inside it.

Eva could not stop herself. She had been mistreated for so long. The relief from torture and pain, the sensuality of the warm fragrant water, and the attention of the delectable Weena were overpowering. She wrapped her arms around Weena's hips and lifted her delightfully taut buttocks as high as she could.

Weena did not hold back. She opened herself completely. She clung onto the opposite side of the bronze bath and pushed herself back against Eva. Her slit, set in a soft wet oval of flesh, came against Eva's mouth. Her anus, tight, dark and perfectly formed, pressed against Eva's flaring nostrils.

Eva inhaled the scent of Weena's body. She pressed her nose against her anus. She slipped the tip of her hungry tongue into the slit of Weena's cunt. Weena gripped the edge of the bath tightly, tensioning her body, pressing back, wanting to be filled. The mounded curve of her taut buttocks glistened with the gloss of the sweetly scented water. Steam rose in a mist around them both. Eva's red hair floated in the water. It clung to Weena's thighs in drawn out scarlet tangles. It was as though the water was on fire, as though their passion had set it alight.

The other girls leant against the bath sides. Some dangled

their hands in the water, some stroked Weena's buttocks or touched Eva's hair. One held her fingers tightly in her slit and sucked the hard nipple of another. One licked another's cunt. She lapped at it eagerly, her face wet with moisture from the girl's crack. Her cheeks dripped with beads of sweat caused by the steamy heat that rose from the fragrant bath.

Weena screeched. She thrashed herself in the water. She took her hands from the side of the bath and slapped them on the surface of the water. She flailed wildly. She set the surface of the bath into a foaming turmoil. Eva would not let her go. She strained her tongue out as far as she could. She delved it into Weena's cunt. She licked at the soft inner surface, tasting the blend of the scented water and Weena's own delicious fragrance. Eva gulped, drinking it in. She lifted Weena higher, delighting in her anus, claiming satisfaction for her appetite. Her inflamed passion was hungry and she fed it eagerly.

Weena's panic increased. She screamed at the top of her voice. Bubbles mixed with her cries. Chokes blended with her breathless gasps. She wriggled in Eva's grip, sometimes pulling herself away from Eva's tongue and enjoying the exposure of loss. Sometimes she pressed hard against it and sucked it in as deep as it would go.

Two of the young girls draped themselves over the edge of the bath, their hands between each other's thighs, their fingers delving into each other's cunts. One of the girls sucked at the handle of a hairbrush. She dribbled her spit across it in sticky strands before opening her legs and pressing it deeply into her naked crack. Another stood above her and urinated on her face. The girl below, opened her mouth and drank it in keenly.

Suddenly, the flaps of the tent doorway were flung open. Calliope marched in. As soon as she saw what was happening, her face filled with fury.

She grabbed hold of Weena and pulled her out of the bath. The frightened girl fell onto the ground. Her firm body ran with steaming water as she writhed and clawed for something to bear against. She twisted onto her back and dropped her legs wide open. Her slit glistened with moisture, her anus was dilated.

Calliope angrily took hold of one of her ankles. She dragged Weena roughly across the tent. Weena's head bounced in the sand, her flowered crown already lost, her safety now in tatters.

'You are here to give pleasure, not to take it!' shrieked Calliope. 'I will teach you your place. And you will never forget the lesson!'

Still holding her by the ankles, Calliope hauled Weena out of the tent.

The other girls quickly helped Eva out of the bath. They dabbed her with towels and fussed anxiously with her hair. They were unhappy not to be accompanying their mistress, fearful that inadvertently they might be doing something to inflame her anger.

'We must follow our mistress,' said one nervously. 'We dare not anger the Lady Calliope more.'

Eva followed Calliope as she dragged Weena along the covered walkways between the tents. Weena writhed and screeched but Calliope took no notice.

Small open stalls lined the walkways. Here, soldiers were entertained by slaves in Praxis' thrall. Some of the soldiers looked up as Calliope went past dragging the screaming Weena. Some could not disguise their surprise at seeing Eva, free and attended by the still fussing girls. Some did not notice anything — they were too involved in the entertainments laid on by Praxis, the blind provider of all perversions.

One burly soldier, his waist tightly strapped by a broad leather belt, caned a naked woman tied forward over a saddle. Her buttocks were striped with red lines. Tears poured in streams from her eyes. The man looked around quickly as Eva passed, but turned back straight away to the vicious thrashing. Another, wearing a leather hood with eye holes, had a slave tied up in a tangle of knotted ropes. She hung on her back, suspended on the ropes, her mouth gagged with a massive ball, her cunt stuffed with a black, ebony cudgel. The man held a tallow candle above the woman's breasts. No sound came from her, but her eyes conveyed her silent screams as he dribbled the melting wax onto her nipples, her throat and along the edges of her broad stretched lips. Six soldiers stood around a naked woman. She knelt before them, a bowl in her hand as if begging. They filled it with their copious semen and, when it was full, she drank it under threats of punishment if she did not.

Calliope pulled the screeching Weena into a large circular tent. For a few moments, Eva could see nothing — the contrast between the bright light outside and the semi-darkness inside was blinding. Slowly her eyes became used to the dimness and she saw the massive bulk of Praxis forming in the darkness. The spider-like Master Wang hung onto his arm. In front of them, in the centre of the tent, a latticework contraption, made of leather and metal. By its side a bath of water and several large leather buckets.

Calliope dragged Weena up to the contraption.

'Meet the "shrinking man",' she said mockingly. 'I think you will come to feel very close to him.'

She threw her head back and laughed.

Praxis stepped forward, holding his hands out, reaching for Calliope.

'You are angry, my little angel? What has caused this?'

'This girl, this slave, Weena. She forgot her place. She thought she was allowed to live so that she could have pleasure for herself. She forgot she was here only to give pleasure to those she served. I found her squirming with joy and writhing with pleasure, my lord. Now, I want her to taste the joy of constriction. I want her to couple with the shrinking man.'

Weena tried to pull away, but immediately fell into Praxis' outstretched arms. He grabbed her instantly, enclosing her forearms in his massive hands.

'Ah, little Weena, you want a closer look at your new lover, I think.'

He pushed her forward so that she was forced to stare at the framework of wet leather and metal.

'I cannot see, but, my wayward slave, I can feel.'

He let go of one of her arms but still held her fast in the other. He ran his free hand across her pert breasts. He felt her hard nipples and pinched them between his finger and thumb.

'Do you like the feeling of tightness my little slave?'

He reached out to the metal and wooden contraption. He ran his hand across the complex framework. He smiled, pleased by what he felt under his touch.

'Look, the shrinking man awaits you, little Weena. See how he is shaped to fit your body. See how he has been constructed to lie close against every limb. See how he is wet and ready to clasp his arms around you in the most passionate embrace. Here are the leather bands that will come across your face. And here the metal framework to hold your head in place. Look how he is perfectly shaped to fit your shoulders and back, your breasts and your stomach. Look how his framework is carefully arranged to clamp around your hips and thighs. See how his leather straps are formed in such a way as to tighten into your delicate slit. Think of that, little Weena, imagine the drying leather pulling into your youthful crack, parting it, opening it, cutting into its centre. Yes, little Weena, when the "shrinking man" dries he will clasp you tighter than any lover. He will hold you so tightly you will not remember what it is to move your body. You will experience complete stillness. He will have perfect control over you. Then, locked into complete submission, you will know why you are being punished.'

Weena struggled in his powerful grip, but it was pointless. Her eyes were wide with fear, her face pale with anticipation of what lay ahead. She kicked her feet out and squirmed, but Praxis only laughed.

'Wang!' he shouted. 'Give the shrinking man a final dousing. We want him to find every curve of his new lover. We want him to fit closely to every part of her nubile body.'

Wang ordered two soldiers to douse the framework with water from the buckets. He made sure that all the leather was wet. He rubbed his hands gleefully along every length of its complex structure to ensure no part was missed. Water dripped from it as he stood back satisfied.

Eva hung back in the shadows. She stood behind a heavy wooden tent pole, still unsure of her place. Seeing the terrible device had suddenly reminded her of the precarious position inhabited by those in thrall to the Greeks. She looked over to Calliope. Calliope looked back and smiled. Eva relaxed a little. Her naked body was still wet, her mass of red hair tangled and hanging loosely around her shoulders. Soldiers moved some torches and their flickering light shimmered across her glistening body.

She stared at the "shrinking man" and shivered. She could see its purpose. She could see how its doused and slackened leather would soon dry and tighten around its victim. She could only imagine the pain of the tightening leather, the fear, the horror of not being able to move. She shivered at the totality of its irresistible bondage. She licked her dry lips. A sudden sense of realisation filled her. She felt a wave of relief that no longer was she a slave, no longer was she subject to the will of others, victim of the caprice of her masters. Yet, this sense of freedom somehow weakened her. Where her servitude had strengthened her, her new feeling of freedom took away her resolve to suffer. She knew that now, even though she had tolerated much as a captive to the Greeks, she could not bear the horror of the "shrinking man". She looked again at Calliope, her tall angular form, her beauty, her smooth skin. Calliope nodded and smiled. Eva felt assured of her new freedom and blessed with the loss of suffering that came with it.

Weena fought but she could not prevent herself being incarcerated in the "shrinking man". The metal frame was opened up and she was forced onto her hands and knees inside it. The leather straps were pulled up tight and the frame closed around her. Her arms and legs were held fast. She could no longer move her slightly bent back. A leather strap pulled up tightly between the lips of her crack and between her buttocks. Her face was laced with the strapping and her head was held firmly in place by the metal framework. The soldiers doused her with water from the buckets. The heavy splashes hit her hard, stung her body and made her gasp. They tightened the wet leather straps as much as they could.

Weena's mouth gaped, her jaw held firmly in the "shrinking man". She tried to cry out but could only make a monotone gurgling groan. Her eyes were wide with fear.

Torches were set in the ground around her. The glistening leather straps and her taut wet skin shimmered in their light. Slowly, the leather began to dry and tighten. Eva saw it pulling against Weena's skin. She saw the strapping digging in, pulling against the metal frame, binding Weena ever tighter within it bonds. A dribble of spit ran from the corners of Weena's mouth.

Eva pulled herself against the wooden tent pole, allowing her legs to fall either side of its smooth surface. The touch of it against the insides of her thighs instantly inflamed her. She imagined it was like the tightening leather against Weena's skin.

Spit dribbled down in long strands from Ween's mouth. Finally, it touched the floor.

Eva wanted to crawl forward and lick it up. She wanted to lie beneath Weena, her mouth upturned and open, gaping, waiting for the dripping spit. She wanted to taste it on her dry lips. She wanted to suck it in. She wanted to gulp it down, and swallow it. She wanted to pull herself beneath Weena, she wanted to lie between her legs, her face beneath Weena's cunt. She wanted to watch the leather tightening into Weena's slit, pulling at her flesh, squeezing it out on either side. She wanted to watch the tightening strap disappear in the moist valley of flesh as its grip grew ever more painful. Lying there, Eva would wait for Weena to urinate. She would let it flow into her mouth, catching it as it dribbled down over the leather strap, and fell in a shower — warm, sharp to the taste, plentiful, moistening, tangy. She would let her thirst be quenched by it.

Eva pulled herself tightly against the tent pole. She opened her legs and squirmed herself against the post, opening her flesh, exposing it to the smooth wooden surface. She felt her clitoris hardening at the touch of the unforgiving pole. She pressed it forward, rubbing herself up and down, exposing it, hurting it, forcing it with painful pressure to engorge and throb. Her flesh was wet, it slipped readily against the wood. She did not put her hand down, she wanted to feel the contact directly. She wanted nothing between her squirming wet flesh and the hard smooth timber.

She could not take her eyes off Weena. Spit was now running freely from her mouth in a continuous stream. She was not moving in any way. Her body was completely held fast by the terrible device of metal and leather. And all the time it was tightening. Still the leather glistened with wetness, still it was shrinking. Weena's eyes widened and spit continued to run from her mouth. A glistening trickle of urine dribbled first on the insides of her thighs then, in a sparkling shower as it bubbled over the ever tightening leather strap between her legs.

Suddenly, the flaps of the tent opened. Achilles and Agamemnon strode in. The blinded Ajax attended by two young girls followed behind. Ajax sniffed the air — he sensed his enemy Praxis, the one responsible for his blinding when Calliope had tripped him forward onto the waiting spears.

The powerful Ajax turned around sharply. The girls hanging onto his arms were knocked over.

'My lords,' he said angrily. ''Have you brought me into the company of the one who blinded me in order to further my punishment?'

Achilles laughed.

'Ajax. It is over. You must let it go. Look, Praxis has something here for our entertainment. A little slave girl is bound within the "shrinking man". Come, feel the tightness of her bonds. Feel her heart pounding. Put your face against the leather straps and feel her panting breath.' Achilles turned to Praxis. 'And what is the poor victim's name?'

'Weena,' said Praxis

Ajax's face filled with anger.

'She is mine!' he shouted. 'I brought her from Troy! Now, this weasel Praxis not only steals my slaves but dares to punish them as well. My lord. I appeal to you. He has already taken my sight. Now he deprives me of my possessions.'

Achilles stepped forward and restrained Ajax.

'It is a slave, my friend. You should not get so attached. I will replace her tenfold.'

Ajax allowed himself to be held back, but his wrath was

not assuaged. He stared out blindly towards Praxis and, under his breath, uttered a cursing revenge that he bound himself to fulfil.

After everyone had left, Eva, stayed. She crept up to the silent girl, still fixed inside the metal tomb of the "shrinking man".

Weena could not speak, the constriction was now too tight, but she could move her eyes. Eva looked into them — filled with fear, panic-stricken by her treatment, terrorised by the unknown.

'Are you in pain, little Weena?' asked Eva. 'Is your new lover, the "shrinking man", holding you tightly enough? Does he have you close enough in his loving arms?'

Weena eyes flashed from side to side. She wanted so much to speak, but it was impossible.

Eva squatted down beside the captive girl. She reached forward and touched her. Weena did not flinch, she could not. Eva felt the tension in the girl's body. Eva opened her legs and exposed her slit to the imprisoned girl.

'Look, Weena. Can you see the glistening moisture on the edges of my crack? Would you like to lick it? Would you like to run your tongue along it? See how it opens at your glance. It is expecting the tip of your tongue to caress it. It wants to feel its heat. It wants to feel its warm fleshiness lapping at it, slurping at it, drinking from it. Would you like to drink from my cunt little Weena?'

Eva moved closer, pressing her knees against the bound girl. The still tightening leather touched her skin. A thrill of joy ran through her. She imagined how Weena must feel — trapped, helpless, out of control. She ran her fingers along the edges of her slit. It opened at her touch. She looked down. Her silky moisture glistened. She parted the sparkling lips. The pink interior scintillated in the flickering lamplight. She prodded the base of her finger against her throbbing clitoris. The contact made her gasp. She ran her finger deeply inside her cunt. With her other hand, she drove two fingers into her dilated anus. As she got them as deeply as she could, and with spit running profusely from her wide stretched lips, she rose, in a massive, heavy and long awaited orgasm.

Chapter 4

Captives of the cruel Polydorus

Sappho's wrists screamed with pain. The thongs had tightened in the blazing sun and now cut deeply into her skin. Sappho and Chryseis were both squeezed into the small cage. The narrow iron bars, heated in the midday heat, pressed against their bodies and held them fast. Neither of them could move. Two spears were pushed between the bars and four soldiers bore the cage high on their shoulders. It rocked from side to side as the soldiers wove their way between the jostling crowd that crammed the crowded, narrow streets of Troy.

Polydorus rode alongside them in his ornate pony trap. Several slaves cleared the way for him and his entourage. Everyone knew he was the king's son, that he was cruel, and that he was to be feared. He held the long leather reins high in his right hand. In his left hand he brandished a long thin whip. Its tip curled in a snapping crack whenever he brought it against his ponies' bare buttocks. He flicked the whip whenever he was dissatisfied with the performance of the two women who pulled him. Sometimes they pulled too fast, sometimes they were too slow, sometimes they were not quick enough to respond to his instructions.

The women's colourful plumed headdresses nodded back and forth as they ran. Both kept their heads up proudly. Both clasped their teeth hard onto the silver bits in their mouths. Their sweat-glistening bodies, taut and well defined, pulled in unison — their paces equal and in concert with each other. Their buttocks, muscular and perfectly shaped, were parted only slightly by the leather strap that was pulled up tightly between them. Their shaved cracks closed around the thin leather strap. It rose up across their lower stomach and was secured to a wide belt at their slender waists. Shiny leather chest collars were pulled tight beneath their breasts. Rings in the backs of the collars held traces which led back to attachments on the front of the cart. Two outriggers jutted out from the shafts just behind the women. Leather pads were wound around them, acting as breaching when the trap slowed and pushed forward against its harnessed ponies' buttocks. Each shaft ended in a curved hook the end of which pointed back towards the trap. Each hook was surmounted by a shining silver ball.

They approached a massive, ornate gateway. Its doors slowly opened under the straining hands of fearful slaves. Polydorus snatched the reins back in his left hand. The two women halted. The padded breaching pressed against their rumps. They let their heads rock back and forward. Their headdresses inscribed a broad flashing curve in the bright midday sunlight. They welcomed the rest, but were already anxious to start again.

Polydorus clipped the whip into a brass ferrule attached to the side of the trap. He jumped down and handed the reins to a young male slave. The two women whinnied, disappointed that they could not continue to serve their master. Polydorus heard their sorrowful moan and walked up to them. He stroked their buttocks and they nodded more emphatically. He stroked them again. He ran his hands up their flat stomachs, over the leather chest collars and, one by one, circled their hard nipples with his fingers. They both thrust out their breasts, eager for his attention, stimulated by their master's touch, still hoping that he would return to the trap and whip them back into action.

He turned and strode in through the huge gateway.

'Bring in the cage!' he ordered. 'Let us see how these priestesses take to the service of Polydorus.'

Sappho looked out fearfully through the imprisoning bars as the cage was carried on the two poles into Polydorus' palace. The high, embellished entrance gave way to a large gardened area surrounded by colonnaded walkways topped with terracotta pantiles. In the shade of the walkways were many doors, some ajar, some tightly closed. Cypress trees and obelisks were placed around the gardens. At its centre, and raised above the height of everything else, stood a small temple with a statue of Polydorus as the entrance. Leading down from the front of the temple was a formal water garden fed from a spring which emerged near the temple entrance. Pools descended in steps and gushing waterfalls flowed down from one pool into the next.

The cage was carried to the lowest pool and dropped to the ground. Sappho gasped as the breath was knocked from her.

Women's faces stared down at her and Chryseis. Some of them poked their fingers into the cage, some giggled. One of them knelt down and started licking at Sappho's breasts, squashed and unmoveable against the cage's bars. Another dribbled spit onto Sappho's face, pressed as it was against Chryseis' breasts.

Polydorus brushed them all aside. They dropped back. Some fell to their knees and clasped their hands together in prayer. Others clung to each other in fear of their cruel master.

Polydorus poked his finger at Sappho, pressing it between her buttocks. She felt its tip against her anus. She could not move. She gasped as he drove it in up to his knuckle. She felt as if her whole body was filled by it. She wanted to open her mouth and cry out, to expel the shock of it, but she could not. She felt the heat of Chryseis' breasts against her face. Chryseis' chest rose and fell quickly. Her breasts absorbed the movement. Sappho could feel her panting desperation. Polydorus pushed his finger harder, probing her rectum, filling her with the heat of it, the driving intrusion of it. She felt her anus contracting against the base of his finger, grasping it, tightening on it in passion.

She could not help it. She knew her body was reacting to him, clamping itself onto him, holding him, showing him that she needed more. She wanted to be free from her captivity in the cage. She wanted to be able to drop down onto it, to squirm on his penetrating finger, to open herself up fully, to allow it to control her. She gasped with frustration and swallowed hard.

She could do nothing to keep it there. He pulled his finger out. She felt the keenness of exposure as her anus was left, open and dilated, still needing, still wanting. She wanted it back inside. She wanted it filling her again. She could not bear the abandonment. She pictured herself on her hands and knees, begging him to fill her again, pleading for his finger, opening her buttocks, spreading her thighs wide, entreating him in every way. She thought of herself dropping back, still on all fours, lapping the ground with her tongue, being obedient to his wishes. She imagined herself waiting as long as he made her, staying on the edge of fulfilment for as long as he decided. She could only see herself under his control, his slave, his victim, his toy. She felt inside herself the joys of letting him control everything she was.

'Release them!' he shouted.

The slaves who had carried them in, unlocked the cage door. It swung open. For a moment, the two women stayed in place, still locked together, pressed against each other's bodies and the cage bars. Sappho was afraid to move. She felt strangely protected in the cage. Even surrounded by the taunting voices and the poking, mocking slaves, she felt safe, embracing Chryseis, feeling the warmth of her body, the sanctuary of her closeness, the soft warmness of her ample breasts.

Sappho's arm was grabbed roughly. They were both dragged from the cage. The soldiers tried to make them stand, but they both dropped to the ground. They pressed against each other, still fearful of letting go, fearful of the world outside their prison.

Polydorus kicked at them. They shrank back. He kicked at them again.

'Get up, my priestesses. Do not be afraid of Polydorus. I will look after you better than your god, Apollo. See what he has let happen to you! Oh! And your wrists are so tightly bound. You must be freed. But it will be impossible to release you without first giving you a wetting.'

Sappho glanced at her wrists. She had almost forgotten how tightly she was bound by the now dried out thongs of leather. She lifted her arms and fiery talons of pain dug into her pain-racked body. She looked at Chryseis as she struggled to pick herself up off the ground. Her face was covered in mud and dust. Her short dark hair was dirty and unkempt. Tears welled from her reddened eyes. Sappho reached out her hands. Chryseis took them. They entangled their fingers, clawing at each other for a safety neither of them could provide.

'Collar them!' shouted Polydorus. 'Come, my priestesses. You can see what the house of Polydorus has to offer.'

Tight leather collars with rings were buckled around their necks. Leads were clipped into the rings. Slaves holding the leads tugged them sharply. Sappho fell to the side, surprised by the sudden yank of the leash. The slave pulled it again and, this time, she followed. Chryseis did not respond so quickly and Polydorus snatched the leash from the slave's hands.

'You will have to learn not to be so slow in the service of Polydorus, my little priestess. Here, let me show you.'

He yanked the lead viciously. Chryseis fell to the floor choking and gulping for breath. He yanked it again. She squirmed on the ground, fighting to get up. He yanked it again and, still coughing and gasping for air, she struggled onto her knees. She tried to get to her feet, but still she was not quick enough. He pushed her over, allowing the lead to tighten first before pulling heavily on it again. He kicked her backwards, just to make sure she was unable to fulfil his order. She fell again.

Sappho could not bear to witness the humiliating punishment. She threw herself in front of her friend, trying to protect her, hoping to save her any more punishment and humiliation.

'Ah!' Polydorus exclaimed. 'What faithful friends you are. This one prepared to suffer for the sake of the other. How sweet. How charming my little priestesses are.' He grabbed Sappho's face, gripping her cheeks with his thumb on one side, his fingers on the other. 'But, my little priestess, I am the master here. You do not act unless I command it. You protect your friend only if I order it.' He pushed her to the ground. 'I think my little priestesses like being on the ground. And so I will be kind to them. I will keep them on all fours. They can follow me like dogs.'

Buckets were brought and Sappho and Chryseis' wrists were plunged into the water. Slaves held them there — on their knees, afraid, degraded. A table was brought and set out nearby. Polydorus had wine and olives served while he waited. Sappho and Chryseis were kept with their wrists in the buckets of water. Slowly, the leather moistened and stretched enough to be cut away.

Sappho gasped as the knife cut the thongs and she felt the relief of release. She rubbed her wrists quickly, trying to relieve the stinging pain that encircled them. But neither Sappho nor Chryseis had time to recover. Polydorus threw down a napkin on the empty table before him. He jumped up and, without a word, they were yanked forward on the leashes held by the obedient slaves.

Polydorus strutted ahead. Sappho and Chryseis were led behind him on all fours. If they went too slow, their leads were pulled sharply. If they went too fast, they were tugged back with a painful jerk. Sappho felt ashamed. How quickly they had fallen. Like angels expelled from heaven they had descended from the priesthood of Apollo. In the temple, surrounded by the worshippers, they had been looked up to by all. Now they were pitiful slaves in the hands of a cruel master — led on all fours, reviled, mocked and dragged along like animals.

Polydorus walked haughtily down through the pleasure gardens. Some slave girls were bathing in one of the pools. They stopped frolicking as Polydorus walked by. They giggled at Sappho and Chryseis as they crawled past on their leads. Sappho did not look up, she felt too ashamed.

The lowest pool was the largest. A fountain, assembled from a tower of crescent-shaped marble bowls stood at its centre. Women stood on each tier, their feet at the points of the crescents, urinating into each other's mouths. Sappho watched them, gaping beneath each other, their mouths as wide as they could make them, licking their tongues out, drinking in each other's fluid. Polydorus watched them for a while, then ordered them down. They scrambled to the ground, and stood before him, glistening with water and urine, panting with excitement, eager for whatever he had planned for them.

He pointed to the smallest, a young girl with pale skin, her head shaved and with no pubic hair. She stepped forward and dropped to her knees. She looked up at him with dark, doe eyes.

'Master?' she asked, showing him in that one word that her whole life was directed towards serving only his needs.

'You may drink my seed,' he said, opening the front of his long robe and exposing his cock. The shaft was hard and venous, the tip swollen and throbbing. 'Yes, you may drink my essence. Here, take it deep. I only want to see you gulping it down. I do not want to see any spilt.'

Without a second thought, the young girl, still on her

knees, turned her back to her master. She dropped her head back, craning her neck as far as possible, resting back on her outstretched arms. She opened her mouth. He stepped forward and placed his cock above her face. She encircled its tip with her eager lips. She held herself there for a moment, feeling its hot swollen tip filling her mouth — absorbing its heat, accommodating its bulk.

Sappho watched the girl's cheeks dishing in as she began sucking on the cock. As she sucked, Sappho watched the shaft slowly entering her mouth. It did not stop. It did not pause. The venous shank went in, further and further, relentlessly penetrating the young, submitting girl.

The girl did not alter her position. As Polydorus' cock sank deeper, Sappho saw her throat thicken, swollen by the intrusion of the massive shaft. The girl still sucked hard, swallowing it down, not gulping, not gagging, not resisting it in any way.

Sappho felt her cunt moistening at the sight. She looked from side to side, wary of the slave who held her leash, frightened by the possible wrath of her new master, Polydorus. But no one was watching her. She brought her hand between her legs and slipped her fingers into the wet slit of her cunt. She dropped onto it, taking it in by moving onto it as much as by pushing it upwards inside. She gasped with pleasure as she felt its intrusion. She felt the moisture from her crack running over her fingers as, all the time, she watched the young girl's lips still pressing further along Polydorus' prodigious cock.

Finally, Polydorus' testicles rested either side of the young girl's nose. Still, she did not move. Polydorus and the girl stayed there for a moment, locked together — still, like statues.

Sappho rose up on her fingers. She pressed her thumb against her clitoris — it was hard and pulsating. But it was not enough. She wanted her mouth filled like the girl. She wanted to feel the bulk of Polydorus' pulsating cock filling her throat, plugging her, delving deeply into her.

She looked at the girl's cheeks, still dished in, still sucking on Polydorus' cock. She saw her throat, swollen and full. The girl gulped, one long swallowing gulp. It pulled Polydorus' cock in even deeper. It drew his scrotum tight against the girl's stretched lips. It squeezed his testicles around her nostrils. He reared his head back in ecstasy but did not pull away. His face tightened as he released his copious flow of fluid deep inside her. Sappho clawed at her cunt, squeezing her clitoris, pulling at the soft flesh that surrounded it. She watched the girl sucking every drop of semen from the throbbing cock. She watched her gulping it hungrily, unable to satisfy her appetite until it was all drawn out and swallowed.

Polydorus let his cock empty into the girl. Finally, he pulled away. Sappho could not believe the length of the cock as it came out. She could not believe it had all been inside the girl. Relieved of the pressure, the girl swallowed again — a long easy gulp.

Polydorus wrapped his robe around his muscular body and strode on. Sappho was pulled up alongside the young girl — still resting back on her hands, her mouth wide open. Sappho stopped, resisting a yank on her lead. She rose up on her arms and leant across the young girl. She looked into her mouth — pink, soft and fleshy. She saw the glint of semen on her tongue. Aware of Sappho's closeness, the girl licked her tongue out. Sappho licked her own tongue forward and lapped inside the girl's mouth. She tasted the semen — salty and sharp. She sucked it back into her mouth. It was still warm. She inhaled Polydorus' fragrance. She swallowed it keenly.

The male slave who had Sappho on the leash, turned and saw what she was doing. He smirked, and yanked so hard on the leash she choked.

Polydorus swaggered ahead. He pushed open doors along the walkway, peering inside, sometimes exclaiming, sometimes shouting orders. Sappho and Chryseis were dragged behind their new master. Sappho looked across to Chryseis. She tried to smile at her friend, to show her that she was keeping up hope, but the tears in Chryseis' eyes only filled her with more fear and desperation.

A painful yank of the lead on her neck told her to pay attention to what Polydorus was showing them.

'Look, my priestesses. See the sorts of pleasure available at Polydorus' house. The aristocrats of Troy are my clients. They know there is nowhere else in the world where their desires can be met. Even my sole surviving brother Paris patronises my house. And he has the most beautiful and obliging woman in the world, Helen, as his companion.'

Sappho was dragged to an open door. She stopped when the tension on the lead was slackened — she had already learned to respond to its commands. She peered inside. A young Nubian woman, slender and tall, sat bound into heavy wooden stocks. Her ankles were fixed on the outer edges with brass clamps, her wrists secured inside them, and in the middle, in a larger hole, her neck was framed by the heavy timber.

'She did not please my brother as he expected. She was too slow to respond. She will stay there for a few more days until she is tried out again. If she does no better, she will return to the stocks.'

He went to the next door. A woman, her head shaved, was hanging upside down, secured by her ankles to a hook in the ceiling. Her mouth was gagged with a large leather-covered ball and firmly secured with thongs tied behind her head. A massive slave stood next to her, twisting the rope to ensure she revolved slowly. Another slave held a short whip and brought to down across her reddened buttocks each time she turned.

'And here, another miscreant,' said Polydorus. 'She was only expected to take a whipping in silence. What could have been easier? But she too failed. She will stay here for a week. She will learn that silence is easily attained if one is taught the lesson in the right way.'

Sappho gaped at the woman, strung up, gagged and beaten. The thought that her suffering was set to continue for a whole week more made Sappho shiver. Her breath quickened. The collar was yanked at her neck. She hung her head. In the corner of her eye, she could see the woman turning on the rope. She heard the smack of the whip against the woman's buttocks. She felt dazed by the emptiness of the enforced silence that followed. She dropped her head completely and looked down at her own nipples. They were throbbing, hard and painful. The collar was yanked and she moved forward on her knees. She felt the moisture in the slit of her cunt as her flesh was squeezed between her thighs. A tingling heat spread into the base of her stomach. Her hard nipples ached.

Another door was opened. A red-haired girl with pale skin was tied backwards over a massive, revolving wheel. Her body strained against the arching curve of the wheel — accentuating the rising mound of her crotch, stretching tightly the slit of her cunt, flattening her small breasts against her ribs, exposing the prominence of her hardened nipples. The wheel turned slowly. The girl gaped. Her eyes rolled dizzily as, on each revolution she tried to orient herself. A black, male slave threw a bucket of water over her face each time she came into view. It splashed across her. She choked and gasped. It ran down her chin and onto her chest. It streamed across her stomach and ran eagerly into the fleshy valley of her cunt. As she was turned on the wheel, the water dripped from her chin, her nose and her nipples. When she was brought up again, more water was thrown over her.

'How long?' asked Polydorus.

'Three days, master,' said the slave.

'Then give her three days more. Her lesson will be over then.'

He turned to Sappho and Chryseis.

'Pay attention, my little priestesses of Apollo. Let these women be a warning to you. Fail Polydorus and only punishment will follow. Whatever pain you are expected to suffer in my service, will be nothing compared to the pain you must endure for failing me.'

Sappho's stomach filled with a rush of nerves. But her anxiety was a mixture of fear and excitement. She had never seen such things, never imagined such things. Yet what overcame her trembling body was not simply the terror of what she might suffer, it was the anticipation of the pleasure that might accompany it. Her mind was filled with images of pain and suffering, but, at the same time, each one produced a wave of need and delight. Everything was mixed up. Her sore knees, the tightness of the yanking collar at her neck, her dirty body and tear-streaked cheeks, all conspired to deliver a sensation of perverse delight. Every pain, every anxiety, every feeling of sullied shame, filled her with a self-disgust. At the same time, it also inflamed in her a desperate need for pleasure and fulfilment. All she had seen, even though it left her shaking with apprehension at the thought of the suffering it might bring, also left her panting with desire for the delights it held.

It was dark when Sappho and Chryseis were thrown into a small stall, used to bed animals. The floor was bare and cold. There was a drinking bowl on the floor. It was dark.

'This will be your home from now on, my little priestesses,' Polydorus shouted after them. 'I will have you cleaned up tomorrow. Then we shall put you to the test. We shall see what pleasures you can bring to my guests. I have a special one here who I know will be interested in you. We shall see if you please me or fail me.'

The door was slammed and they were thrown into darkness.

Sappho reached out for Chryseis. She touched her face and threw herself forward, clinging to her tightly, sobbing and shaking with fear and excitement.

'Dear Sappho,' said Chryseis, unable to hold back her tears. 'At least we are together. We will be each other's strength. No matter how bleak our future seems, we must trust in Apollo. He is the only one who can save us. Sappho, hold me close.'

Sappho ran her hands across Chryseis' shoulders. They were smooth and shapely, square and still proud. She squeezed them, and felt Chryseis' warm breath against her cheeks. She let her fingers find their way to Chryseis' breasts. She encircled their roundness and wound her fingers around her erect nipples. She felt safe so close to Chryseis. She opened her legs and Chryseis plunged her hand between them. Sappho's cunt opened at her touch. Without applying any pressure, its moistness allowed the tips of Chryseis' fingers to penetrate her flesh. Sappho moaned and rose up. She stiffened and held her breath before dropping back, her legs still wide apart, and ready for Chryseis' delving, eager tongue.

Chapter 5

Sappho's humiliation

Sappho sat up, her eyes wide. A sudden noise outside had woken her. Chryseis lay by her side, still asleep, her eyelids dark, her legs open, her fingers pressed into her crack.

Sappho nudged her insistently.

'It is Polydorus! He has returned. Quickly! We must be ready or we will be punished.'

Sappho helped Chryseis to her feet. They stood in the darkness, unable to see the door, frozen with fear at the sound of fast approaching footsteps.

The heavy iron bolt was drawn back and the door flung open.

Sappho and Chryseis rubbed their eyes and stumbled back. Sappho held her hands against her forehead. She peered out of the door into the blinding light. She could just make out Polydorus descending from his pony trap.

The two women who pulled it, their athletic bodies glistening with sweat, stood nodding their heads. They wore the same leather strap pulled up tightly between their buttocks and fixed to the wide leather belt at their waist. Their chest harnesses had been freshly burnished and their colourful headdresses teased out and combed. When Sappho had seen them before, they were barefoot, now they wore back leather boots, shiny and smooth and reaching up to the middle of their smooth thighs. At the heels of the boots were sparkling metal spurs with rotating silver wheels, faceted to reflect the sun as they spun. The fine plumage of their headdresses shone like rainbows in the shimmering morning sun. They relaxed on the loose traces, getting their breath back, kicking at the ground in their eagerness to move on again.

Polydorus marched over to the open door.

'Bring them,' he ordered. 'Tie them to the rear of my trap. They will travel at the pace of Polydorus. And pain will be theirs if they fail to keep up, or if they hold my beautiful ponies back.'

He fed his ponies from his hands as he watched Sappho and Chryseis secured by their wrists on ropes tied behind the ornate trap. Sappho waited fearfully as he took the reins from a blonde haired slave girl, and removed the long whip from the brass retaining ferrule. He flicked the whip. It cracked across the taut buttocks of the woman harnessed on the left of the trap. She stiffened and bent her head slightly, ready to move, waiting for her companion. Polydorus flicked the whip again. It cracked stingingly across the tightened buttocks of the other woman. He snatched at the reins and shook them. The women closed their teeth onto the metal bits in their mouths, lifted their heads and trotted forward.

Sappho hurried behind, afraid that she would not keep up. Her wrists were snatched and she was jerked forward. She nearly fell over, but just managed to stay on her feet.

Polydorus drove his trap beneath the covered walkways. The women's black boots clicked on the decoratively tiled surfaces beneath the shading pantiled roofs. The shiny wheels on their spurs scattered beams of multicolored light.

Polydorus peered in through some of the doors as they passed. At one particular one with a red painted door he stopped and entered. He took his whip with him.

As Sappho stood struggling to get her breath, she heard the cracking of the whip and the cries of pain that were produced by its savagery. Again it cracked. Again a fearful cry. Then it was silent. Suddenly, Polydorus emerged from the doorway. His face was red with fury. He kicked the side of the trap before stepping up into it. He shook the reins angrily and flailed his cracking whip across the women's buttocks. They both flinched and reared back, shocked. Their buttocks pressed against the padded breaching on the shaft outriggers and the trap jolted backwards. Sappho and Chryseis shrunk back fearfully.

Polydorus brought the whip down heavily across the buttocks of the woman on the left. A red mark appeared instantly on her skin. She made to move forward just as his whip cracked across the buttocks of the other. The women lost their sense of unified action. The trap lurched forward unevenly. Sappho stumbled again, but this time, Chryseis fell to the floor. She hit the tiled surface of the covered walkway hard. The trap slewed sideways and crashed into one of the marble columns that lined the walkway. Polydorus fell forward onto the front of the trap. The harnessed women were yanked back. They struggled as much as they could, but were unable to move the wedged trap. They breathed hard and whinnied in panicky frustration.

Polydorus jumped down. He strode over to Chryseis. She recoiled, holding her bound wrists in front of her breasts and struggling to get to her feet.

Polydorus raised the handle of the long whip in his hand. He flicked it. The shiny leather strand bent backwards in a slow curl. He brought the handle forward and the tip cracked loudly. A burst of smoke erupted from it as its tattered end snapped with fire. He threw it back again, but this time working the angry tip closer to his victim — the cringing Chryseis. Again it curled back. Again it cracked. This time even closer.

'Hold her!' shouted the angry Polydorus. 'I could have been injured. My ponies are distressed. Let her buttocks feel the heat of my fury.'

Two slaves grabbed Chryseis' arms. They dragged her to a marble table and bent her forward over its edge. They held her arms on its surface while another slave bent beneath the table and held her ankles.

Polydorus brought the cracking whip down immediately, and with complete accuracy. It snapped against the taut skin of Chryseis' buttocks. A flame red mark appeared straight away. She screamed in pain. Her whole body filled with the agonising fire of the burning leather tip. The whip came down again. Another mark, another scream, another tide of pain. She pulled against the restraining hands of the slaves in agony and panic. The whip came down again. A louder crack than before. A whiff of smoke heralded a bright red smudge on her skin. Her terrifying howl of pain was tribute to her anguish and terror.

Sappho watched as Polydorus whipped the captive Chryseis relentlessly. She screeched until she could screech no more. Her cries turned into whimpers, her whimpers into silence. In the end, she slumped in the hands of her captors. Her legs bent and buckled beneath her. Polydorus kept beating her for a while, but, in the end, he tired and stopped.

'Take her away for more appropriate punishment,' he ordered. 'I do not want to see her again until she is able to follow my orders.'

Sappho's heart dropped as Chryseis was hauled away, her legs still bent, her head hanging down, her buttocks reddened and angry, her whole form dissipated with overwhelming pain.

The trap was released from the column and the progress continued.

They passed two women being trained as ponies in a cleared ring in the ornamental garden. They were both Egyptian, tall and noble with smooth sallow skin. Although their pubic hair was shaved, neither had their head shaved. The dark straight hair of each was worked into a heavy plait which fell down between their shoulder blades. Both had golden rings piercing their nipples through which were attached red silk tapes. A tall woman with a black, ankle length cloak held the tapes in one hand and a long whip in the other.

Polydorus stopped to watch as the two women were led by the red tapes around the training ring. First they walked. The woman in the black cloak coaxed them with the stinging whip, making them keep their heads up and their arms by their sides. Then she made them trot. One lagged behind the other for a moment, and the woman with the whip cracked it angrily across her buttocks. Finally, they cantered, their heads high, their heavy plaited hair swinging against their sweating backs.

Polydorus was pleased with their performance. He went to them and held out something sweet in his hands. They bent their heads and took it, nodding to him as eagerly they chewed their reward. He strode up to the woman with the whip and thrust his hand between her thighs. She rose up stiffly. He took her whip and pushed it across her mouth, holding her fast, her eyes wide, pinioned on his powerful hand. Sappho felt her own cunt moistening as Polydorus pushed the woman to her knees and thrust his heavy cock into her gaping mouth.

Further on, another door was open. The trap was stopped. The women were tied to a hitching post. They knelt and drank thirstily from a large earthenware bowl of water.

Polydorus went inside the room and ordered Sappho released from the trap.

She was led inside. A young girl, an Abyssinian — lean and small breasted — knelt in the centre of the room. She held a bowl in her hands, just below her mouth. It was empty. Six men stood around her, each holding his stiff cock in his hands. The girl looked up at them as they slid their hands along the shafts of their cocks. Her brown eyes dwelt on their cocks, watching them throb and expand as the men's hands ran up them, seeing the skin tighten and redden as they drew their hands down. Behind them, stood more men, all naked, all waiting.

Sappho shivered. Polydorus called for a chair. A large ornamented throne was brought. He dropped himself into it heavily and motioned Sappho to sit on his knee. She held back, unsure, but he waved his hand at her insistently and she approached.

'Sit here, my little priestess. Make yourself comfortable for the exhibition of buk-ka-ke. I am interested to see how it affects you. Yes, sit on my knee. I want to feel your squirming buttocks against my skin. I want to feel the moistness of your crack against the top of my thigh.'

He lifted his purple robe and exposed his naked thighs. She sat nervously across his left knee. She felt her naked flesh squeeze down against his muscular thigh. Its moistness allowed the soft flesh to flatten and tighten against the crack at its centre. She felt fearful and embarrassed. She pressed her hands between her knees.

The motion of the men's hands was hypnotic. She watched their gripping fingers sweeping along the venous shafts of their stiff cocks. The ends swelled and reddened with the rhythm of their hands. She pressed her hands between her knees. She stroked her fingers lightly against the silky skin on the insides of her thighs. She found herself moving her fingers in time with the motion of the men's hands. Polydorus lifted his thigh slightly and she slipped along it, closer to his groin and to the heat of his own burgeoning cock. She felt the heat from his testicles rising against her skin. She felt the teasing sideways tension of his muscular leg against her crack, pulling at it, opening it a little, allowing its moisture to run against his skin.

The first spurt of semen splashed on the young girl's cheek. She opened her mouth in response to it, licking her tongue out to catch any that ran down onto her lips. She held the bowl outwards, ensuring the remainder was spilled into it. It ran down the insides of the bowl and collected in a sticky pool at its centre. The next spurted into her eye. She blinked as it ran around her lids. It spread on her eyeball and stuck to her long black lashes. That too ran down her cheek, this time, streaming over her top lip and onto her waiting tongue. The rest she took in the bowl.

Sappho kept moving her hands between her legs. She could not stop herself. She watched Polydorus' cock engorging. It rose and strained against the side of her leg. Its heat burned her with excitement. She wanted to reach out and grasp it in her hand. She wanted to work her hand along it as she watched the men with their hands on their own cocks. She wanted to keep up with their rhythmic movements and bring out Polydorus' semen in the same way as the semen of the men which was filling the girl's bowl.

She could not stop herself. She grabbed his thick cock in her hand. It swelled more as she grasped it. She tightened her grip and pulled the venous skin beneath her hand.

'Show me, my little priestess. Show me how you fill the bowl. Show me how you nourish yourself on its contents. Show me your taste for buk-ka-ke.'

Sappho released her grip on Polydorus' cock. The palm of her hand felt cool as she pulled it away. She eased herself on his knee — getting ready to stand up. Her cunt felt wet and the soft flesh stuck to his skin as she lifted herself off. She stood and moved forward. No one stopped her. She was acting under her master's orders. It seemed as though she was in a dream, an ecstatic dream, a dream filled with discipline, joy and the overbearing excitement of unknown pleasures.

She took the bowl from the girl's hands. There was still semen in it. She lifted it to her lips and drank it. She let it slip over her tongue, holding it in the centre for a second before taking it to the back of her throat and gulping it down. It stuck to her lips. She left it there, glistening and gluey. The girl got to her feet and stepped aside. Sappho stood in place of the girl and slowly knelt. She held the bowl up in front of her, offering up her wrists, wanting them bound.

A slave brought some wet leather thongs and wrapped them around her wrists. Sappho did not move. The slave wound the leather several times. Each binding circle increased Sappho's excitement. Her nipples hardened and ached. Her chest pounded in time with her racing heart. Her slit throbbed and swelled. The slave pulled the ends of the thongs into a tight knot and stood back.

Sappho brought the bowl up beneath her chin. It still shimmered with the sticky white semen collected by the girl. Sappho opened her mouth and looked up at the circle of men that surrounded her. She looked at their cocks, thickened and pulsating under the tight grip of their hands. She watched the veins on their stretched surfaces throbbing. She turned to each one. She cupped her hands beneath the bowl and held it out. She begged for their semen, showing them she was waiting for her bowl to fill, showing them she only wanted to drink it down, only wanted to feast on its nourishment.

She glanced over to the Abyssinian girl. She stood beside the men, her face still dripping with semen. Sappho squirmed her buttocks together and felt the wetness of her cunt between the swollen folds of flesh. She pulled her wrists against their bonds. The feeling of tightness, of constriction, sent thrills running deeply inside her. She held the bowl out further, pleading with her eyes, imploring the men to feed her.

She did not blink as the first splashed into her eye. It ran silkily around her eyeball. She could see it hanging onto her eyelashes, dripping down. She felt its heat as it trickled onto her cheek. She breathed deeply as it ran down into the corner of her lips. She licked at it. Its tang filled her with shivering thrills of excitement. She sucked it in as the next splattered into her open mouth. It covered her waiting tongue. Running from its end and dripping down into her bowl. More came, some spurting directly into the bowl, some running over its edge onto her fingers. Some splattered onto her head, some on her cheeks, some in her mouth. She drank any that went into her mouth, and collected as much as she could in the bowl. She wanted to fill the bowl. She needed to provide herself with enough to quench her ever growing thirst.

The first men stood back and were replaced by those behind. Sappho was awash with their hot semen. Her bowl was filling with the creamy mixture. It slopped against the sides and stuck to her hands as it ran over the rim. It flowed down her forearms, dripped off her elbows, and dribbled onto her knees.

The last man stood back and another took his place. It was Polydorus. His purple robe was wide open. His massive cock throbbed in his hand. Sappho held her bowl up to him. He looked down at her in contempt. She lifted it higher, wanting him to fill it to overspilling, wanting him to add his fluid so that at last she could drink it down.

He lifted his cock's weighty end in his hand and held it above her. She could feel its heat on her face. Semen ran from her chin, and dripped into the bowl. Polydorus pulled his hand the full length of his cock. The end swelled and reddened. A sudden massive spurt of semen shot from it. It hit her face, her cheek, both her eyes. It ran into her mouth and then, as she held it up, it filled her bowl. She waited until there was no more left.

'Now,' said Polydorus. 'Now, you may drink, my little priestess. Do not stop until your bowl is empty.'

Sappho did not nod, she simply stared, the moment had

arrived. At last she could quench her desperate thirst. She opened her nostrils wide and inhaled the scent of the semen. She breathed it in deeply. Her master had told her what to do. She wanted nothing else. She only wanted to follow his instructions. She only wanted to do the thing he instructed. There was nothing else in her life except her master's will, the contents of the bowl, her thirst.

She lifted the edge of the bowl to her lips. The semen on them slid against the wet, gluey rim. She sucked a little, she wanted to take the first sip slowly. She drew it into her mouth — soft, salty, slippery, delectable. She sucked in more, not removing the bowl for a second. She slurped at it, filling her mouth with its viscid fullness, swallowing it, gulping it, devouring it. She tipped the bowl, emptying it, quenching her thirst yet still not having enough. She tipped the bowl right back, licking her tongue into it, lapping up all she could, cleaning the rim, slurping around the outside edges. Finally, she had taken it all, she had drunk it all down. Still, she wanted more.

Sappho looked up at Polydorus. She opened her legs and exposed her wet slit. A trickle of semen ran down from her mouth. It dribbled between her breasts and onto her stomach.

'Take her!' ordered Polydorus. 'Tie her. She can watch the beast chase. I have had enough of her. I will decide tomorrow what to do with her.'

A rope was tied to Sappho's ankles and, with her wrists still bound with the leather thongs, and glistening with the soaking of still wet semen, she was dragged back along the covered walkways.

She bounced on the tiled surface. She saw the pony girls eagerly setting off with the trap behind them. They looked so clean and bright, so eager and beautiful. Sappho, felt the bonds around her wrists and the rope tugging at her ankles. She felt dirty, shamed and humiliated. She thought, for a moment, of her time as a priestess. She pictured her own splendid robe, of Chryseis beside her, of the worshippers of Apollo bending on their knees before her. She saw their faces, waiting for her instructions and, as she realised what she had sunk to, she felt a deep inner sense of self-disgust and worthlessness.

She was dragged through the gardens and secured with ropes to a post. Girls draped in lion skins and with the head of lions as masks, roamed on all fours amongst the bushes. They stopped and cocked their heads to the side if they thought they heard something. They dropped down if they thought they had been seen. Sappho saw men with the skins of male lions and with masks with heavy manes drawn across their faces. They stalked the lionesses, prowling around the garden, sniffing the air, growling and roaring and scratching at the earth with their hands. Suddenly one of them charged towards a lioness. He wrapped his arms around her waist and thrust his cock beneath her tail. She cried out, a screaming growl, and he howled loudly as he thrust into her wildly. Another came and he too thrust the lioness from behind. She howled again, this time louder. Then another came, and another, until she was surrounded. They clawed at her menacingly and she cowered in fear before them. Each one in turn clung to her waist with his arms and thrust his cock into her from behind — sometimes into her cunt, sometimes into her anus. Her screams got louder. Even when they all left her, seeking other prey, she continued to whimper and cry out, howling occasionally, growling and panting rapidly.

When the sun had set, Sappho was untied from the post and flung back into the dark stall. The door was slammed behind her, She had not seen Chryseis since she had been taken away. She felt around in the darkness and realised she was not there. Her stomach filled with fear. Her heart starting beating fast. She felt desperately alone. She wondered what could have happened. She feared she might never see her friend again, and that she was doomed to a life of loneliness, captivity and suffering.

She dropped down in the corner of the room and stared blankly into the darkness. She thought of Chryseis' beating, of the cracking whip, and her cries of pain. She saw again the reddened skin of Chryseis' buttocks as they had suffered blow after blow from the smoking tip of the leather whip. Sappho let her legs fall open. She could not get the image out of her mind. A trickle of spit dribbled from her mouth. She could still taste semen on her tongue. She licked her lips, but let the dribble of semen scented spit run freely. It fell onto her crack. It ran along its length, mixing with the moisture already there.

The image of Chryseis' beating flashed back into her mind, the sound of her cries resounded in her ears. Sappho's heart raced. She licked her lips and again tasted the semen in her mouth. She thought of the girls in the lion skins, and of the men chasing them as beasts. She saw their tails rising up in the hot sun, and she heard their cries of pain and pleasure as the men-lions mounted their prey from behind. Sappho gasped for breath and, with the only pressure against the flesh of her cunt the drip of succulent semen and spit, she strained back in an unstoppable and contorting paroxysm of ecstatic joy.

Chapter 6

Calliope's humiliation — Eva's redemption

Young female slaves, wearing only light, pleated tunics, opened the entrance to the large tent as Praxis and Calliope arrived. Calliope looked haughtily at a nervous Weena who held one of the flaps. She grabbed it in both hands to stop it fluttering in the wind. As Calliope came closer, Weena shrank back, aware of the temper her mistress had, and barely recovered from her last punishment at Calliope's hands. Calliope hesitated at the door, checking the anxious girl with her eyes, hoping to find something wrong that could warrant punishment.

'Show me your teeth, girl!' she ordered. 'Quickly! Quickly!'

Weena dropped the edge of the tent flap and stepped forward uneasily. She opened her mouth and exposed her fine white teeth.

'Wider! Wider!'

Calliope peered into the girl's mouth.

'Push out your tongue. I cannot see for it!'

Weena pushed out her tongue as far as she could. Calliope poked her fingers inside Weena's mouth. The girl gagged as Calliope's fingers pressed against the back of her throat. Calliope kept her fingers where they were, and looked disapprovingly at the anxious, choking girl.

'Why are you choking, girl?' she demanded. 'Why do you gag when my fingers enter your throat? Can you not take a man in there? Have you not been trained to swallow the shaft of a man? Speak! Speak!'

Weena's face reddened. She dipped her head and swallowed hard in an attempt to stop acrid vomit running up her gulping throat.

'Mistress, I — ' she heaved and choked again.

Calliope thrust her fingers deeply inside Weena's throat. Vomit ran up onto them. She pulled them out and shook the vomit onto the floor dismissively. Vomit bubbled from Weena's gasping mouth as she continued to choke and heave.

'My lord, Praxis,' Calliope said disdainfully. 'This girl needs checking. I fear she may be unable to carry out her duties. I think the training Master Wang has given her has been inadequate. I shall have to correct it.'

Praxis turned to her. Master Wang tugged urgently at his arm. Calliope looked annoyed at the man's intrusion.

'Lord,' said Master Wang as he pulled more insistently. 'They have brought the "brazen bull". It has been set up outside the main tent. None will dare stand against you now, lord. All will fear the punishment of the "brazen bull". All will fear the wrath of the great Praxis.'

Praxis held out his arms. Both his massive biceps were banded with tight leather straps. He moved forward blindly.

'Take me to it. I need to feel its power. I need to run my fingers over its muscular form.'

Master Wang took his arm and led him towards the entrance of the tent.

Calliope rushed forward, seething with jealousy.

'But the girl, my lord. Are you not concerned about the girl? Her training?'

'Later. Later,' said Praxis dismissively. 'If you cannot deal with it, Master Wang will deal with it later.'

Calliope scowled angrily, but followed nevertheless. She was not going to let Master Wang get the better of her. She grabbed hold of the still choking girl.

'Be quiet, girl. Follow me.'

Master Wang led Praxis outside the tent. He stood him in front of a massive statue of a bull. Its prodigious shoulders and muscular hindquarters, beautifully cast from shining bronze, shimmered in the scorching midday heat.

Its huge curved horns glistened in the dazzling sunlight. The effigy had been fixed to the floor with heavy iron nails. A fire had been set beneath its belly. A door in its side, just big enough for a man to be squeezed through, testified to its use as a torture device.

Master Wang held Praxis' hands against the hard bronze flesh of the tremendous beast.

'Feel its strength, my lord. Feel the line and curve of its mighty muscles. Master Epeius, the statue maker and pugilist, has built it exactly as he promised. It is truly an amazing invention. A punishment device to rival any other in the world. Everyone who sees it, is in awe of its power. Epeius has installed the system of tubes and stops exactly as he pledged. They run from inside the body of the ox into outlets at its mouth and nostrils. When the victim begins to scream — and scream he surely will when the fire is lit beneath him — the screams will issue from the beast in tremendous bellows. Then, Epeius says, we will call the beast the "infuriated ox". When it announces its fury, he says, we will think it is enraged and angered because the gods themselves have torn out its innards.'

Calliope shrugged and turned back to Weena who was shivering at the sight of the terrifying "brazen bull".

'Not me, mistress. Please, not me. I could not stand being shut in. I could not stand the heat. The pain. The sound of its fury. Please, mistress. Not me.'

She tugged harder, squirming to get away.

Calliope grabbed her ear and pulled her forward.

'Follow me, you ridiculous girl,' she said. Weena scuttled behind still shaking with fear. 'I will see if Master Wang has done his job with you,' Calliope said loudly, and with emphasis, so that there was no mistaking her intention to embarrass Praxis' Chinese henchman.

As she was dragging the young girl through the entrance, Achilles arrived. His elegant, princely bearing made her drop back. Straight away, she regretted her loudly announced exit. Now, she wanted to return to the tent, to impress Achilles. But it was impossible — she was committed to leave.

'Are you having trouble with one of your pretty maidens?' Achilles asked, running his hands across the shaking Weena's pert breasts.

'No, sire ... yes, sire. She is causing trouble, sire. But it is not of my making. It is caused by — '

'But you will correct the problem. I am sure of that.'

'Yes, yes, my lord, I will. Have no doubt of that.'

'Good. I could be very pleased by a well-trained maiden such as you have there. Pleased by the maiden and ... ' he lifted Calliope's chin in his hand. ' ... pleased by the trainer.'

Achilles marched into the tent. Calliope went out. She stared back at Master Wang, annoyed and brimming with anger. She tossed her head back and smiled at the promise in Achilles' words. She dug her fingers deeply into Weena's already bruised ear.

'Master Praxis! What have you here for me today?'

Praxis swung round to the sound of Achilles booming voice.

'Anything you please, my lord, anything you desire.'

'I desire some distraction. I need some pleasure that will make me forget the worries of this war. Something that will put the misery of being stuck here, year after year on the Trojan beach, to the back of my mind.'

'Then you are right to visit the tent of Praxis, my lord.'

Praxis clapped his hands together loudly.

Eva came in. She was naked except for a shiny leather belt around her waist. She was fragrant and bathed. Her body was oiled. Her long red hair had been combed up into a massive fiery mane. A line of male slaves followed her. In pairs they carried poles borne on their shoulders. On each pole was slung a net, and tightly held inside each net, was a captive girl.

'Who is that woman at the head of the line?' asked Achilles.

'She is the German noble, Eva. I have offered her some of my favour. She is splendid, do you not think? Wang tells me she is the most beautiful woman he has ever seen. He says her head is ablaze with fire. Is he right, my lord?'

Achilles nodded in agreement.

Praxis listened for his reply.

The netted captives were paraded once around the tent. Achilles was invited to choose one. He pointed at the one closest to him. Two slaves ran forward brandishing knives. They slit the net and the girl fell out.

She struggled to get up. Her mouth was filled by a leather ball. It was drawn tightly into her mouth by attached thongs tied behind her head. Her wrists were bound with leather straps. A leather collar encircled her neck. A leash led from a ring bound into the collar. A slave grabbed the leash and yanked it hard.

'Now, my lord, you may choose her punishment.'

'Ah, but what is her crime?'

'She has stolen drink from the kitchen, my lord.'

'Then bring a bowl, and a whip!' ordered Achilles keenly. 'And remove the gag!'

The gag was removed. The girl was forced onto all fours in front of the bowl. Two slaves were made to urinate in it. They filled it to overflowing. The girl's head was bent down to the bowl. The slave holding the leash placed his foot on the back of her neck to keep her there. Achilles took hold of the whip — a short stout leather flail with a strong handle and six individual tails all of which ended in a thin tattered end.

'Make her drink!' he ordered.

The slave forced the girl's face into the bowl. She spluttered as she tried to lap hopelessly at the urine.

'Aha!' mocked Achilles. 'Look, Praxis, one of your slaves is stealing drink. I think she needs punishing.'

'You are right, my lord. And there is no better hand to take on the task than my lord Achilles.'

Achilles brought the flail down sharply onto the girl's buttocks. She reared back. Her face came out of the bowl and she screamed with the painful shock. Straight away, the slave pressed his foot harder against the back of her neck and forced her face back down again. She choked and coughed. Foaming bubbles of urine overflowed from the bowl. Achilles whipped the leather flail down again. It struck her buttocks fully. Its ends cut her skin and laced it with red stripes. Again, she pulled back and screamed. Again, she was forced back down.

Eva watched the punishment. She ran her fingers around her leather belt, feeling its smoothness, its tightness against her skin. Every time the flail slashed across the girl's buttocks, Eva felt a shock of excitement in her swelling crack. Every time Achilles lifted the flail, she held her breath as she anticipated the moment of contact — the slap of leather against skin. Every time she saw the girl's face dipped into the bowl of foaming urine, she moved her fingers further down from her belt towards her aching, moistening cunt.

The girl spluttered as the beating continued. Her face was red and, when she lifted herself back, urine and spit ran freely from her gaping mouth. Her buttocks were an angry smudge of red — all the lines inflicted by the flail had melded into one. Eva closed her eyes and let the girl's screams fill her head. She clawed at the top of her cunt, letting her fingers probe their way into her delectable crack. It opened easily and, within its soft moist folds, she found the tip of her throbbing clitoris.

But the girl's screams were not loud enough. The flail did not inflict the pain it promised. Achilles was dissatisfied.

Suddenly, he ordered the girl thrown into the latrines.

'She can feast there all she wishes,' he said as, tired of the punishment, he tossed the flail to the ground. He threw himself down in a massive chair.

Eva gasped, her fingers massaging her aching clitoris, her head yearning for the sound of pain, her eyes searching for the vision of servitude and punishment. She wanted to rush forward and plead with Achilles to continue. She wanted to throw herself at his feet, and beg him to take up the whip and thrash her instead. Anything that would fill her with the torment of punishment. Anything that would allow her own pleasure to flow.

Suddenly, Calliope strutted back into the tent. She held Weena by the ear and pulled her along on her knees.

'Praxis, what is this?' asked Achilles, pleased with the diversion. 'Has your beautiful assistant been planning something for us? And I thought, when she rushed out of the door with her little slave, that she was hiding from me.'

'My lord, she has trouble with that very slave.'

'You surprise me, Praxis. That a young slave like that should be trouble to your beautiful assistant.'

'Some of these slaves are wilful, my lord, and difficult to control.'

'Then, I think, if the slave is stronger than the master, the master, or as in this case, the mistress, should be the slave.'

Calliope scowled at Praxis. Achilles saw her anger and smiled.

Master Wang ran forward, preening at Calliope's discomfort.

'There, sire, you have it. A trial of strength. That's what it is. Perhaps the beautiful Calliope can show you how she has taught the young girl the lesson she accused her own master of not providing?'

Calliope scowled again. She dragged Weena forward, released her ear with a final yank, and kicked her down onto the ground. Weena shrank back, nursing her ear, terrified.

'She has been no trouble to me, my lord Achilles,' Calliope said, barely able to disguise her trembling anger. 'I quickly cured her. She is a puny maiden — easily subdued. I do not know why Master Wang had difficulty with her. It was such a simple matter. Perhaps my lord would allow me to demonstrate. I'm sure my training will not be found wanting.'

'As you will. Show your chieftain how you have subdued this terrible foe.'

Achilles laughed loudly.

Calliope pursed her lips.

'Here, girl! On your knees!'

Weena scuttled forward and knelt where Calliope indicated.

'Ah, yes, you have trained her to be a dog,' mocked Achilles. 'She kneels at your command. I am impressed. But I have lots of dogs. And they are cheaper to keep than slaves.'

'Yes, she kneels, lord, but now I will show you what I have taught her. You will soon see she is worth more than any dog. Look up, girl! Attend to your mistress's orders.'

'I hope your promises can be fulfilled, my lady. I have no more patience for disappointment today.'

'They can, sire. They can.'

A strongly built male slave was brought in and stripped. He stood, naked before Calliope. She ordered him to stretch his arms out wide. Weena was lifted up and placed with her back against the slave's. Her arms were stretched wide and her wrists were bound with leather straps to his muscular forearms. Her ankles were tied to his calves with thin leather thongs.

She hung on her bonds, panting with terror, glowing with the sweat of fear. The moisture on the edges of her crack glistened. Her hard nipples gleamed.

The male slave was told to bend forward. As he did, Weena was bent backwards against him. Her body arched tautly against the naked man. Her small breasts flattened against her ribs. Only her nipples stood out, hard and throbbing. Her hips were forced out prominently — her stomach was flattened and dished in between them. Her delectable pink slit, shaved and naked, was stretched so tight, its edges brought together so closely, that only the finest crack was visible. She lay against the back of the athletic man, unable to move, stretched out as though she were on a crucifix.

'She is ready for you, sire. She will take everything you have. Yes, even the mighty Achilles. I have ensured she will swallow it to the hilt.'

Achilles smiled and walked forward. Weena lay bent backwards over the slave's back, her face upside down at the height of Achilles' groin. He opened his tunic and lifted up his weighty cock. It swung heavily against her open mouth. Her eyes widened as she saw its size. She felt its heat against her skin. Her smooth cheeks flushed with anxiety and terror.

Achilles pressed the tip against Weena's lips. She opened them as much as possible. It entered her mouth. Her cheeks filled as its end ran across her tongue. Her eyes widened more. The slave that held her on his back, brought his arms forward so that she was stretched even tighter. She tried to express the pain of the tension in her body with a scream, but her mouth was plugged completely. Her wide, fear filled eyes were the only signal of her building terror.

Eva, still holding her fingers around the tip of her clitoris, stared at Weena. She watched Achilles' cock thickening and entering her mouth. The heavy venous surface slid between Weena's stretched lips. Weena's eyes widened as it entered. Eva watched it going in further. She clawed at her clitoris, squeezing it between her fingers, sending shooting pains of joy deeply into her body. She rose up as she felt the pent up pressure inside her body beginning to release.

Weena's body tightened as the cock continued to slide into her mouth. Its tip reached the back of her throat. Her face reddened more. Still, it continued to enter. Weena gagged and tightened against the shaft but she did not stop. She swallowed it down.

Eva watched Weena's throat thicken as the tip of the throbbing cock entered it.

Weena tightened more against the slave's back. She pulled against the bonds which held her wrists and ankles.

Eva opened her legs then tightened them again. Her head filled with the picture before her. In her mind, she could see nothing else.

Weena strained and squirmed. Suddenly, she tightened on Achilles' cock. Her face reddened more, her eyes bulged, her chest rose and she heaved. Vomit was in her throat. She tried to hold it back, to swallow, to let his cock continue going in, but she could not. She choked. Achilles pulled out his cock. He held it in front of Weena as vomit and spit ran from her gasping mouth. She coughed and choked as the naked male slave, not ordered to do otherwise, kept her stretched tightly backwards against his back.

Eva gasped and bit her lips. Her body was seized with the unreleased tension of her ecstasy. She shivered with frustration. Her body was throbbing with her pent up ecstasy but she could not liberate it.

Achilles stood back and stared hard at Calliope.

'I think that you have lost control of your little empire, my dear Praxis. Perhaps it is time to start looking elsewhere for my entertainment.'

Praxis looked around blindly. He was filled with anger and worry. He could not afford to lose Achilles' patronage. Without it, and with Ajax as a sworn enemy, he knew he could not survive. Now, he sensed Achilles' anger brewing, and, like others, he had learned in the past to fear it. He did not know what to do. Beads of sweat ran in the heavy furrows of his forehead. He dropped his arms to his sides, somehow admitting that there was nowhere to turn.

A figure pushed up beside him.

'Let me, my lord. I think the mighty Achilles will not be disappointed with me.' Praxis recognised Eva's silky voice. 'Perhaps, if I please our lord Achilles, I will also please my lord Praxis?'

Praxis nodded.

Eva smiled and walked into the centre of the tent. Weena was released from her bonds. She slumped to the floor, still choking. Calliope scowled at her, and kicked her viciously before spitting on her.

Achilles shook his head disapprovingly.

Eva stood with her back against the naked male slave. She opened her arms out wide and waited, She was quickly bound to the slave in the same way as Weena. When the slave bent forward, Eva took a deep breath and allowed her body to be bent backwards until she was taut and her face was hanging upside down.

She waited, her head hung backwards, her mass of tangled red hair hanging down around her cheeks. Her throat was open and stretched. She felt the tension in her slit, the swollen edges pulling at her clitoris. The tightness accentuated its throbbing, allowing the imprisoned pleasure within her to build again.

Achilles approached her, his massive cock in his hand. Eva opened her mouth. He slipped the end between her lips. She lapped her tongue against its upper side, running its tip around the hard throbbing glans. She felt its bulk filling her mouth as he pushed it in further. She swallowed on it, lubricating her throat in readiness. She felt it against the back of her throat. She swallowed again, this time encouraging it to enter, allowing it down. She dropped her head back completely and let the shaft go down.

She felt her clitoris pulsating against the stretched edges of her slit. She tightened herself as her stored up passion began to flow. Achilles' cock slipped further. Eva could no longer swallow, she could only be filled. She felt the heat of his testicles. She felt his fleshy scrotum parting at her nose. She felt the weight of his testicles against her nostrils. Her eyes bulged — she could not stop them. She felt the naked slave tensioning her more as he bent forward under the strain of her weight. She heard Achilles' groan. She felt the searing surge of heat in his cock. She felt the splatter of his hot semen deep inside her. She held onto it until it was empty. She felt her own orgasm flooding inside her at the same time. It mixed with the taste of his drenching semen, saturating her, dousing her with heat, drowning her with joy and overpowering ecstasy.

Calliope stamped across the tent looking for something upon which to vent her anger. She kicked angrily at Weena. Weena did not care any longer. She simply lay on the ground, not even bothering to cover herself. Calliope kicked harder, but still there was no response. She ordered her thrown into the latrines with the others. She scowled as the girl was pulled past her. In an effort to redeem herself, she kicked Weena hard as she was hauled out of the tent entrance.

'Your young slave seems to be ignoring you,' joked Achilles. 'Perhaps she has already forgotten the lesson you taught her. Perhaps too, she has forgotten that she is your slave.'

Calliope's face reddened. She spat onto Weena. It

dribbled across her face.

Calliope looked over to Eva.

'There is another who is difficult to control. My lord, Praxis. Let me discipline her and ensure she pleases her masters.'

Praxis, held his arm out in front of Eva.

'No, my lady Calliope. She has pleased our lord Achilles. Eva will not be the subject of your vengeance. I think she will be better suited as a lady, not a slave. Do you not agree?'

Calliope tossed her head back haughtily.

'Of course, my lord. You are right. Of course.'

Calliope smiled at Eva. Eva was not sure whether it was a smile of complicity, an acknowledgement of agreement, or a forced attempt to disguise her boiling hatred.

CHAPTER 7

EVA'S BARGAIN WITH PRAXIS

Eva sat next to Praxis. Weena, held on a lead by her mistress Calliope, crouched on all fours. Her head was bent, and her buttocks held high as she lapped milk from a bowl on the floor.

'Give me your hand, my lord,' said Calliope. 'You might like to stroke my little slave. You will then know how she has become tamed. How she has bent entirely to my will. You may feel her purring, or pushing her neck against you as she tries to curry your favour. You will think she is your faithful pet. But, if I snatch her lead, if her collar tightens around her neck, she will quickly jump back to my side. Even though she has the chance to purr for her lord Praxis, and the opportunity to rub her neck against his leg, she will still respond to the will of her mistress when she feels the tightening leather pulling at her neck.'

Praxis allowed Calliope to guide his hand onto the back of Weena's shaved head. He smiled as he listened to the young girl lapping at the bowl of milk. He ran his hand around the side of her face — her skin was perfectly smooth. He stretched his fingers out then let them curl back before opening them again. He ran his fingertips around the taut, silky skin of her cheeks, dished in as she sucked at the milk in the bowl. He felt the motion of her lapping tongue and the contractions in her delicate throat as she swallowed. He stretched one of his fingers forward and stroked the edge of her protruding tongue.

'She is a pretty thing is she not, my lord?'

Praxis smiled and nodded.

'Watch, my lord. I will parade her for you. She will prance and sit and wait if I tell her. Watch my little beauty, my obedient little animal, perform for her mistress.'

Praxis sat back in his chair. Calliope yanked the lead attached to Weena's collar. Her head was pulled back. Milk ran from her lips and down over her chin. She looked round nervously, as if she had been unaware of anything as she had drunk from the bowl.

Eva leant against Praxis. She ran her hand across his thigh and gripped his weighty cock in her hand.

'Mistress Calliope asks you to see her pet. But, my lord, she forgets your suffering. She forgets how you must endure blindness. She forgets how you must prevail in eternal darkness, cruelly injured by the vengeful Ajax.'

'But he too is blinded. By my own hand he now lives in the darkness like me.'

Calliope strutted around the tent with Weena on the lead.

'Look, my lord. See how she prances. Look how I have taught her to lift her paws. She is the most elegant little beast do you not think? And see, the lead dangles only loosely at her neck. I have no need to remind her of the control her mistress has over her.'

'Again, Mistress Calliope mocks you, my lord,' whispered Eva, as she tightened her grip on his stiffening cock. 'She asks you to see a world to which you are blind. She taunts you as Ajax does.'

'How do you know he still taunts me?'

'Can you not understand, my lord? He is taunting you through Mistress Calliope. She is teasing you. She is mocking you.'

Eva pulled her hand up his cock, feeling its stiffening shaft expanding under her massaging grip.

He lifted his hips, pressing his burgeoning cock harder into her hand. She responded by slipping her encircling palm along its length. She stretched the skin of his scrotum as she drew her hand towards its tip, then tightened the skin against the back of his throbbing glans as she drew it down again.

'Tell me,' he said.

'Look at her, my lord.' Eva kept drawing her hand up and down the shaft. 'See how she parades her prancing slave. But Calliope herself should be on that leash. I could make her prance better than the one she holds on the collar. Sire, if only I had the chance, I could train her better than any beast. Calliope would purr at my feet. She would lap at her bowl in the evening. She would lie by the great fires on the beach until I tied her to a post for the night. Sire, if only I had the chance. The chance to please you.'

Eva let her head fall onto his shoulder. Her tangle of red hair curled down onto his massive chest in a fiery tangle. He inhaled its scent. She lifted her face to him. Her wet lips glistened in the torch light.

'Sire, Ajax plots against you. Even now, he hatches his plan to overthrow you. I can help you, master. I have his confidence. He confides his plans in me. Sire, if only I had the one who prances before us. The one who leads another. If only I had Calliope on a leash. If only I had her to control, then, my lord, I could help you vanquish once and for all, the mighty Ajax. Even now, lord, his hatred for the one who tricked him, your prancing favourite Calliope, feeds his anger. It is not to your benefit to have her as an ally. Give her to me, lord, and I will make Ajax my pet as well. We will overthrow him together. At last, you will be revenged, my lord.'

Calliope led Weena across to a young male slave. Weena's taut buttocks squeezed together as she moved. Calliope pulled back the leash and brought Weena to a stop. Weena waited silently on all fours, nodding her head slowly. She looked down at the young slave's feet and licked her lips.

'See, my lord,' said Calliope, seemingly ignorant of Eva's attention to Praxis. 'See how my little pet serves even slaves. Here, girl! Lick this slave's feet. I want to see your tongue between his filthy toes. I want to see his feet cleaned. I want to see them shining with your saliva. I want to see how my little animal is so humble a beast that she cleanses a slave's feet with her tongue.'

Calliope pushed her foot against the back of Weena's neck and forced her face against the slave's foot. Weena licked her tongue out and drew it across the young slave's dust-covered foot. Her spit soaked up the dust and dried straight away. She tried again but the same happened. She bowed her head and squeezed as much spit into her mouth as she could but, when she tried again, the same thing happened. She turned and looked up nervously at her mistress.

Calliope scowled.

Eva saw Calliope's anger. She dropped her mouth onto the tip of Praxis' cock. She encircled it with her full lips and flexed her fleshy tongue around its throbbing mass. She pulled away. Bubbling spit dripped from her mouth as her bright blue eyes turned up to him appealingly.

'There, my lord. See how your Eva needs your seed.' She sucked back the spit noisily. 'Listen how my excitement fills my mouth with spit. Hear my wetness for you. Hear my desire. But listen to your other servant, sire. Hear how she taunts you, mocks your blindness. Hear how she begs with a slave who will not attend to her orders. Master Praxis, let me draw out your semen. Let me suck it all into my mouth and swallow it down. I need to feed on it. I need to mix it with my spit and drink it. It is my elixir. And let me attend to your needs of vengeance too. Let me help you vanquish your foe, Ajax. All I need is the one before you, the one who battles for control of her own pathetic slave. All I need is Calliope to be my own, leashed pet. All I want is to take her on a lead. To train her properly. To make her obey. To train her to give you pleasure.'

She dropped her mouth back around his cock that

throbbed stiffly in her grasping hand. Again, she enclosed its tip with her full, wet lips. She took it in, as deeply as she could. She did not pause, did not hesitate. She took it into the back of her throat and held it there, letting it swell. She swallowed on it, but it was an incomplete swallow, it gripped his shaft into her throat and held it in place, tight and fixed. She felt the stream of semen building at its base. Still, she kept it tight. She felt it flooding up the shaft. She gulped at it. She swallowed again. Her already contracted throat tightened even more. Its narrowing constriction tightened around the end of his pulsating cock as it splattered her innards with its searing, hot fluid.

Calliope watched Eva as her body rose and fell. She watched her squirming, her face buried deeply into Praxis' groin. She saw her thighs opening, revealing her glistening crack. She watched the breathless swelling of her chest and the thrashing of her desperate limbs. She saw the strands of her fiery hair sticking sweatily to her smooth drawn cheeks.

Calliope snatched viciously at the lead in her hand. It yanked against Weena's neck. Weena cried out weakly. She could do nothing to satisfy her mistress's command. She could not respond to her mistress's orders. She hung on the lead, transfixed, gripped with fear and inaction. She wanted to save herself from pain, but she did not know what to do to achieve her aim. She was frozen in the dizzying confusion of her hopelessness.

Calliope yanked at the collar again. She pulled it hard, snatching it angrily. Weena reared up against the tension. Calliope held the lead taut and dragged the slave sideways. Weena slid on her hands and knees but still, she did not know what to do. As the tension increased, she became rigid, still crouched hopelessly on all fours, still a frozen victim of her own terror.

Eva filled herself with Praxis' semen. She closed her

eyes and let it flow into her. As his cock began to beat less strongly, she pulled back a little, finding again a gap between its massive shaft and the sides of her throat. She swallowed heavily and let him draw it out. But she was reluctant, and sucked hard at the still dripping end before finally letting it go.

She took a long slow breath. She looked up at Praxis, his empty eye sockets staring ahead into incessant darkness.

'That is all I need, sire. To serve you. To have Calliope to call my slave. To bring you vengeance against your enemy, Ajax.'

Again, Calliope forced Weena's face down against the slave's dirty foot. Again, Weena could not keep her tongue from drying. Again, her confusion prevented her from serving her furious mistress.

Eva held Praxis' flaccid cock in her hands, massaging it, licking it. She watched Calliope calling for a cane. She licked at Praxis' cock as Calliope forced Weena to bend over a bench. She licked it more as she watched Calliope bringing the cane down repeatedly on Weena's smooth, taut buttocks. She watched Weena flinching with shock, tightening her body with pain, crying out with fear and suffering. Eva drew her tongue along the heavy soft flesh of Praxis' cock as Weena was turned over on her back and caned across her small, hard tipped breasts. Eva watched the red lines appearing on the suffering girl's pale skin. She licked harder as Weena cried for mercy. She produced more spit to drool across her lips as Weena was spread eagled and caned across her tightly defined crack.

Calliope punished the helpless girl relentlessly. Eva felt her own cunt heating with excitement as she witnessed the fear, the pain, and the torment of suffering before her. She had suffered so much herself. She knew what the pain of a beating felt like — the searing shock of the cane's strikes, the hot anxiety of the degradation that came with them.

She understood the empty feeling of humiliation at the hand of a dominant. She knew the confusion of inaction brought about by suffering too much to be able to please. That knowledge only increased her excitement. Each stroke of the cane inflamed her more than the one before. Each scream of the terrified victim sent surges of heat along her swollen crack. Each red line that appeared on the girl's skin, hardened Eva's nipples more — made them ache, made them throb, made them feel as though they too were being beaten by the thrashing cane.

Eva cradled Praxis' heavy testicles in her hands, weighing them, squeezing them, toying with them.

Calliope had water fetched in buckets and thrown over Weena. The water splashed noisily against her skin, first between her legs, then her face and breasts. Weena had to be held down. She squirmed so much, and she was so wet, that once she escaped her captor's clutches. They caught her and tied her wrists together with leather straps to prevent her fighting against them. But, after her outburst, her strength was exhausted and she was easily subdued.

'Now!' shrieked Calliope. 'Now, let me see you lick the slave's feet! Now, let me see you clean the dirt from them with your tongue! Now! Now! Now!'

Weena was held by the shoulders and forced face down against the slave's feet. Water ran across her back. It glistened on her shaved head and dripped down her cheeks and off her nose. She tried to lick her tongue out, but she was shivering so much she could not control herself.

Praxis sat up but did not move Eva away. Eva again dropped her mouth around his cock and felt it hardening against her eagerly licking tongue. She stared at the helpless Weena and pressed her hand down between her own legs. Her swollen crack opened at her touch. She ran her fingers along it, prising it apart, feeling its warmth, its heat, its need.

Calliope's anger increased. She grabbed Weena by the ears and dragged her to her feet. She spat on the girl's face and spread it over her cheeks and eyes with her hands. She screamed at her and again forced her to her knees and commanded her to clean the slave's feet with her tongue.

Weena fell to the side exhausted. Her small frame shivering, her breasts rising and falling with her short, panting breaths.

The young male slave shuffled his feet uncomfortably. He was unable to hold himself back any longer. He had seen Weena before, even exchanged glances with her. He had hoped they would be put to serve together, that someday he would be able to talk to her, even touch her. He could not bear to see her suffering anymore. He bent to help her up. He knew it was wrong, but he could not stop himself.

Calliope exploded. She screeched at the top of her voice. She pushed the young man back angrily. She kicked Weena. She took up the cane again and thrashed at them both in a torrent of uncontrollable fury.

The young man fell back whimpering, realising his mistake.

Praxis suddenly jumped to his feet. He knocked Eva aside. She fell back, her mouth dripping with spit, her fingers still wedged into her fleshy cunt.

Praxis stood, his temples throbbing with anger, his pulsating cock still dripping with Eva's spit.

'Calliope! You have let me down. Even a poor weak slave betters you. If you wish to stay in my service, you will have to suffer some training yourself. From this moment, you will be the slave of Eva.'

Eva grinned broadly. She could hardly believe what had happened. Calliope set her jaw. She dropped the cane from her hand and squeezed up her eyes.

'And do not expect any special favours from me until

you learn better,' he said. 'I will ask for daily reports on you. From now on, your future relies on your new mistress.'

He turned blindly towards the moaning slave who had tried to help Weena. 'And take this young slave I hear whining for mercy to the brazen bull. I shall listen out for its song. Yes, feed him to the brazen bull. I will soon hear if the beast is pleased with his feast.'

Eva stood up and walked to Calliope. Calliope was quaking with anger. She looked to Praxis. His face was fixed. There was no sign of mercy on it. She dropped to her knees and allowed the collar to be placed around her neck. She looked up under her eyes as it was tightened. Her snarl turned to a grin as she responded readily to Eva's tug on the lead.

Eva sat on the chair next to Praxis. She held Calliope proudly on the lead. Calliope knelt by her side.

Eva listened to the young slave's pleas for mercy. She imagined him struggling against his captors. The picture she had in her mind of his tense straining muscles sent waves of searing heat through her trembling limbs. She imagined how he had been overpowered, how he had not the strength to fight against his persecutors. She pictured his sweat-covered face. She imagined the veins bulging on his forehead, his eyes wide with fear, his mouth agape. She heard his continuous, despairing screams. She cocked her head and listened as his voice became an echo — a hollow, ethereal cry of hopelessness, a feint distant counterpart of the man he had been.

She followed what was happening in her mind. She saw him being pushed, still fighting, inside the bronze beast. She heard his muffled cries being stifled. She heard the heavy thud as the door in the side was slammed shut. She listened to the bolt being closed as the man's begging screams were finally and completely shut in. Then she heard the crackling of the fire as it was lit beneath the massive statue. She cupped her hand behind her ear as she listened to the first gasps of anger as the brazen bull released its furious cry.

'Listen to the bull, master,' said Master Wang excitedly as he ran into the tent. 'It is truly infuriated. It glows with heat and calls out to the gods to save it. Hear its cries. It is as though they come from hell itself.'

Praxis cocked his head to the side. The poor young slave's cries resounded around the tent. Praxis sniffed the air, smelling the heated bronze, the flames of the fire beneath the brazen bull, the aroma of the slave inside its inflamed carcass.

Eva felt the warmth of Calliope's body against her leg. She thrilled at the thought of her waiting at the end of the leash for instructions from her new mistress. But the excitement that filled her body was produced not by the captive Calliope, but by the suffering of the slave she could not even see. Her head was full of the roaring of the brazen bull. Her ears rang with it. Her head pounded. Her mind was a panic of thunder and lightning and images of hell from which the beast had been born. Her whole body quivered to its song. Its clamouring bellows overpowered her. She was a victim to its fury. Herself, a slave of its savage power.

Eva tugged Calliope's lead. She pulled Calliope's head between her open thighs. Calliope smiled and opened her mouth. Eva pulled her closer. Calliope's tongue reached out from her wet lips. Eva drew her in until the tip of her tongue touched her wet, waiting crack. Calliope licked along its length. It opened to the warm contact. Eva pressed herself forward onto Calliope's tongue, allowing it to reach inside and lick at the soft wet interior of her waiting, needy flesh.

Eva dropped her head back in ecstasy. Calliope pressed harder against the soft, wet flesh. Eva felt Calliope's tongue lapping inside her. She felt its tip searching out the deepest parts of her flesh. She felt its edges squeezing against its insides. She felt her clitoris swelling against it, throbbing to the rhythm Calliope's tongue set up as it moved to the tempo of her own desire.

Eva pulled harder on the leash, tightening the collar, bringing Calliope in closer. She felt Calliope's cheeks against the insides of her thighs, the heat of her face against her taut skin. She saw a slave standing with the cane Calliope had used to beat Weena. Eva motioned to him. He moved closer. Eva nodded. He lifted the cane behind his shoulder. He waited for her instruction, for her command. She held back for a moment, savouring the control she had over the slave, his action, and the sway she had over Calliope's pain.

But she could not stand waiting for long and nodded to the slave. He brought the cane down quickly. It struck Calliope's smooth buttocks with a sharp, cutting snap. Calliope tried to rear back, to act in response to the sudden, shocking pain. Eva held onto the leash and Calliope could not move. Eva gasped as she felt the shock passing through Calliope's body. She felt the thrills of excitement surging through her as she realised she had Calliope under her control. She shivered as she saw that she could restrain her, hold her close against her cunt, prevent her even from rearing back from the pain Eva herself was responsible for inflicting.

The cane came down again — another quick slicing cut as it fell against Calliope's exposed buttocks. Again, the shock, the suddenness, the penetrating pain. Again, Calliope reared back against the restraining collar. Again, she was held in place — forced to stay with her face buried between Eva's thighs, her tongue, lapping inside Eva's cunt.

The cane was brought down repeatedly — each strike at Eva's command, each blow a surprise to its victim. Each shock of pain it brought was a demand for Calliope to rear back. Each tensing response from its victim was a reason for Eva to hold onto the leash that much tighter, to restrain her captive that much more.

Eva closed her eyes as she felt the rush of oncoming ecstasy within her.

The slave held the cane above his head, waiting for the next command.

'Do not stop until I tell you.'

Foaming bubbles of spit dribbled from her quivering lips.

'Do not stop!'

She held Calliope in place. She kept her thighs firmly around Calliope's head. The leash pulled tightly against the collar at her neck. Each blow of the cane brought more thrills of heat. Each smacking contact increased the pressure of her building joy. Each breathless, prevented reaction from Calliope, brought the resolution to Eva's effort that much closer.

Eva opened her mouth wide and gasped as it finally flowed. She held onto the leash and groaned — jerking, panting, listening to the cracking cane, the stinging blows against the tight flesh of Calliope's taut, upturned buttocks. Eva screamed as it ended — a final rush of heat, a final clenching of pressure inside her quivering body. She fell back listening to the sound of her gasping breaths. Then, like an accompanying orchestra, the cries of the brazen bull came back into her head. Its angry bellows were still issuing from its fiery nostrils. It filled her again and she reared up, drawing the leash as tightly as she could, as another wave of ecstasy surged through her in a massive swelling tide.

Finally, Eva relaxed the pressure on the lead. Calliope did not pull back. She stayed where she was, licking the moisture from Eva's cunt. She purred, pushing herself against Eva's thighs, wallowing in the joy her mistress had succumbed to, drinking from its source, quenching the thirst she had for her own satisfaction. Calliope was a willing pet.

Chapter 8

Suffering in Polydorus' brothel

Sappho held her hands up to her eyes as the doors to her cell were opened. For a moment, she was confused — she did not know where she was.

Blinking against the dazzling light of the sun outside, she saw again the images of the women in lion skins being chased by the men, themselves covered in the skins of beasts. She felt the thrill it had aroused in her. She saw again Chryseis cowering beneath the ferocious whipping that Polydorus had given her. She saw again the burning tip of the cracking whip, and Chryseis' reddened buttocks. Her stomach filled with nerves as she realised that her friend had been taken away from her, and that she was alone.

'Bring her out!' shouted a guard. 'Polydorus wants to see her. And he is impatient.'

A hand grabbed Sappho's arm and pulled her to her feet. Another hand forced itself between the tops of her thighs. She felt a silky line of moisture along her crack, and she felt it being squeezed onto the probing fingers of the powerful hand.

'Quickly! Bring her!' shouted the guard. 'She has seen enough pleasure from us. And she did not even wake! Quickly! Our master will be furious if we keep him waiting.'

Sappho stumbled forward. She ran her own hand down the front of her stomach and onto her wet crack. Her fingers slipped along it easily. She took her hand away and held it against her nostrils. She smelled the aroma of semen on her fingers.

'Yes, come, my sleeping beauty,' urged the guard. 'Your master, is waiting.'

They pulled her into the bright sunlight. She wiped her

bleary eyes with her semen soaked hand. She inhaled the musky aroma. She realised what had happened. Even as she had slept, she had not been safe from the attentions of her guards. Even as she had dreamt of Chryseis and their time together, the soldiers had been thrusting their cocks onto her and splashing their semen into her soft, wet cunt.

She saw Polydorus standing between his pony-girls. He fed them titbits from his upturned hand. They nuzzled against him, pushing gently at each other for a position closer to their master. He stroked them as they fed. He ran his free hand down their backs and across their rounded buttocks. Their plumed headdresses shimmered in the sunlight. Their leather harnesses gleamed. Their slightly sweaty, smooth skin glistened and shone. Their eyes burned bright with enthusiasm to serve their master.

He looked up as Sappho was dragged forward. She felt ashamed of herself compared to the fine pony-girls. She looked down in embarrassment at her filthy feet. She stared at the streaked dirt on her thighs where the semen from her unknown lovers had been spread and smudged.

'Wash her down!' shouted Polydorus. 'And be quick. My important guest will be here soon.'

He turned back to feeding his pony-girls.

Sappho was pulled along a covered walkway to an open door. She was too confused, and too weak to struggle as they dragged her inside a high-ceilinged square room.

Women hung on ropes around the walls. Their strained bodies shimmered in the dancing red light from spluttering flares set on poles at each corner. Others were held cowering on their knees under the overbearing threat of canes and whips. Some were hooded, some bound by the ankles, some gagged. All shivered with fear. Each of the guards held a cane or a flail above their heads ready, at any time, to bring it down in punishment for some transgression or simply to gratify their need to inflict pain.

They pushed Sappho down in the centre of the room. She looked at the captives. On the one side of the room, three women hung from ropes bound around their wrists. They hung freely, swinging slowly in circles, their bodies taut under the strain of their weight. All three drooped their heads, but whether in shame, despair or exhaustion, Sappho could not tell. A long strand of glistening spit dribbled from the mouth of the woman in the centre. She looked up slightly and stared for a moment at Sappho before dropping her head back heavily. The strand of spit stuck to one of her nipples and dripped onto her feet.

On the next wall, three women had their wrists tied together behind their backs and then to their ankles. They were gagged with large leather-covered balls secured behind their heads by leather thongs. A strap was fitted across each of their foreheads and this was led back to the bindings behind their backs. In this way, their heads were pulled back, continuing the half circle described by their bent back bodies. Leather straps had been used to bind them. These were wound into a metal ring which was attached to the end of a rope suspended from the ceiling. The women spun around giddily. Their bodies bent agonisingly. Their breasts pressed flat against their chests. Their slits were tightened by the pressure. Their gagged mouths stretched their jaws into a gaping yawn. Their eyes were wide and dazed, unable to focus on anything for a second. They reflected the terror of captivity and the anxiety of a future which could only hold more pain.

On the third wall, three women were each secured to a timber crucifix. Their arms were lashed to its cross beam, their ankles secured tightly to its upright. Their bodies curved to the side so that their knees bent slightly. The woman in the centre had her nipples pinched between two wooden slats clamped together at each end by tight bound leather straps. The women on either side of her had upturned buckets over their heads. Water ran down their bodies and dripped from their feet onto the ground.

On the last wall, three more women hung suspended by their ankles on ropes. They all had hoods over their heads. One of the hoods had worked down over the woman's chin until it rested against her nose. Her mouth was clearly visible. Sappho's heart started pounding as she recognised Chryseis. She wanted to call out to her, to let her know she was there. But, as she strained forwards, she was knocked sprawling onto the ground. She thought of running to her friend, of rescuing her, saving her from the terrible ordeal. But she shivered with fear. She lay on the ground, looking away, unable to move — too afraid to go to the aid of her suffering friend.

'Wash her down!' shouted one of the guards. 'She's filthy!'

Sappho struggled to sit up and see what was happening. She did not have time to look around before a heavy splash of water hit her in the face. It knocked her over and she fell backwards. She gasped with the shock and struggled to pull her legs together, to get up, to protect herself. Another bucket of water was sloshed over her. It hit her full in the chest. She gasped for breath, dropping her jaw wide, trying to wipe the flooding water from her face. Another, between her legs, sent shivers of pain along the exposed crack of her cunt. Again, she tried to bring her legs together, but two guards held them wide. They pinned her ankles down and laughed as bucket after bucket of cold water was sluiced over her. Her head was knocked from side to side by the force of it. Her nipples ached, her skin tingled, and her mouth bubbled with spit as she struggled to get her breath.

She was dragged to her feet. They did not dry her. She was led, dripping and shivering through an adjoining door into the next room. She glanced back to the hooded women. She saw the pitiful figure of Chryseis. Just to know she was there, reduced her fearful loneliness. Perhaps Chryseis would forgive her, understand why she could not help? As she stared, her face was gripped in powerful hands and turned away from the sight of the friend she had let down.

The room was dark. No torches lit it, no shadows were reflected from the suffering bodies of captives.

'Aha! At last. My little prize.'

Polydorus walked towards her out of the gloom.

'Light!' he shouted.

Torches were brought in hurriedly. Their flames reflected a turmoil of wriggling shapes on the dark walls.

Sappho shrank back in terror.

'Do not be afraid,' said Polydorus. 'They are merely shadows.' He took Sappho's face between his hands and pointed it towards the ceiling. 'Of these!'

Sappho stared upwards terrified. Many ropes were suspended from the ceiling, all different lengths, different thicknesses. Between them were leather slings and tapes, some shining with moisture, others glistening with silver studs and buckles.

Polydorus laughed loudly.

'Secure her! Make her ready for my special guest. I do not want to disappoint my own dear brother.'

A guard lifted her up in his muscular arms. He held her high, her slit close to his face. First her arms were stretched out and her wrists secured to leather slings. The pressure on her chest was almost unbearable. She squirmed from side to side to try and relieve it. The guard holding her up was so strong that, for all her twisting and turning, he still held her firmly in his grip. Next, her legs were pulled wide and her ankles laced around with wet leather loops. She felt her crack open as her legs were stretched apart. A coolness ran along her slit as the moisture along its edges made contact with the air in the room. Then she felt a warmth against it. The guard had drawn her close to him, close enough to reach her slit with his probing tongue.

He drew the flat of his tongue along the full length of her crack, first from front to back, then the other way. As he pulled it back toward the front, the full width of it pressed against her swelling cunt. She allowed herself to drop onto his hands, hoping to relieve the pressure on her wrists, hoping to let him take the full weight of her body. But the slings on her wrists were stretched so tight they kept her fast, stretched out, strained and racked with pain.

Sappho shivered along her arms. The weight of her body strained them so much they picked up all the sensations that were running through her. The guard's tongue lapped again along her cunt. He drew its underside against her clitoris, pressing at it, circling its base. He pulled it down to the rear, stopping for a moment before letting the tip enter her dilated anus. She wanted him to bring it back to the front. She wanted to feel its fleshy warmth against the softness of her cunt. But she also wanted its tip delving into her anus. She wanted to drop down onto it, to wriggle herself over it, to take it in as far as possible. She wanted him to taste her very innards. She wanted him to feed on her, to delve into her rectum, to lick its inside, to feast on her. She wanted him to exploit her exposure fully, to stretch her wider, to probe her deeper with his wet tongue. She wanted him to use her, to deny himself nothing, to consume her completely in any way he chose.

She tightened her arms against the leather loops at her wrists. She lifted herself against them. She pulled against the tension of her own weight on them. She stretched herself in an effort to make herself more open to him. He took the swollen flesh of her cunt in his mouth, sucking at it, wetting it, drinking its wetness. She felt her body filling with heat, a fiery overpowering heat which consumed everything she was. She tightened her buttocks and felt her nipples pounding. A final lapping contact of his tongue against her throbbing crack, just the touch of its tip, and she felt the flood of her ecstasy beginning to flow. She tightened herself more, bracing herself for it. Then suddenly, it stopped. The tongue was not there. The heat was abating. The fear returned.

A slashing cut across her stretched buttocks made her wince with pain. She squirmed against her bonds, her legs wide, her arms outstretched, her cunt exposed. Another cutting slash of the cane and she shrieked in agony. Another, and she twisted hopelessly, contorting in confusion, frustration and terror.

'Leave her be!' shouted Polydorus. 'Save her for the wishes of my brother. Let him decide her punishment'

Sappho hung in her bonds, the straps around her wrists cutting painfully into her skin, the loops at her ankles stretching her legs wide. Her heart was pounding as she gasped for breath.

She blinked her eyes as the door was opened. A line of young girls was marched in. Each was naked except for white cotton material pulled up between their legs. It was sewn to fit tightly around their buttocks and pulled up closely between their cracks. They all had their heads shaved and each had a colourful garland of flowers resting forward on their foreheads.

Each of the girls was bent forward and their wrists brought down to their knees. Their wrists were secured by leather thongs to their knees. The thongs were led up around their necks so that they were forced to stare down between their legs. A ring was attached to the strap behind their neck and they were hauled up on ropes until they were suspended, squatting, from the ceiling. They were each pulled up in a line from the door to where Sappho was suspended at the far side of the cavernous room.

A figure appeared at the door.

'What have you for me, brother?' asked a deep voice.

'A rare beauty, Paris. A girl from the temple. A priestess no less. See how she waits for you. See how she stretches her legs wide for you.'

Paris looked to the far end of the room and smiled.

'And the others? In the far room?'

'They all await your inspection. But, they have been there for several days. They can wait a little longer.'

'Like fine wine, brother Polydorus, they improve over time.'

They both clutched each other and laughed.

'Yes, the longer they suffer, the more tasty they become.'

Two naked young girls ran forward and straightaway starting removing Paris' tunic. They slipped it from his shoulders and folded it carefully. They took his wide leather belt and removed the garland of green ivy which was placed around his head. He stood naked. Paris, the most handsome man on earth — envy of the gods themselves. Paris, prince of Troy and lover of the most beautiful Helen, princess of Sparta, wife of Menelaus and the reason why the thousand ships of the Greek army were beached on the shores of this foreign land.

'Here, brother,' said Polydorus. 'As always, the maidens of rain are ready for you.'

Paris stepped forward beneath the line of suspended girls crouching in their bonds. He looked towards Sappho.

'Ah, brother. She truly is a beauty, this priestess. You look after me so well. You cater to my needs so precisely. I will walk to her through the delectable rain of sensuality. I will approach her through the golden rain that washes me and prepares me for my ultimate delights. Yes, I need to bathe before my pleasure.'

Sappho stared at Paris as he stepped forward. He stood beneath the first woman and turned his face upwards. Sappho watched the first droplet squeezing through the tight pulled, thin cotton material at the woman's crotch. It fell gently towards Paris. Then another, before the first one touched his face, appeared on the surface of the white cotton. Another. Another. Then a shower, of perfectly separate droplets, rained down on him. He turned his face into the shower that doused him. He opened his mouth and licked his lips as the drizzling rain of urine fell into it. He stepped forward a pace. Sappho watched the droplets of urine coming through the next tight pulled piece of material. It rained down like the first — soft and slow. Individual droplets fell gently onto the welcoming face and naked body of Paris below. He walked forward and savoured them all. He wiped his face with his hands, washing himself in the delectable soaking. He opened his mouth wide and drank from all of them as they showered him with their gentle rain. Sappho watched his glistening body approaching. He was like a golden statue, beautiful, shimmering — a god.

He stepped out of the exquisite mist and stood before her. His wet body glowed.

Sappho felt herself shivering with fear. She looked from side to side, as if there was some power waiting in the shadows to save her.

'Do not be afraid, my little angel. Yes, for that is what you are, a little angel hanging in the sky, sent by the gods as their messenger. Yes, a delectable angel, bearing your succulent gifts, your sensual treasures. No, do not be afraid, my little angel. It is I, Paris. The one you have been waiting for.'

He held out his right arm and waited. An attendant ran forward and placed a thick spear into his hand. At its end, instead of a point, was a thick leather-covered model of a heavy cock. Its end was formed as a glans — swollen and flared. Its shaft was ribbed and venous, its length, prodigious.

He held it out in front of him.

'No, my little angel, do not be afraid.'

Sappho quivered as he moved the tip of the spear towards her. She looked at its black ribbed surface, its bulging end, its rigid length. For a moment, she turned her head, afraid to look any longer. But she could not take her eyes off it — it had transfixed her. Even though its bulk was terrifying, its shiny surface, its swollen end and her exposure to it, made it irresistible.

Paris lifted it higher, raising it on the spear so that it was between her open legs.

'Are you ready for it, my angel?' he said smiling. 'I see you are open. I see you are wet. But here, taste it first.'

He held the leather cock up to her lips. He pressed it against them. She smelled the leather — the scent of an animal. Her lips parted. She could not resist it. The heavy bulging end slipped inside her mouth. She closed her lips around it. She sucked at it feverishly. It filled her. She wanted it. She licked it. She covered it with her saliva. Bubbles of spit ran from her mouth and down ths shaft. She made more and let it run copiously along the shiny, ribbed surface.

Paris drew it back slightly. Sappho gripped it, sucking hard, using her lips to encircle it, desperate to keep it there, unwilling to release it.

'Ah, my angel, you must release it. Your moisture has inflamed it. Your sucking has filled it with a desire of its own. Release it, my angel. You will not be without it long. It will not disappoint you.'

Slowly, she let it out of her mouth. Bubbles of spit followed it. They stuck to its surface and dribbled in gluey strands from her lips. She drooled at the side of her gaping mouth. She felt her cunt swelling. She felt her slit open for it — hungry for its moisture. She stared at it, unable to think of anything else.

Paris held the tip of the leather cock against her wet crack.

He rubbed it against her flesh, wetting it more, moistening its edges, lubricating its entrance.

Sappho felt herself rocking on her bonds, swinging slowly forward and back. The edges of her cunt touched the leather cock as she rocked forward, and pulled away from it stickily as she rocked back. She dribbled more spit down onto it. It glistened in the torchlight as it ran down onto the leather cock. She was transfixed. She wanted more.

Paris held it more firmly against her. He allowed it in whenever she rocked forward, but still let it out when she rocked back. She stared down at him, hoping he would not pull it back, hoping he would allow it to stay. Slowly, he gave her more. Slowly, he kept a little more inside each time. Slowly, she took it. Slowly, her heat increased. Her eyes were blurred, her head spun, she was taken over by it. She felt her heart racing, her veins pulsating. Her temples throbbed, her mouth ran freely with spit. She was set on fire and nothing would cool it.

She rocked back and forth, each time taking more. She looked down at its black shiny mass between her legs. She saw it go inside bit by bit. She watched less of it come out. She saw less of it exposed.

Suddenly, she screamed. She could not help herself. It was a loud, screeching howl. She knew she had it all. She howled again. It was fully in. She belonged to it. She was the object of its desire. She was pinioned by it. Her body was on fire. Her ecstasy was released. It was as if a dam had burst, as if the tide of the universe was running inside her. Spit ran from her mouth like water. It drained down between her legs. But now it only ran onto the spear. There was nothing more to be seen of the huge leather cock at its end. She was filled with it, overtaken by it. She was a slave to it.

Paris handed the spear to one of the attendants.

'Cut her down,' he said. 'Bring her to my bed.'

Sappho lay back on top of silk sheets. Their cool smoothness sent shivers across her skin. She breathed in deeply. The scent of frankincense filled her nostrils. She felt giddy with its heavy aroma. She reached her hand out and felt the warmth of Paris beside her. He turned over lazily. A cup was placed in her hand. She sat up startled. A young girl in a thin, pleated tunic knelt on the floor beside her.

'Do you need a drink mistress?' she asked smiling.

Sappho took the cup and sipped from it. It was sweet and sticky — like fragrant honey. She sipped again and swallowed eagerly. The sweetness ran though her body. It filled her with warmth, with softness, with a sense of safety and ease.

She held out the cup for more. The young girl filled it.

Sappho drank the whole contents of the cup. She felt sleepy. She passed the cup back to the young girl. She lay back on the bed. She could not keep her eyelids open. She licked her dry lips and let her head rest back heavily on the massive bed.

A tall female figure appeared at the door. Her blonde hair curled around the smooth skin of her perfect face. She wore a long sheer dress of translucent silk that trailed lazily on the ground. It was Helen.

She took the cup from the young girl and smelled it. She smiled. She motioned with her finger. Two guards came in and removed Sappho. The naked Helen climbed into the bed alongside Paris.

'What shall we do with her?' asked one of the men holding Sappho.

'Throw her into the street,' said Helen, used to disposing of her lover's entertainment. 'We will hear no more of her.'

Chapter 9

The omen of destruction

Sappho was not sure what was happening to her. She felt hands grasping her arms, she felt herself being pushed, or carried, but nothing felt normal. Everything was a blur, a mixture of murky images, distorted sounds, flashing lights and shapes and forms she did not recognise.

She tried to concentrate on what had happened to her. She tried to picture the women suspended from the ropes, Chryseis, the golden shower of urine, Paris, the leather cock. But it was hopeless. She could not keep any images in her mind long enough to see them clearly. Every time she tried to form something, it became misshapen, deformed into something else, or it slipped away altogether. She felt her heart pounding with anxiety. She felt the wetness of sweat on her arms and legs. She felt herself trembling with fear. At least that was real. But it was not a consolation — it only fed her terror.

She smelled the scent of frankincense in her nostrils. Her head filled with its thick aroma. She felt herself choking. She tasted semen in her mouth. She swallowed and felt the shape of a cock against the back of her tongue. She sucked at it. She hoped to feel its venous shaft against her cheeks. She hoped to feel its throbbing mass against the back of her throat, But, as she closed her lips around it and drew it in, her mouth was empty, there was nothing there. She felt her cunt being filled. She felt the heat of a huge cock inside it. She felt her wetness running against it, bringing it in, allowing it to fill her completely. But when she reached down to grasp it, to feel its base, to feel its throbbing weight, there was nothing in her hands and her cunt was empty.

She was in a panic.

She saw lights around her. Torches — red, flaming, sparking, smoking, dithering in drafts of wind, burning higher, spluttering to smoke. She heard the voices of chanting worshippers — rhythmic, monotone, endless, hypnotic. She felt the heat of their bodies as they pressed around her. Their cloaks shimmered in the torchlight. She saw a naked young girl borne on their shoulders. They carried her between their ranks, displaying her, holding her up for scrutiny. They pawed at her as she was carried past. Hands ran along her naked legs. Fingers poked along her shaved crack. Her nipples were pinched and pulled. Her mouth was prised open. Her tongue was pulled forward and twisted at its tip. Hands stroked her shaved head, while others found the delectable curve that dished down between her prominent hips.

Sappho closed her eyes, but could not shut out the images. The dirge of the chanting worshippers filled her head. She shrank back as the naked girl was brought closer. She tried to crouch down, to hide, to make herself invisible, but it was hopeless. The crowd parted as the girl was offered alongside Sappho. Sappho watched the pawing hands clawing at the girl, pinching her, poking her, invading her privacy. She saw that the girl was bound, her wrists held tightly together with leather straps and laid on her stomach. Her ankles, restrained by a single leather thong.

Sappho reached up and touched the girl. Her skin was smooth and silky, unblemished and pale. The girl looked at Sappho. Her eyes were dark and doe like, her face calm and resigned. Sappho reached up and touched the girl's lips. They parted. Sappho let her finger inside. She felt the softness of the girl's tongue, its warmth, its fleshy wetness. She put her finger in further. She ran its tip along the inside of the girl's cheeks. She felt their tension, their wet velvety surface. The girl's eyes remained fixed on Sappho — staring deeply into her, penetrating her with a vacuous stare.

Suddenly, the girl closed her teeth on Sappho's finger. Sappho screeched and pulled her hand back. The girl would not let go. She bit down harder. Sappho screeched in pain. She howled and yanked her hand desperately. The girl lay motionless, her eyes still fixed on Sappho, her teeth still clamped firmly onto Sappho's finger.

The worshippers started shouting. Sappho was jostled. Suddenly, opening her jaws like a spring trap, the girl released her. Sappho fell to the ground, clutching her finger. Feet stamped around her in panic. She twisted to escape them. The noise of their frantic pounding filled her head. She felt as if it was going to burst. She thought she would get trampled. She panted breathlessly.

She fell onto her back. A man in a cloak bent between her legs and ran his tongue along her exposed crack. Another joined him and did the same. The first one poked his finger into her anus. She gulped as it went in deeply. He felt inside, twisting it against the lining, finding his way ever deeper. Still, the second one licked at her cunt. She felt his tongue around its wet edges, spit dribbled from his mouth and ran down into her filled anus. The finger in her anus slopped with spit. It twisted more. It went even deeper. She felt its tip in her rectum, exploring her innards, invading her completely, stuffing her full.

Suddenly they were gone. She felt hollow, empty. Her cunt was wet, cool, exposed. The worshippers were crowding around the young girl who had bitten her. She was lifted down from the shoulders of the men. They pulled at her frantically. She stayed still, apparently not noticing their grasping hands, their probing fingers, their prying eyes. They dragged her towards a shining white marble altar.

Sappho rushed to join them. She jostled with the crowd, pulling at their robes so that she could push her way to the front.

The young girl was carried to the altar and laid on its smooth top. Still she stared at Sappho, as if beckoning her, as if she had a message. The clamour died down. The worshippers fell back. They lowered themselves onto their knees. They clasped their hands together and started muttering in fearful prayer.

Sappho worked her way closer to the altar. She reached up to the beautiful girl and touched her arm. The girl did not respond. Sappho climbed up and looked down at her.

'Speak to me,' she said.

The young girl raised her head. She parted her sweet, full lips.

Sappho leant down and placed her ear by the young girl's mouth.

'I have a message,' she said. 'Troy will be destroyed. The columns of the temple will fall. Fire will consume everything. The women will be raped. The men killed. Only a few will be saved. There will be nothing left. But you will find your friend again and you will find new power in the kingdom.'

Sappho's heart pounded at the thought of finding Chryseis again.

'My friend. Tell me about her. Tell me about my friend.'

'You have seen her already. She needed your help, but you did not give it. She will come to you here, in the temple. That is where you will find her. It is in the house of Apollo that you will be reunited. That is all I know.'

The girl dropped her head back and sighed. Sappho sensed something was wrong. The worshippers starting wailing in a fearful dirge. One, brandishing a staff, ran forward and started waving it at Sappho.

'You have transgressed the law of the temple. You have broken our sacred rules and violated our sacrifice. The girl is worthless now. She has spoken. She has spent all her life in silence preparing for this moment. Now, it is lost.

The spell of silence has been broken. Only the wrath of the demon himself, the satyr of Apollo, can follow from this. Yes, he has been roused by your blasphemy. Listen! Already, he comes.'

Sappho climbed down hurriedly from the altar, but there was no escape. She heard the sound of hoarse breathing, like a dragon. She smelled the heavy aroma of frankincense. Her mind went into confusion. The columns of the temple seemed to bend as he approached. Smoke filled the air and then, as if stepping out of hell, he appeared.

He pounced up onto the rostrum where the marble altar stood. He had the head of a goat. Twisted horns curled out from each side of his forehead. His eyes were like red globes. His face was wrinkled and dark. His hands were horny and clawlike. His fingernails were long and yellow. From the waist down he was covered in coarse hair. He had thin bent legs, a long tail and cloven hoofs. His erect cock stood out from his groin, bent upwards and bulbous at the tip. His testicle hung heavily in a pendulous scrotum.

The worshippers fell back as he moved around the altar. He sniffed at its edges, then at the girl.

'She has spoken!' he cried in a broken, hollow voice.' I can scent that she has spoken! Who is responsible for this?'

One of the men in robes edged forward nervously.

'Have you an answer?' asked the demon. 'Can you explain this sacrilege?'

The man bowed and dropped to his knees.

'Speak!'

'Master. It was all as you expect from us. The girl had been kept since childhood in silence. We bore her here as you instructed. She was placed on the altar for your delectation. Then ... '

'Then what?' boomed the satyr.

'Then ... my lord, she was approached. She was approached and questioned. And she spoke.' The man fell prostrate on the ground. 'Forgive us, my lord, forgive us our wrongdoing.'

Sappho quaked with fear. She had never seen anything like the satyr. She had heard of them, had seen images on vases, but she had never imagined them in real life. She hid behind a robed worshipper, clinging to his cloak, hoping she would not be seen.

'Then who is responsible?' demanded the satyr. 'Who has caused this blasphemy? Bring whoever is responsible to me. Deliver this blasphemer to me and I may postpone my wrath on you all.'

The man crawled forward on his belly.

'It is a woman, master. She is here. I have her ready to offer.'

The satyr pranced forward. His hooves clicked on the smooth marble floor. He screwed up his wrinkled face.

'Then bring her! Let me see her!'

The man scrambled to his knees and scanned the worshippers. They moved aside and exposed Sappho.

Sappho cringed with fear as the satyr's eyes fell on her. She fell to her knees and clasped her hands together beseechingly.

'Please, master,' she begged. 'I did not mean to — '

'Silence!' he shouted.

He trotted around the altar and stood in front of her.

He sniffed at her hair. He clawed at her breasts with his long yellow talons. She pulled back. He stamped his feet in annoyance. She dropped her face and stood still. Her heart pounded. She gasped for breath. She felt as if her chest would explode.

He bent his head and sniffed her nipples. He took one of them between his yellow teeth. He bit down hard onto it. Sappho pulled back. She could not help herself. The satyr kept his teeth where they were, and looked up at her with his huge red eyes. She froze with fear. He closed his teeth harder around her nipple. A rush of pain erupted from it. It ran through her like a scorching fire. It throbbed in her breast, filled her chest, flowed up her throat and stuffed her mouth. She wanted to open it, to let it out in a scream, but his red eyes were still on her. She was too afraid to act. She was frozen with fear.

He released her and sniffed down the front of her body. He stopped at her navel and circled his nose around it. He bent and ran his nostrils between her hips, then down onto the front of her crack. He inhaled deeply. Again, he looked up with his red eyes and stared at her. He licked his tongue out. It was long and pointed, its fleshy form like a snake, angling itself in all directions. He laid its tip against the front of her crack. She gasped. The heat from his tongue was intense. It was like a scorching fire. She felt as if she was being branded by it. She drew back. Instantly he grasped her buttocks with his clawlike hands. He dug his nails into her flesh and brought her crack back close to his mouth. He exhaled loudly. She smelled his acrid breath.

'You must punish her!' he shouted to the murmuring crowd. 'I will enjoy this slit with my tongue. But it is you who must punish her. Only then will your terrible sacrileges be forgiven.'

The satyr twisted Sappho in his hands. She felt like a feather in his beastly grip. He lay on his back, bracing his hooves against the side of the altar. He brought her open legs across his mouth. Her face fell against his huge, bent cock.

'Now!' he screeched. 'Punish her!'

She felt his long talons digging into her buttocks as he pulled her cunt onto his mouth. His fleshy lips sucked at its edges, wetting them with his spit, heating them with his own fire. His long tongue delved inside. She held her breath. It was as if it would never stop. It probed inside her. First its tip examined the entrance — it licked the sides and sucked in the moisture. Then its writhing body, snaked into the deepest parts. It searched out its secrets. It found its untouched flesh. She rose onto it then dropped herself fully down. She wanted him inside her completely.

The heat of his cock against her cheek was almost unbearable. It rose and fell as it throbbed. Its angular curve accentuated its stiffening beats. Its bulbous end swayed under its own prodigious weight. She rested against it, sniffing at it, savouring the promise of it, not knowing if she dared take it into her mouth. Spit dribbled from her lips. She knew she must — it was irresistible. His tongue stroked her cunt. She lifted her face back a little and placed her lips around the heavy end of his pulsating cock.

It tasted sweet. She sucked at it. A dribble of semen oozed from it. Its salty stickiness increased her appetite. She sucked harder. More semen oozed out. She closed her eyes, relishing it, feeding on it.

Her jaw tightened as a sudden smack came down across her buttocks. One of the worshippers brought the cracking end of a leather whip sharply across her skin. The satyr kept his grip, his clawing talons digging deep, his clasping arms not giving way.

Sappho gasped, but it was hopeless. Her mouth was filled with the satyr's cock and she could not draw breath. She arched her back. Another cracking smack hit her hard. It laced both her buttocks. She felt the fiery tip snapping at her skin, burning her, scorching her. The pain shot between her hips and up into her chest. She gasped again. Again, it was an empty effort. The satyr pushed his cock deeper and she gagged as its bulbous end entered her throat.

Again, another snapping crack and the pains of fire filled her once more. Her head spun as she fought for breath, but the satyr would not release her. He held her buttocks tight, exposing them to the snapping whip, opening them to its scorching fire. And he kept pressing his cock down ever further into her throat. The further it went, the more it expanded against its sides, the more it choked her.

The whipping stopped. The satyr gripped her tighter. His tongue delved further. His sloppy mouth sucked more eagerly at her dripping cunt. His cock went deeper. She swallowed on it again. She felt its end swelling in her throat. He gripped her buttocks tighter, opening her to his mouth, exposing her for more punishment.

A lashing cane fell across her upturned buttocks. It cracked against her skin. Its sharp penetrating sting spread through her whole body. Its intensity filled her mind. She could feel nothing else. She could imagine nothing else. She had become a product of the pain itself. Another slash, another burst of pain, another massive sting. She was saturated by it. Her head spun. She sucked harder. She tasted the satyr's semen. Another lashing crack across her buttocks. She rose as much as she could. Her body could not stop itself. She swallowed hard. Another burst of pain — another shudder of anguish as the suffering took complete control of her.

She felt a moment of relief. There was a pause. The caning stopped. She let the satyr's cock down as deep as it would go. It was inside her fully. She swallowed on it again. She felt its venous surface against the inside of her throat. She did not gag anymore, she simply fed on him. He was nourishing her with his seed. She was hungry for it.

She felt a heat against her anus. The satyr's clawing hand pulled her buttocks wide. The heat intensified. It burned against her. Suddenly, it thrust inside, penetrating her completely in one surging entry. Her rectum filled with it and the burning cock filled her throat. She swallowed in shock and felt the scalding splash of semen from the satyr's cock. It ran into her stomach — a massive gluey flow. Her anus felt on fire. Her rectum was burning, full and stuffed. She swallowed hard and drank the satyr's flow, as her rectum was filled by the thrusting of the satyr's clawed finger.

She was released and fell to the ground. Her legs dropped open. Sticky flows of semen ran from her mouth. Her cunt was wide and wet. Angry red lines patterned her pale buttocks.

She stared up to the ceiling of the temple. It was glowing red. Flames licked around the massive columns. Braziers were overturned. Their hot coals spilled on the floor, setting light to the huge drapes and curtains that hung from the ceiling. Air was drawn in through the entrance in a massive gust. It fed the flames which quickly raged into an inferno.

Everything was coloured by the fiery glow of the conflagration. Worshippers, their robes ablaze, ran in panic to escape. Others flung girls to the ground. They parted their legs and drove their cocks inside them. They thrust at them wildly, desperate to reach their ecstasy, desperate for fulfilment before they were consumed by the inescapable flames.

Sappho could not see the satyr. The altar sank into the ground. A hole appeared where it had been. Instantly, it filled with muddy water. Fires broke out around it.

Sappho was pulled into the filthy pool. Flames licked around its edges. The men who had dragged her there, held her down. They pinioned her wrists and ankles and held her still. She choked as the muddy water splashed over her face and into her mouth. Worshippers jumped into the foaming pool and took their turn with her. Each one fed his stiff shaft into her — some in her cunt, some in her anus, some in her mouth. Sometimes two took her at the same time, sometimes three, sometimes four. The muddy water splashed around her, wetting her cheeks, cooling her heat as the flames burned around her and the temple crumbled to the ground.

Sappho suddenly opened her eyes. She looked down at her naked, mud stained body. Her legs were apart, a beggar dressed in filthy rags lay with his roughly bearded face between them. His tongue was licking at her cunt. She stared up at the ornate ceiling of the temple of Apollo. She did not know how she had got here. She squirmed herself onto the beggar's tongue. His slow, lapping licks were hypnotic. She drifted on the rhythm. It was as if she was rocking on the swell of a warm ocean. She thought of what she had seen and heard — the demon, the young girl, the portent of impending doom, the terrible fire, her humiliation. She looked again to the ceiling. The temple was still there. It had not been destroyed. A surge of relief ran through her body. She reached down and pulled the beggar's face closer. The images of destruction, of her degradation by the satyr, faded as she gripped his hair tightly between her fingers. She yanked at it viciously, pulling him as close as she could, tightening herself onto his delving tongue. She opened her mouth, but did not cry out. She lay silent, gripped in an ever tightening seizure, as she rose on the beggar's tongue in a massive, jerking and ecstatic orgasm.

CHAPTER 10

THE WOODEN HORSE

Master Wang held onto Praxis' arm and led him out between the beached ships and into a clearing amongst the dunes.

'Lord Praxis, this is the mighty wooden horse which is being built by Epeius the Persian. It is so fine, I can hardly describe it to you.'

'Try, Wang. I must know of this wonder.'

'It is huge, sire. As high as twenty men. It glistens like the sun itself. Shiny scales of metal hang as armour about its massive frame. Its wooden structure is brightly painted — red, blue, white, green. Its neck is decorated with garlands of fresh flowers. Naked girls stand high on ladders hanging them like pendants about its mane. They are so excited to be close to it, they press their cracks against it and smear its body with their moisture. Colourful flags dangle on its bridle and reins. In its belly, a heavy trap door hangs open. Inside, it is dark and empty.'

'It is like the brazen bull, Wang. It has a hollow belly.'

'Yes, my lord. That is where the soldiers will lie in wait. And women too, I hear. When the great horse is inside the mighty gates of Troy, then they will spring their trap. The women will slip down the ropes which will fall like entrails from the beast's belly. They will slide the bolts back on the gates. Once the gates are open, our troops will flood back across the plain and into the city. Master, victory will be in the hands of the Greeks at last. The city of Troy will be there for the taking.'

'How do you know all this, Wang?'

'I listened to the great lord Achilles as he hatched the plan with Menelaus and Ajax.'

Praxis scowled at the mention of his enemy's name.

'What part has Ajax in this?'

'He sails to Teredos with Agamemnon. It is Achilles who leads the raid from the horse. There will be many spoils from this enterprise, my lord. There will be slaves aplenty for anyone in a position to take them.'

Praxis understood what he meant. He was not going to miss this opportunity to increase his wealth and influence.

Eva stepped forward and stood alongside Praxis. Calliope crouched on all fours beside her, the tight collar around her neck. The lead attached to it pulled tautly in Eva's hand. Eva looked down disapprovingly at Calliope. She snatched the lead quickly. Calliope straightened her arms, bent her back, and raised her taut buttocks. The oval of her cunt was squeezed between them, the crack at its centre, tight and well defined. The slightest hint of moisture glinted on her luscious slit. As she moved, her flesh squeezed open. The faceted golden ring in her clitoris flashed quickly as it caught the sun's bright rays.

'That's better, my little pet,' said Eva haughtily.

Eva stepped forward towards the horse and pulled Calliope behind her.

A young girl was holding a pot of paint for an artist working on the huge construction. She wore a cotton smock, it was torn and splashed with paint. One tear in the fabric exposed her left breast — small and pert with a hard pink nipple. A smudge of red paint was smeared across it. Another rip, just inside her left hip, revealed the shallow line of her stomach as it dipped down towards the front of her delectable crack. Her head was shaved. The pot tipped in her hands as, tired and exhausted in the hot sun, her eyes closed and she lost concentration on her task. The red paint dribbled over the edge and ran onto her exposed thighs.

'What is this girl doing?' asked Eva arrogantly.

Epeius ran forward. Used to the scrutiny of his Greek masters, the sculptor and former pugilist was always ready to cater to their demands. In keeping with his own training as a prize fighter, he was strict and cruel and treated his slaves with sudden and vicious brutality. If they slacked, he punished them with no mercy. If they were defiant, he had them removed and they were never seen again. If they worked hard, and showed the proper respect, they were fed.

'My lord, Praxis. It is an honour to have you visit.'

'What is that girl doing?' asked Eva again. 'She looks like a woman of leisure. Surely she sleeps. And she spills the paint she is supposed to be holding. Is that how slaves act who are in the service of the great Persian, Epeius?'

Epeius looked over at the girl and scowled.

'Bring her to me!' he shrieked.

A rope was wound around the young girl's waist and she was dragged over to Epeius. She pulled as hard as she could against the restraining rope, forcing the muscular guard who held her to brace himself against her effort.

'I shall be interested in how you punish her,' said Eva. 'Do you have some shade for me and my pet?'

A male Nubian slave was ordered to bring a large parasol of ostrich feathers. He stood, holding the massive parasol in his huge arms. His loins were barely covered by a carefully worked gold coloured scarf. The outline of his genitals pressed against the soft material.

Eva beckoned him. She stood motionless as he brought her beneath the parasol's welcome shade. She tossed her head back disdainfully.

Master Wang led Praxis forward. He sneered at Eva. She ignored him. She considered herself immune from any threat.

Suddenly, the girl took hold of the rope and snatched it out of the muscular guard's hands. She placed her feet wide apart, bent her back and stood ready to evade recapture.

'I really cannot believe how some of these slaves are out

of control,' said Eva. She threw back her mass of tangled red hair. 'I could not tolerate such behaviour. See how my pet responds to my every wish.'

Eva slackened the tension on the leash and tapped her foot on the ground a little ahead of Calliope. Calliope bent her elbows and dropped her face against Eva's sandalled foot. She licked it carefully, allowing her tongue to move slowly along the leather straps of Eva's sandal. She poked the tip between each of Eva's toes. The leather of the sandal glistened with her spit.

Eva yanked the leash tight again. Calliope sat back on all fours. Her lips glistened.

Epeius lunged forward and grabbed the rope that hung from the girl's waist. She was shocked by the suddenness of his action. She clung to the rope as he pulled her over. She fell in a heap on the floor. Dust billowed up around her. She thrashed her feet on the ground in a frantic effort to pull against him and escape.

'She is indeed furious,' mocked Eva. 'But surely tameable?'

Epeius pulled the girl along the ground. She kicked her feet and twisted her body as she held firmly onto the rope with both her hands. He dragged her to some heavy wooden stocks. A large hole in the centre was flanked by two smaller holes on either side. The top bar of the stocks was lifted and, with two male slaves helping, the girl was forced to kneel down before it. They held her neck over the large hole and forced her wrists into the holes on either side. She was still kicking and struggling as they dropped the bar and finally trapped her between its confining jaws.

Epeius bent down and squeezed the girl's cheeks between his thumb and fingers.

'You will not shame me again, girl. You will receive a lesson that will be impossible to forget.'

The girl twisted and kicked. She was frantic. She spat at

Epeius. It dribbled over his hand. He shook it off. She spat again. It splashed on his leg. He wiped it away. All the time, he struggled to keep his temper under control for fear of more embarrassment in front of his visitors.

He grasped her cheeks again, pressing them in as hard as he could. She tried to spit again. It just splattered out over her lip and onto her chin.

'Impossible to forget!'

The girl kicked her feet in a frenzy. Some slaves fetched a wooden bar and lashed it between her ankles in an effort to stop her squirming. Still she twisted and turned. She lifted both her feet and kicked them back against the ground fiercely. Dust billowed up around her in clouds.

Eva laughed and bent to stroke Calliope on the back of her head. Praxis held his hands out, stretching his fingers forward as if they would somehow give him sight. Epeius kicked dust up at the girl's face. She spat at him again and kicked all the more wildly.

'What is happening?' asked Praxis. 'It sounds as though a wild animal is loose.'

'A slave out of control, my lord,' said Master Wang. 'Completely out of control.'

Praxis edged forward and reached down to the spitting girl. He held his hand in front of her face. She bared her teeth. He moved his hand closer. She parted her teeth and bit him viciously. He did not move his hand. His face froze. He set his jaw. With his other hand he opened her mouth and drew out his fingers.

'Bring my whip, Wang. I will show you how to subdue a slave. Even a wild one like this. She has bitten my flesh. She will find out that it was a mistake.'

He had two slaves kneel in front of the stocks. He gave them a thick piece of timber. He told them to hold it between them, in front of the girl's mouth, but not touching her. Two more male slaves were made to kneel and hold the girl's ankles for, even though they were pinioned onto the wooden beam, she still struggled and thrashed her legs up and down.

'When she has been subdued, she will take the wooden bar between her teeth. I promise you she will be gripping it soon. It will remind her of my hand. It will ensure she remembers my lesson. It will prove her obedience to Praxis.'

The girl spat at the bar. Her spit dribbled from it in gluey strands. She gnashed her teeth and bared them like an animal.

Eva leant the side of her knee against Calliope's shoulder. The warmth of Calliope's skin excited her. She watched the girl struggling against the entrapping stocks, the hands that held her down, the bar between her feet. She saw her anger and panic. She saw her pride and unwillingness to be subdued. She saw her fear, and she saw her willingness to tolerate suffering.

Eva saw herself in the girl. Already, her plight had set off the heat of excitement within her. Now, as the girl faced her punishment, Eva's anticipation was building like a growing fire. It released its heat within her. It softened her cunt, wetting its edges, making her ready. She pressed harder against Calliope. Calliope leant back, returning the pressure, signalling her own excitement.

Praxis took the whip in his hand. Master Wang positioned him.

'Master, she is yours,' he said.

Praxis flicked the whip and let its end drift lazily onto the ground behind him. Its length curled slowly then settled easily. It lay still, his wrist cocked, his arm flexed and ready.

Eva breathed in deeply. She sensed the locked up tension in the whip. She could see its power. She knew how much anger it had to release. She could already feel its sting.

She looked at the wooden bar in front of the girl's mouth.

She saw the resistance in the girl's face — her refusal, her defiance. Eva imagined herself in the girl's place. She felt herself locked in the stocks, pinioned, held down and, all the time, tantalised by the bar of wood that was held so close to her tight shut mouth.

Eva heard nothing as the whip curled for the first time. It lifted off the ground in a long slow swirl. It tightened into a curl, the curving loop rubbing against itself as it gathered all its unleashed fury in one tight pulled coil. As it crossed Praxis' shoulder, it released its ferocity. Its tip reached out eagerly for its target. It snapped as it coiled again at its fullest extremity, cutting into its target, precisely, perfectly, punishingly.

The girl howled. It was the cry of an animal in agony. The pain reached her whole body instantly. The small point of contact against the taut skin of her buttocks, was the key to everything she was. What emanated from it, suffused her in an instant. The level of pain did not diminish as it spread. The cracking snap of torment that was delivered to the point of contact by the whip, was the same when it reached her fingertips, her toes, her tongue, her mind.

Eva gasped with the shock of it. She could read the instant journey of sustained pain on the girl's terrified face. Eva felt her cunt moistening. She needed contact against it. She needed something pressing against her swollen flesh. She needed pressure against her throbbing clitoris. She needed something to cool her heat. She lifted her leg and straddled Calliope. Straightaway, the proximity of Calliope's body beneath her, filled her whole body with a surge of pleasure. She felt the promise of satisfaction. She was anxious, but she did not rush. She dropped herself slowly, seeing the oncoming contact in her mind but keeping it in abeyance, stalling it until the perfect moment.

Another slashing crack and the whip hit its target again. The girl shrieked. Spit spayed from her mouth in a storm.

Her whole body tightened as the wave of intense pain spread through her. Every part of her body felt the cracking tip of the whip. Every part of her mind was filled with nothing but the pain it inflicted.

Eva dropped lower. She felt the warmth of Calliope's body beneath her. She tightened the lead, pulling on the collar, straining herself against its tension. She gripped the leather loop tightly in her hand. She let it cut into her skin. She imagined it was the tip of the whip — the burning end of the slashing scourge, the punishing messenger of delectable pain that Praxis was meting out to the agonised girl.

The whip cracked again and again. Each time it found its target precisely. The girl's buttocks were quickly covered in red blotches and streaks. The cracking end of the whip left a red burning smudge, the lace thin filament behind it, an angry stripe. Praxis knew where it landed by the sound of the crack and the feel it delivered through the leather handle. Sometimes, he lowered it so that it slashed against the backs of the girl's thighs. Sometimes he let it drift higher onto the base of her back. Sometimes, he brought it down time and again in the same place. When he did this, the pain intensified until the girl could feel noting more of her body than that one particular part. Her whole being was drained into the source of her suffering. The pain had overwhelmed her.

Eva licked her lips. She let her free hand drift down the front of her stomach. Her fingers reached down and found the opening of the front of her crack. She parted the slit and slipped her fingers in against her clitoris. It throbbed at her touch. She massaged its base. She felt its swelling hardness and the excitement it was delivering to every part of her. Spit trickled over her bottom lip. She let it run onto her chin then she sucked it back.

She closed her eyes for a moment and listened only to

the slashing cracks of the vicious whip. Her head was filled with its anger. When she opened her eyes and looked at the girl, she saw she still had her mouth tight shut. She was still resisting the sanctuary of the bar that was held before her. The girl's refusal to accept the bar's refuge only fanned the flames of excitement that licked within Eva's smouldering body.

Praxis threw the whip down. It had done its job.

The girl bit hard onto her lips. She absorbed the pain which still pulsated through her in heavy, rolling waves. Eva could not believe that she had resisted taking the bar in her teeth. She could not imagine how she had held out against the pain. She could not understand how she had stopped herself from biting on the bar, how she had resisted dissipating the agony which was filling her, by clenching her teeth around its unforgiving thickness.

Praxis stood behind the girl. She clenched her jaws shut. She panted and gasped through her flaring nostrils. She squeezed her eyelids together and clenched her teeth again. She knew her suffering was not over.

A slave rushed forward with a long rod. At its end a massive black leather cock. It was perfectly shaped, its shaft ribbed, its tip bulbous.

Praxis took the rod on his hands. Master Wang held the cock and placed it against the delectable oval of flesh between the girl's upturned buttocks. The red streaks and blotched marks on her skin contorted as she tightened herself against it. Praxis pressed the bulbous leather tip of the massive cock against the slit at the centre of her cunt. The crack opened at its touch. He felt the moist softness as he pressed the cock against the girl's flesh. He held it there for a moment, then slid it in. He did not hold back or wait, he pushed it inside in one long thrust.

The girl yelped. She choked. It was as if it had reached her throat. Her fullness mixed with the still burning pain from the whip. She yelped again.

Eva increased the tension on Calliope's lead. She felt her weight, the stiffness of her body, the tightness of her collar. She tightened her knees around Calliope's waist and lowered her buttocks until at last they touched. Calliope's back pressed upwards. Eva felt its warmth against her splayed cunt. The moisture on her flesh spread against Calliope's skin. Eva felt a fresh fire inside her. Its flames licked her from inside — she was being consumed by her own passion.

Master Wang came forward with another rod. Again, it had a huge leather cock at its end. Praxis knew he was there. He leant his weight against the rod that was inserted in the girl's cunt. He nodded. Master Wang smiled with relish. He placed the bulbous tip of the second leather cock against the girl's exposed anus. She tightened her buttocks as much as she could, as she felt the threatening contact.

Master Wang pressed it against her dilating anus. She kicked her feet on the ground — a last wild demonstration of resistance, a final frenzy of hopeless opposition.

Eva watched the girl's feet kicking at the ground. She let herself drop heavily against Calliope's back. The second huge leather cock was pushed deeply into the girl's anus. A screech exploded from her mouth. Spit sprayed out as her teeth unclenched, as she admitted defeat. She gripped the bar between her teeth and held it, while the leather cock was drawn back before being thrust inside again.

Eva tightened her knees against Calliope as hard as she could. The tension increased between her thighs. She held herself there, watching the girl's teeth biting deeper into the bar of wood. She watched the girl relinquishing her defiance, giving in to her master's control as, finally, Eva's own orgasm was ignited and a raging inferno burned through her every nerve.

Epeius stood back proudly. The massive wooden horse was finally ready.

Naked women had leather belts tightened around their slender waists. Metal rings at the back were clipped into more rings on long ropes that extended from a trailer of wheels beneath the mighty horse's feet. The women stood in long lines waiting for the command to move. Their naked bodies shone in the heat of the midday sun. The hot air shimmered around them and dust rose in small whirlwinds around their feet.

Agamemnon organised the withdrawal of the army. The men clambered into their ships and rowed back out to sea. Within the hour they rounded the island of Teredos and anchored in its lee. From the beach at Troy, they could not be seen. Anyone watching from the shore would conclude they had returned to Greece.

Sinon, chosen for his rhetorical gift, stood at the head of the long lines of women. He waved them forward. Slowly, with slave masters wielding their whips on the backs of the naked women, the mighty wooden horse began to move. The whips came down in terrifying cracks, burning into the captives' backs as they were forced to muster all their strength and pull the huge horse forward. The huge wheels rumbled and groaned. Gasping for breath and sweating with the effort, the lines of naked women hauled the great horse out over the dunes and onto the plain of Troy where so many brave warriors had died.

CHAPTER 11

A GIFT FROM THE GREEKS

At sunrise, the massive horse was hauled by the naked women out across the plain of Troy. Flinching beneath the vicious whips of the harsh slave masters, they toiled for hours in the quickly building heat. None of them escaped the biting wrath of the leather tips. All bore the red lines inflicted by the cutting flails on their sweating bodies. In the midday sun, some fell exhausted to the ground, unable to go any further. The progress was halted. The unconscious women were hauled up on ropes into the body of the beast. There, they were thrown down — consumed by their efforts. Others, kept in reserve to take their place, were unchained, let down and secured to the ropes. At a signal from one of the slave masters, the women bent forward and began their task again. The cracking snaps of the relentless whips kept them at their labour until, again, too many dropped to continue the terrible journey without others being brought to toil in their place.

The sun dipped onto the western horizon. It dropped behind the island of Teredos, outlined as a dark shadow by the crimson glow that now lay behind its rocky form. At last, as the daylight disappeared, the wheels at the horse's feet finally ground to a halt at the mighty gates of Troy.

Some of the women collapsed to the ground. Even the whips could not bring them back to their feet. Some knelt and drew sand up to their mouths, so confused by delirium they drank it as though it were water to quench their thirst. Others stood, bemused, gasping for breath, staring into a distance that they could not see, a future they could not foretell.

Sinon marched forward. He stood beneath the towering walls and spoke.

'Citizens of Troy. I bear a gift for you all. Agamemnon has led his army back to sea. Your shores are empty. The Greeks have returned home. They have had enough of this terrible war, now, they seek only peace. To mark their respect for you, they leave you this mighty wooden horse. They wish you to accept it as an offering. Present it to your gods as a favour. I beg you to receive it, take it into your city. There it can remain; forever an emblem of the peace between our nations. Citizens of Troy, the war is over.'

Guards ran frantically along the mighty walls of Troy. Messages were passed, orders received. As dusk turned to darkness, all fell silent.

It was stifling inside the mighty horse. Exhausted slave women were packed in tightly, their naked bodies crammed together in a smothering heap. Eva crouched nearby. She held Calliope tightly on her lead. Calliope, on all fours, looked up at her, waiting for instructions. Eva bit her lips anxiously. She had been sent by Praxis to find suitable women for slavery. He said her future depended on her success. He had spent a great deal on bribes to get her into the horse, and he would not tolerate her failure. If she was successful, however, her reward would be beyond her wildest dreams.

Achilles and his men crouched amongst the wood and iron scaffolding that was the framework of the mighty beast. Huge timber uprights were clamped with iron bolts to cross members upon which an internal floor was laid. Soldiers stooped in the confined space, weighed down with their armour, anxious to see battle. Pensively, they ran their fingers along the edges of their sword blades. They tested the sharpness with their nails, satisfying themselves that they had done everything possible to prepare for what lay ahead. Achilles rested on one knee, waiting for the moment to break free from the innards of the horse. His piercing dark eyes reflected his single-minded preoccupation with victory and destruction. He was a warrior created for action. He had no other purpose. Two oil lamps burned in the horse's eyes. The light from them reflected back into the beast and cast a greasy yellow glow onto its silent occupants.

Some soldiers, restless for action, moved about silently in the belly of the beast. They appeared like wraiths in the half light cast from the oil lamps. They prowled amongst the sleeping women, stepping between their sprawled out legs, lifting their feet over the women's entangled arms. One of the men bent and circled one of the women's erect nipples with his fingers. She lay exhausted, unconscious, stifled in the heat, unaware of his touch. He circled her nipple again, this time offering more pressure. Still, she did not respond. She lay on her back, sleeping deeply, her legs wide apart, her arms pulled up above her head. The slit of her cunt could just be seen in the half light — the dark indentation between its swollen edges, a delightful invitation to what lay within. The soldier looked at his comrades. They came closer. One of them bent and ran his hand down the woman's flat stomach. He felt the curve of her thighs and followed the delicious line along her slender waist. Still she did not move — she was completely unconscious. Another let his hand fall between her legs, near the top of one of her thighs. He felt the soft skin, its tension and smoothness. He moved his hand up until it touched the exquisite flesh of her cunt. He pressed the palm of his hand against it. It was firm, but gave under the pressure. Still, she did not move. He let his finger press against the slit in her flesh. It opened to reveal a glistening line of moisture. He traced it with his fingertip. The crack opened more.

The two men knelt beside the woman, both aware of Achilles nearby, both conscious of the need to remain quiet inside the horse. Eva watched them. She saw their furtive eyes, their surreptitious movements, their grasping hands. She saw the heavily closed eyes of the woman, her mouth, half open, her chest rising and falling with her slow breaths. She listened to the rhythm of the woman's breathing. She reached down and stroked Calliope, picking up the tempo of the soldier's hand as he began massaging his finger along the woman's glimmering cunt. Calliope responded to Eva's touch. She rested her head against Eva's leg and purred.

The man pressed his finger against the woman's clitoris. Eva saw it raised between the fleshy lips of the woman's open cunt. She watched its throbbing end against the man's probing finger. She saw the woman's hips lifting against his touch. When she looked at her eyes, they were still closed tightly, still testimony to her sleepy oblivion.

The man was emboldened by her lack of response. He let his finger inside her cunt. Still she lay, silent, exposed, unmoving. He moved it up and down, as if it were a cock. She parted her lips slightly. He stopped for a moment, checking to see if she would rouse. But she did not. She remained quiet and still. The other soldier took his sword from its scabbard. He held the shining blade in his gloved hand. He offered the butt end of the handle, the pommel, against the woman's cunt, just beneath where the other man's finger was still inserted. She squirmed against it slightly but quickly stopped. The one with his finger in her cunt, pulled it out and presented its tip to her anus. He pressed it against the tight circular muscle. Eva watched it dilating under the pressure. It opened up for what was being offered, welcoming it in. Still, the woman did not awaken.

Calliope tugged on her lead. Eva held her back. The strain on the lead sent a quiver of excitement through Eva. She wanted it tighter, She pulled Calliope back, just to sense the excitement of the increased tension. Calliope eased herself against the lead's restraint, but slowly, not allowing the tension to decrease, keeping the pressure on her collar and on the loop of the leather leash in Eva's hand.

Eva licked her lips again as she watched the thick handle of the sword entering the swollen flesh of the woman's glistening cunt. The leather work on the handle glinted at the fleshy entrance. It soaked up the moisture that ran from it. It picked up the yellow light from the oil lamps in the horse's eyes. The man forced the handle in slowly. It entered up to the hilt. Still the woman remained motionless, completely at rest, her sleep undisturbed, her dreams uninterrupted. The other man pressed his finger into her anus. He kept the pressure up until his knuckle stopped it from entering any more. The moisture from the woman's cunt ran down the palm of his hand. It shone with wetness as he pressed his finger harder, just to test that it could go no deeper, just to be sure it was at the limit.

Calliope pulled against the lead. Eva held her back. This time the pressure was greater. Calliope's enthusiasm to pull against the restraining collar was increased. Eva felt spit on the inside of her bottom lip. She sucked it up onto her tongue. She swallowed it. She let Calliope have some slack in the lead. Calliope pulled forward, moving first her one hand then the other. Eva tugged at the lead, but only teasingly, not with any true purpose or intention to restrain. Calliope pulled against it.

A third man crouched above the woman's face. He held his cock in his hand and pressed the swollen end against the woman's still parted lips. She opened her mouth more as it touched. He waited and watched. She did not wake. He pressed it in. She reared up a little, opening her mouth wide, allowing it fully in. Still, she was asleep.

Calliope pulled more. Eva let her go forward — enjoying the movement as well as the tension. Calliope moved her one knee then the other. Slowly, she crawled another step. She stopped behind the man with the sword. Eva held her there, pulling the lead tight — waiting, expectant, filled with the excitement of anticipation.

Calliope pressed the side of her face against the man's thigh. He turned and saw her. He looked up at Eva, unsure what to do. Did he have her approval? Should he speak? Eva looked down at the woman and opened her mouth. She licked her tongue out and drew it back slowly. Calliope pressed harder and moved her head up and down against the man. She curled herself against him, bending her body so that her waist squeezed against his thigh. He removed the handle of his sword from the sleeping woman's cunt. He realised he did not have to ask for approval.

Calliope pulled harder on the lead. Eva allowed her some slack. Calliope crawled forward until she was by the side of the sleeping woman. She dropped her head and took the woman's erect nipple in her mouth. She raised her buttocks and allowed them to part enough to display the delectable shape of her fleshy cunt. The crack at its centre glowed in the yellow light. Moisture ran along its length. It parted more as she dipped her back. Eva pulled the lead back until it was tight, but she had no expectation, no desire, that Calliope would do anything other than brace herself against its tension,

Eva felt Calliope's panting breaths through the taut lead. Each tightening tingle in her hand told her of Calliope's growing excitement. She pulled it in front of her so that the loop of the lead in her hand was against the crack of her own cunt. The man with the sword held the pommel of the handle against Calliope's anus. It shone with the moisture from the sleeping woman. Calliope lifted herself to it. Her panting gasps increased. Eva held the tightened lead closer against her own crack. Calliope's breaths sent shivering shocks through the taut lead. They passed directly into the flesh of Eva's swollen, throbbing cunt.

Calliope's anus dilated and welcomed the handle of the sword. The rounded butt went in first, opening up the anal muscle, pressing past its elasticity, allowing it to close tightly behind its bulbous shape. Calliope's breathing quickened. The pulses in the lead increased. Eva's cunt tingled with excitement. The ribbed handle went in deeper. Its grip, bound with leather and wire and covered with sharkskin for a better grip, tugged against the silky flesh. Calliope started gasping. Eva held the leather loop of the lead tightly between the folds of her crack. She pulled it up between her flesh, tightening the shiny leather against her own moist softness. The handle went deeper, the shagreen tugging at the fleshy sides that it penetrated. Calliope panted so quickly than one gasping breath ran into the other. The tautly pulled lead vibrated with her effort. Eva clutched the loop against her cunt. She watched the sword handle go in up to the ornate cross guard — the whole of the hilt was inside Calliope's anus.

Eva looked over at the men with the sleeping woman, one with his heavy cock in her mouth, another with his finger deep inside her anus. Everything was silent except for Calliope's gasping breaths. Eva dropped to her knees. She wanted the handle of the sword penetrating her cunt. She wanted the man's finger deep in her anus. She wanted the throbbing cock in her mouth. She wanted to be in Calliope's place. She wanted to feel the collar tightly around her neck. She wanted to feel her mistress pulling at the lead, controlling her movements, taking away her will. She wanted to feel the restraining hand of another. She wanted to sleep while she was violated. She wanted to wake and find herself sore with the penetration of which she knew nothing. She wanted everything that was before her. She wanted every image in her mind to become reality.

Suddenly, she felt the powerful hand of Achilles on her shoulder. She jumped back startled and terrified. He held his hand across her gaping mouth, ensuring she did not cry out, making sure she knew she must be silent. She did not move. He let his hand drop. She remained still, overcome by the sensation of his powerful body, his closeness, his strength. He nodded slowly. She took his nod as an order to remain silent — to keep still until he told her otherwise. She thrilled at being in his control. She kept the strap of the leather leash close to her cunt. Shivers of joy ran through her whole body in a massive, surging tide.

Achilles looked at the man who held his sword handle deep in Calliope's anus. The man pulled it out. Calliope gasped and dropped forward. Spit ran from her mouth. It stretched down in gluey strands to the boarded floor. Achilles knelt behind her. He lifted his leather tunic and took out his weighty cock. He held it in his hand as it stiffened and grew. Eva stared down at it, unable to move, hardly able to breathe. Achilles held the swollen end of his swelling cock between Calliope's buttocks, just touching them, just allowing them to feel the heat of his pounding shaft. Calliope, still panting, responded to its searing heat. She raised up on her arms and strained her head back. She tightened her throat, squeezing the exit for her panting breaths, making them even louder. Achilles held the throbbing tip of his pulsating cock against her open anus. Eva saw it widen as it sensed the heat. The tip pressed against it. Calliope's anus opened. The burning glans of Achilles' cock went in. Calliope drew breath in one sudden gasp.

Achilles picked up a rag and held it in both hands. He pulled it across Calliope's mouth. She let it in between her teeth and grasped it tightly. He pulled it back and, as he tightened it against her bite, he thrust his hips forward and buried his cock deeply into her anus. She breathed in suddenly and heavily through her wide nostrils. She bit down hungrily on the tight pulled rag. Achilles forced his cock in as deep as it would go. Calliope held her breath.

Eva saw it was fully in, its whole length had penetrated Calliope. She had it all.

Eva watched the sleeping woman, still the unconscious victim of the men. She watched the still swelling cock in her mouth as the one man massaged his hand along its length and coaxed his semen to run. Achilles thrust again into Calliope's welcoming anus. He held the rag as tightly as he could. Calliope inhaled and exhaled like a beast — a wild animal, brought to the ground, tied to a stake, and defiled by her ruthless captors. It was the desperate panting rasp of a panicked victim. A captured prey, unable to escape, with no will of its own. The terrible sound filled the carcass of the wooden horse. It reverberated through its mighty framework. It echoed inside its hollow limbs.

Still Achilles thrust deeper. Eva pulled hard on the lead. She felt the tension in Calliope's body. She felt the thrusting of Achilles. Her head filled with the gasping breaths of the ecstatic, out of control Calliope. Eva desperately wanted to get down in Calliope's place. She wanted to kneel before the great Achilles. She wanted to feel his prodigious cock buried deeply inside her anus. She wanted him to gag her with a rag and pull it back against her locked jaws. She wanted to feel her chest rising and falling against the heavy breaths she struggled to get through her wide, flaring nostrils. But she did nothing. She kept silent. It was his command. She hardly breathed. She watched and did nothing.

But the punishment continued to feed her passion. Her stillness infected her mania. She could not hold herself back. She felt it boiling inside her — sending her into delirium. She drew the leash loop close into her flesh. She pulled it around her clitoris. She tightened it. She pulled at it. She yanked at it. She felt the pain it delivered — the throbbing anguish it wrought. She rose on it. She tightened her jaws. She clenched her teeth. She fixed her stare.

Suddenly, it started to flow. She was drowned by an orgasm so massive, so overcoming, that were she able to move she would have collapsed at Achilles' feet, drooling, gasping, foaming at the mouth.

Still, she held it in. It exploded within her, and she did not let her body respond to its power. Her mind was full — of colours, of noise, of franticness. She was giddy. Her head spun. She shivered. Her skin tingled. She felt hot and she felt cold at the same time. She could see only Calliope and the sleeping woman, and what was happening to them. Everything was caught in a whirlwind of confusion. Achilles reared back and let his semen flow into Calliope's rectum. Eva imagined its flow — massive, hot and splashing. At the same time, she watched the sleeping woman — still unaware of her violation. The man's cock flooded his semen into her open mouth. It ran in a pool onto her tongue. It flowed over the edges of her lips. It dribbled on her chin and poured down her neck. It ran up into her nostrils, along the sides of her nose and into her eyes.

Eva stood rigidly, consumed by her joy — silent, still, on fire.

The horse's nostrils boomed with the gasping breaths of Calliope. Its eyes glowed with the yellow oil lamps in their sockets. The plain of Troy echoed with the noise of Calliope's ecstasy. The citizens, safe inside their walls, peered out over their ramparts and listened to the bellowing beast that lay before them. Its magic infected them. They were beguiled by it. The order was given to bring it into the city.

The mighty gates of the city creaked back on their massive hinges. It took a hundred men to haul them open. The women, some lying on the ground, some asleep in each other's arms, were brought back to their feet by the slave masters. They leant against the rings in the backs of their belts, tensioning the ropes, urging the heavy wheels to turn. Slowly, as the whips cracked loudly against the women's naked backs, the huge horse began the last part of its terrible journey.

The women dragged it to the centre of the city's main square. There it sat silently, its eyes still glowing in the dawn light. The women were unclipped from the ropes and carried away by citizens eager to taste the delights of Greek slaves. The cruel slave masters were themselves driven back outside the gates, the inhabitants of Troy fearful that they might be impossible to control, or that they might bring disorder to their wonderful city. The slave masters gathered outside the walls, refusing to leave until spears finally drove them back onto the great plain.

The sun rose. The heat of the sun burned down on the horse's mighty carcass. Shimmering swirls of heat curled up from its back as it baked in the relentless inferno of the day. Citizens of Troy came out to view the great statue. Some poked at it, some hung back fearful of its size and overbearing majesty. Some discussed what to do with it. Some even said it was a trick and should be taken back outside the city. Polydorus rode up to it on his ornate trap. His pony-girls reared back and whined as they approached and, even though he lashed their buttocks with his cracking whip, he could not get them to go any closer. As dusk came, the horse was surrounded by a large crowd but, as darkness encroached, they left it silent and unwatched in the middle of the empty square.

Chapter 12

The trap is sprung

Above the deserted square, guards stood on the walls looking down onto the silent wooden horse.

Polydorus drove his trap into the square. He had been with his brother, Paris, who had criticised him for being too soft with his pony-girls and he had driven them out into the city in a fury. He galloped them through the streets and tight alleys. He thrashed them relentlessly with his cracking whip. He yanked their reins, brutally pulling back the hard silver bits in their clenched teeth.

The beautiful pony-girls were covered in sweat and gasping for breath. They reared back and whinnied when they saw the mighty wooden horse. Polydorus pulled back hard on the reins and brought them abruptly to a halt. They slipped on the dusty ground, barely manaing to keep their balance. The trap pushed forward and the leather padded breachings pressed hard against their taut buttocks. Their plumed headdresses glittered in the light from the torches placed in the ground around the great horse. Their sweating bodies glistened, their shiny leather bridles and chest harnesses glittered and flashed. The leather thongs attached to their waistbands pulled tightly into the cracks of their cunts.

Dust flew up into Polydorus' face. He coughed and choked. He jumped down from the trap, his face red with anger. He cracked his whip in time with his furious cries.

'Halt! Halt! Halt!' he screeched. 'You have embarrassed me once tonight. I will tolerate no more insolence from you! My brother is right. I am too lenient. I am too kind!'

The two pony-girls bowed their heads. Their heavy headdresses — one yellow, one red — described two wide curves in the flickering torchlight. Dust billowed up around them in a cloud. They were exhausted. They could not calm down. They had been overrun and now were startled by the shock of seeing the mighty horse.

Polydorus ran to the front of them and grabbed both their bridles. He yanked them angrily. They reared back, frightened by his outburst, hurt by the pain of the bits between their teeth. He pulled them back, intolerant of their seeming defiance, unconcerned about their pain and anxiety.

'You defy me once too often!' he screeched.

He gripped the bridles tightly and drew their heads down. Their headdresses tipped forward heavily.

'On your knees! On your knees! On your knees!'

He pulled hard on the bridles. Both of them started to lower their bodies. The trap moved forward. The shafts tipped. The extra weight made the terrified pony-girls gasp. Their terror took hold of them. Polydorus struggled to keep his grip on them. They started to panic. He held their bridles tight. He shook them, trying to steady them, trying to bring them under control. They both whinnied and twisted. Each pulled against the other, each further startled by the movements of the other. They moved backwards and forwards. The shafts of the trap reared up and down. They were lifted off the ground as the trap tipped back, then bent over by the weight that bore down on them as it tipped forward. Polydorus grasped the ends of the shafts. He held onto the silver balls that crowned the curved hooks at the shafts' ends. He dropped his weight on them in a desperate effort to curb the trap's frantic bouncing buit could not control it. The two women were seized by a frenzy of fear and confusion. He tried to release them. He struggled with the rings on the back of their chest harnesses. He could not free them — the traces had become tangled in the shafts. He tried to pull the reins from their bridles. They had twisted around the backs of their heads and he could not liberate them from the snarls. They both became hysterical.

Polydorus took out his knife and cut through some of the tangled traces. The woman with the yellow headdress fell forward, a tight knot of leather strapping still wrapping her in its coils. The sudden movement of freedom frightened her more. Her eyes rolled upwards. She was driven into a giddy state of uncontrollable fear. Polydorus cut frantically at the other traces. He sheered them all, but the woman in the red headdress was so entangled in them, and they were so tightly twisted, that still she remained enmeshed in its snaking whorls. She threw herself about wildly. She thrashed from side to side. Suddenly, the trap twisted up on one wheel and threatened to tip over. It pulled forward and trapped itself in the opening to a narrow alley that led from the square. Polydorus could not move it. The pony-girls began to scream.

He looked around for help. There was no one else in the square. He looked up onto the ramparts of the mighty walls. He saw the guards staring down.

'Guards! Guards!' he shouted. 'I need help. Come down here and help your lord, Polydorus.'

The guards looked at each other in consternation.

'My lord, we dare not. We are commanded to guard the city. We cannot leave our post for fear of our lives.'

Polydorus struggled with the bucking trap.

'Only King Priam and the gods themselves dare speak against your lord, Polydorus. I order you to my aid. Do not incur my wrath. The outcome of defiance would be more than you dare imagine. Come down from the walls at once! Here! To my aid! To Polydorus' aid!'

The frightened guards hurried along the high ramparts and climbed down the steep stone steps to the ground. They ran across the square into the neck of the narrow alley.

Eva watched through a crack in the boards of the horse's side as the guards ran over to Polydorus. The sight of the pony-girls' panic inflamed her. The constriction of the tangled leather traces around their bodies, the tightness of the twisted reins around their heads, sent shivers of excitement through her tense body. She tightened her hold on the loop of Calliope's leash. She pulled it against the collar around Calliope's neck. She could feel Calliope's rapid breathing through the taut leather leash. She pulled it tighter. She could feel the beating of Calliope's heart. She pushed the side of her knee against Calliope's slender waist. She could feel the blood racing in Calliope's veins.

Eva pressed her face against the crack in the timbers and stared at the plight of the terrified pony-girls.

'Lord Polydorus. What can we do?'

'These defiant ponies have let me down. I invest in their training. I feed them and give them warm dry bedding. They feed from silver bowls. They are washed down and oiled each day. Look at their finery. Look at their beauty. But my kindness is wasted. That is the problem. I am too kind and wrestle with my conscience. I try to act with virtue. I am benevolence itself. But kindness does not lead to obedience. It is a sorry tale. I must punish them. They must learn that serving Polydorus is their only aim in life. They must learn not to take advantage of his kindness. It breaks my heart to do so but it is the only way.'

'Yes, lord. What can we do?'

'Bind them to the shafts. I want them to feel the pain of disobedience. I want them to know why they are being punished. I want them to suffer from the thing they need to serve. It is the trap itself that will form the framework of their punishment. And they will know who makes this demand upon them. It is the hand of Polydorus that will wield the tool of their suffering. Lift the first one. Bring her here. And hold the other. Do not let either of them free from the bonds that entwine them. The feel of the leather will remind them of their duty. They will learn to obey the reins that now encircle them. I will teach them that their response to the tension of the leather traces is what I demand. That their aim in life is to serve Polydorus, and nothing else. Here! Here!'

The guards took hold of the woman with the yellow headdress. She pulled back in fear, unused to being handled by anyone except Polydorus, fearful of their grasping hands, their closeness.

Eva saw the look of panic on her face. She pressed her knee harder against Calliope's waist, and tightened the lead in her hand.

'Tie her to the shaft. She will know the thing she has to serve before she knows the hand she must obey.'

They lifted the beautiful woman up. Her eyes were wide with terror. She had never been treated so roughly. The knotted leather thongs of the reins were still tangled around her head. Several of them were pulled tightly across her face. One of them was stretched between her teeth. It dug into the sides of her mouth and indented her cheeks before running behind her head. Several pieces of the cut trace still led from the ring at the back of her chest harness. Two of them had become twisted and had wrapped themselves around her breasts. The twists that they plaited were tightened around one of her nipples, squeezing it agonisingly between their twining strands.

The guards held her above one of the shafts of the trap — face down, her head towards the trap, her buttocks towards the silver ball which topped off the curled hook at the end.

'Lace her to it!' shouted Polydorus. 'And make it tight. I do not want to see her able even to squirm. She will not avoid my punishment in any way.'

They placed her over the shaft. Her arms and legs hung down. Her face, contorted in the mesh of tangled leather, rested hard against the timber shaft. Her buttocks were high, taut and beautifully curved. The delightful oval of her cunt, split by the delicious crack at its centre, no more than a hand's distance from the large silver ball that surmounted the bent hook.

Eva caressed Calliope. She ran her fingers down from her shoulders, into the curved dip of the small of her back, and up onto Calliope's taut, curved buttocks. She fondled them both, allowing her fingers to rest at their centre, before widening her stroke out across Calliope's right hip and down the side of her right thigh. Calliope moaned slightly, then started purring.

Eva stared through the crack in the timber boarding. She watched the guards strapping the woman with the yellow headdress tightly onto the shaft of the ornate trap. They drew some of the loose ends of the traces around her chest. They pulled her arms up tightly until she was grasping the shaft as she would a lover. They tied her thighs together so that the shaft was pinioned between the tops of her thighs. Her cunt pressed against it so that the crack at the centre was forced open.

'And now the other! They disobey as a pair. They shall suffer and learn as a pair!'

The woman with the red headdress was still tangled to the traces that led back to the trap. Her elbows were bound tightly at her back. Her hands thrashed about in panic. The guards pulled at her but could not free her. Seized with terror, she twisted and turned against the intrusion of their grasping hands. She screamed out. One of them tried to cover her mouth with his hand. She bit him. He lashed out at her angrily. She kicked at him in blind panic.

'See how they act!' screamed Polydorus. 'That is how they bite my hand. The hand that feeds them. The hand that cares for them. Cut her free! Lash her to the shaft like her ally in this war of defiance they wage against me.'

The guard she had bitten took a knife from his belt. He

held it in front of her face. She shrank back, frightened by the sight of the flashing metal. He let the blade dip towards her breasts. He held its point against her left nipple. She froze with fear. He pressed the sharp tip against the throbbing flesh. She winced with the pain. She bit her lips. She held her breath, but she could not stop her chest rising and falling and, as it did, from pressing rhythmically against the stinging point.

Eva led Calliope around so that her face was between Eva's legs. Calliope looked up, her eyes wide, her pupils large and black. Eva pulled on the lead and brought Calliope's face upwards. Calliope opened her mouth and poked her tongue out. It was wet and full, its fleshy tip seeking the crack which was so close above it.

The guard pulled the knife down onto the tangle of traces which wrapped around the woman's chest. He sliced the first.

Eva pulled Calliope's face upwards. Calliope pressed her tongue forward.

The guard sliced another of the bonding leather lashes. The woman twisted herself, fearful where the blade might go next. The leather trace fell free.

Eva pulled the leash tighter. Calliope rose up on its tension. Her tongue licked out keenly, following the sweet aroma of Eva's beckoning flesh. Calliope dropped back against the lead, allowing it to tighten against the collar at her neck. She stared at the object of her desire — Eva's glistening cunt.

The guard sliced through the next trace. The woman fell back free. Others grabbed her straightaway. Even though she fought against them, they quickly tied her, like the other woman, onto the other shaft. Both of them lay, tight bound and straddling the shafts, their faces pressed down against the wooden beam, their raised buttocks poised above the silver balls on the ornate hooks.

Polydorus took his whip into his hand. He tested it. He threw its length backwards over his shoulder. He let it rest, as if allowing it to gather its strength, then pulled at it so that it curled off the ground. He reached his arm forward to its target. The looping curl followed his command. He snatched it back and, in its eagerness to obey, it snapped back so viciously its tip burnt with a harsh, cracking snarl.

Polydorus stood well back, facing the women's exposed buttocks.

'Raise the shafts. My whip is keen to find its prey.'

The guards lifted the shafts. The trap tipped back. The women were raised on the shafts and flung forward until the back of the trap hit the ground and came to a stop. They both gasped, their heads now lower than the rest of their bodies, as the shock of the sudden stop took their breath away.

Polydorus threw the whip back. He waited. The gasping breaths of the terrified women echoed through the empty square. He brought the whip forward and released it at the woman with the yellow headdress. The tip shot forward. It touched her buttocks and, as it made contact, Polydorus grabbed it back. The tip cracked cruelly. It burned the woman's flesh, marking her, punishing her for her transgression against her powerful master. She tightened her buttocks in a pointless reaction. She screeched in pain.

'Now lower it!'

The guards hung onto the shafts and brought them down. Their ends hit the ground with a crash. The women were jerked on the shafts. They slipped slightly down them, their exposed buttocks coming a little closer to the silver balls that were attached to the curling hooks.

Eva heard the women gasp as their bodies were stunned by the sudden shock of the shafts smacking on the ground. She pulled at the leash and felt the touch of Calliope's probing tongue.

'Again! I have only just started!'

The guards tipped the trap up again. This time it was the turn of the woman with the red headdress to feel the burning anger of the cracking whip. She screeched when it made contact. Again, they pulled down on the shafts. Again, their ends hit the ground with a sickening thud. Again, the women slid closer to the silver balls.

'Again! Again!' demanded Polydorus.

The guards raised the shafts again. This time, the whip struck the woman with the yellow headdress. She jerked as it hit her exposed skin. A red welt appeared straight away. Again, the shafts went down. This time, as they hit the ground, the silver balls touched the women's buttocks.

Calliope lapped at Eva's cunt. She drew her fleshy tongue across its moist softness. She tasted its fragrant flavour. She savoured its delicious piquance. She inhaled the delightful aroma and was drawn even closer by its inviting delectability.

Eva watched the women on the shafts. She watched their cruel beating. Each crack of the whip excited her own passion. Each thud of the shafts on the ground, fed her own desire. She watched the red smudges on the women's buttocks spreading until they covered them completely. She watched the silver balls first touching their buttocks, then pressing between them. As Polydorus reached a frenzy with his pitiless whipping, she saw the silver balls prising against the women's anuses, opening them, then entering them. She watched the cruel whip lashing the hopeless victims. She heard their gasps as the shafts hit the ground. She watched their jerking bodies, tightening with pain as the silver balls pushed ever deeper into their anuses. Nothing stopped them, the lengths of the hooks upon which they were placed the only regulator of their penetration. Nor did Polydorus stop — his ravening harshness was never ending. The long hooks allowed their crowning silver balls to reach ever inward, for as long as the ferocious beating continued.

The square was filled with the screams of the suffering women.

The wooden horse stood as if silently on watch — the only guard protecting the city.

Unseen, and as if the cries of the tortured women were a signal, the trap door in the belly of the horse dropped open. Achilles peered through the opening. He saw Polydorus and the guards continuing the punishment of the women in the alley alongside the square. They were no longer concerned about the massive horse. The way was clear.

A rope was let down. One of the naked women inside the horse slithered down the rope. She held it tightly between her thighs and let her hands up one over another as she slid down. The rope pulled between the crack of her cunt. It prised it open. It picked up her fragrant moisture on its heavy plaits. She kept her legs tightly entwined around it. When she reached the ground, she was reluctant to part from it. She pulled its coarse braiding between her flesh and only moved aside when the next woman started her descent.

The women gathered silently beneath the belly of the horse. They stood in a cluster, naked, anxious, waiting for a command from Achilles.

His powerful arm signalled from above.

They ran in a flock towards the mighty gates of the city. They hung onto the massive bolts. They strained with all their weight. The torchlight picked out the curves of their taut bodies as they laboured. They braced their feet against prominent features in the walls, or on the timber work which made up the frame for the huge gates. They struggled to lever the mechanism apart. Slowly, the bolts drew back. The first bolt freed. The women pulling on it dropped to the ground exhausted. The second slid back. The women on this one stood gasping for breath, too depleted even to fall to the ground.

A ladder was let down from the horse. Achilles climbed down. His men followed. They ran silently to the gates.

Eva looked down through the trap door. Her heart pounded. She licked her dry lips. She knew she must not hesitate. She felt the wetness of Calliope's tongue still lapping at her cunt. Eva's pent up excitement boiled inside her. She was seized with it, filled with it, but she knew she could not release it. She eased the tension on the leash. Calliope pulled away.

Eva took a deep breath.

'We must leave. It is time.'

With Eva still holding Calliope's lead, they both clambered down the ladder and ran off across the square.

Achilles and his men stepped over the exhausted naked women. They reached up and pulled on the mighty gates. First, a crack appeared between them. Slowly, they swung back. The Greek army stood outside the yawning gates. They had returned from Teredos during the night and brought their ships back up onto the beach. Fully armed, they had crossed the plain and assembled silently beneath the walls of Troy. Now, they stood in the opening left by the gaping gates — shadows of death in the iniquitous darkness of their hatred.

They all drew up to their full height when they saw Achilles before them. His long black hair streamed out behind him, glistening red like flames in the flickering torchlight. He raised his arm and pointed to the inside of the city. A clamorous cry went up, and the Greek army surged behind him into the unguarded square.

Chryseis swung helplessly, upside down on the heavy rope. She could see nothing through the hood pulled tightly over her head. She breathed heavily. The heat from her breath warmed her cheeks, filled her nostrils, moistened her dried her lips. She did not know how long she had been there. She had thought she heard Sappho's voice. Her heart had thumped with excitement as she imagined her friend again. But the sound of her voice had passed and Chryseis had been thrown again into the darkness of despondency.

She widened her eyes, staring into the blackness of the enveloping hood. Sounds filled her head — crying, moaning, screeching. The world seemed in a terrible turmoil. She twisted her ankles against the rope. She felt slackness, some movement. She twisted again. Her ankles moved more. Incensed by the thought of release, she squirmed frantically. She felt herself coming free from the bondage of the binding rope. One last effort and she fell to the ground.

She was stunned by the fall. She rolled about confused, unsure which way was up or which down. She tore the hood from her head. She blinked giddily in the light of lamps and torches. Other captive women still hung from the heavily beamed ceiling of the great room. She did not look back at them as she ran in panic. She chased down the covered walkway of Polydorus' palace, out through the heavy gates. She ran towards the temple of Apollo — the only place she knew where sanctuary might be found.

The city was ablaze. Women were being dragged away, naked and screaming, by Greek soldiers taking their revenge for years of frustration on the beach at Troy. They were savage and ruthless. No woman was safe from their brutality. They thrashed them with canes, and beat them with whips. They bent them over fallen pillars and drove their cocks deeply into their cunts and anuses. They forced them to suck their cocks and drink their semen. They tied them by the wrists and dragged them along the dusty streets by their ankles. There was no mercy for the inhabitants of the great city. There was screaming everywhere. It was as if the gods themselves had come down to earth to take revenge.

Chryseis managed to find her way to the temple. She crawled into a small cellar and cowered between the heavy pillars that supported its low ceiling. She pushed herself into a cage in the darkest corner. Her whole body quaked with fear. She squeezed her hands together tightly, dropped to her knees and prayed to Apollo for deliverance from this hellish nightmare.

Chapter 13

The sacking of Troy

Achilles led the Greek army through the streets and alleys of Troy. Nothing stood in their way. The frustration of years of stalemate was finally released in their vengeful brutality. King Priam was killed on the steps of his palace. The invading army burned buildings, set fire to grain stores, polluted water supplies, desecrated temples, stole treasure. They dragged terrified occupants from their houses and lined them up in the streets. The men they chained, marched out of the city, and drove back to the beach as slaves. Women were herded together and taken into the great square. They stood in rows beneath the shadow of the wooden horse — the beast which had brought their destruction. Their hands were tied in front of them. Some were hooded. Some were gagged.

Eva stood with Calliope behind a half-fallen wall. Her mission to find slaves was foremost in her mind. She watched the women who had been captured. She was interested in the desires of the Greeks, keen to know more about how they were best satisfied. She tugged at Calliope's lead. Calliope went down on all fours. She looked up at her mistress with wide eyes. Eva rewarded her with a sharp tug at the collar around her neck.

The captured women were filed between the forelegs of the mighty horse. They were made to kneel and were branded with the sign of the bronze tipped ash spear — the emblem of the mighty Achilles.

The blind Ajax, led by a young girl, chided Achilles for the branding. He feared the wrath of Agamemnon.

Achilles dismissed his worry.

'Achilles fears no one. Not even the gods. There is no man who can better the great Achilles. Even kings and princes must bow before the one who has taken the great city of Troy. Let the world know. Achilles is indestructible. Now, Ajax, come. We shall celebrate our victory.'

Agamemnon and Menelaus joined them. A great table was laid out. Huge chairs were brought. Soldiers of the victorious army gathered around. They toasted the wooden horse. They congratulated their own bravery. They demanded pleasure from their captives.

'Let the entertainment begin!' cried Agamemnon.

Five women were brought forward for approval. They stood, naked, their wrists tied before them, their heads bowed. Two were red haired, two were dark, one was blonde. Their hair was long in the Trojan style — scraped back tightly from their face and hanging down between their shoulders in a heavy plait. Soldiers with sticks prodded them underneath their arms and made them raise their hands. They poked them in the back and made them bend over.

Achilles ordered the blonde haired woman caned across the buttocks because he thought her too slow to bend over. She yelped loudly with each stroke. He went and inspected the red lines that the cane had cut but was not satisfied that she had suffered enough. He ordered her to be thrashed more. She screamed loudly and, because she squirmed, she had to be held in place tightly. In the end, she fell silent under the beating and was dragged away.

The two red heads were forced down on all fours. The two dark-haired women were bent down across them. The buttocks of the dark-haired women were lifted high. Their knees were secured to their already bound wrists by leather straps passed beneath the arched bodies of the red heads. They both had well-rounded buttocks — curved and taut and brought together with a tightly defined crack. Their cunts were exposed — pink and soft. Their slits glistened with thin lines of moisture,

Eva wet her lips with her tongue. Calliope nuzzled close against her leg

Two men stood behind the women. They held long thin canes in their hands. They shook them to show how thin and whippy they were. They held both ends and bent them almost double. They released them to demonstrate how they sprang back with a snap. The two dark-haired women both closed their eyes and pushed their heads down as low as they could. The heavy dark plait of one of them fell into the crook of her neck. The other one's hair dropped forward over the top of her head and touched the ground.

Eva thought of walking forward, of joining the gathering of the chiefs, of sharing in the victory, but she did not. Watching secretly, observing without anyone seeing her, was more delightful. Looking in on what was happening, without being seen, had more piquance, was more tantalising to her senses. She looked at the women's heavy plaits of hair. She imagined rubbing her cheeks against them, pulling them between her legs, allowing her crack to open against their silky, folded ribs. Calliope purred, sensing the heat of her mistress's excitement. Eva wondered again about striding out into the square, but again she stopped herself. She knew that, at the moment, her needs were best fed from the delightful secrecy of anonymity. She stroked Calliope softly and wet her lips again.

The two men pulled the canes back behind their heads and waited. Agamemnon raised his arm. The men brought the canes down. They bent as they descended through the air, but straightened just before they touched the taut skin of the women's buttocks. There was a stinging crack as they fell against their targets. The women both reared back together. They opened their mouths at the same time. They screamed in unison. They were twinned in suffering. The canes went back again. There was a moment's pause, a moment's silence. It was broken by the swishing sound of the canes as again they were pulled down. The stinging crack fractured the air as they laced across the taut skin of the women's upturned buttocks. Another long red line arose against the first.

Eva pulled the loop of the leash against the crack of her cunt. Calliope pulled back slightly, increasing the tension, making the leather loop slip more cuttingly against her mistress's soft flesh. Eva tightened her jaws as the stinging canes flashed through the air. They were raised back at the same time. They were held for a second. They were brought down together. They worked in harmony, cracking in a measured rhythm against the jerking skin of the women's buttocks. Eva rubbed the edge of leather loop against her flesh. She pulled it into her crack. She probed its sharp rim against her clitoris, causing it to throb, teasing out her growing need for satisfaction.

The women stopped screaming — their pain had drained them. They were untied from the backs of the other women and changed around. The canes came down on the redheads. They lashed them mercilessly, covering their buttocks with a mass of angry red stripes. They too jerked and screeched but, as the others had slowly faded away, in the end they also went silent. When they lay limply on the other's backs, not jerking, not crying out, they too were untied.

The four of them lay on the ground, gasping for breath, shivering, hopeless. Buckets of water were thrown over them to rouse them. It splashed on their exposed bodies. It slopped onto their faces. It doused the cunts of the ones whose legs were lying wide open. They were dragged to their feet and made to stand in a line. They stood, their hands held up to their faces, water running from their heads and down their shivering bodies. A soldier threatened them with the cane. They cowered before it as he forced them to bend over. Their reddened buttocks, wet and dripping from their soaking, glowed in the sunlight. Water ran down between their legs, over their feet and onto the ground in puddles.

Soldiers came forward and stood in front of the women. They lifted the women's heads in their hands and forced their cocks into their victims' gaping mouths. The soldiers with the canes started the thrashing again. They brought them down with increased fury. Each slashing cut made the women lurch forward against the cocks in their mouths. The men held onto their shoulders. They kept them fast, allowing the shock of each caning slash to be transmitted through their bodies and into their sucking mouths.

Eva put her fingers into her mouth. She wanted desperately to walk out into the square. She could hardly hold herself back. She bit down against her knuckles, keeping in time with the jerking bodies of the pitiful women. Each thrashing slash of the canes made her bite harder. Each jerk forward made her suck more. Each tightening of their buttocks brought more spit onto her tongue. As the women's heads were knocked forward, Eva dribbled more. As the stiff cocks went deeper into their gagging throats, she moaned louder. As she heard her own spluttering moan, she thrust her fingers deeper into the back of her throat. Eva could not stop herself. She rose against her delving fingers as she gagged. She tasted vomit in her throat. She pushed her fingers further in.

Eva watched one of the women falling sideways. The soldier held her shoulders tightly. He kept his cock deep in her throat, but still she fell. Her knees bent. With the cane flailing her buttocks, she crumbled and fell to the dusty ground. The soldier's cock pulled out. Its ribbed shaft pulsated. Its swollen end throbbed. Semen spurted from it — a massive soaking surge. It ran into the woman's mouth as she fell. As she hit the ground, it splattered over her face and down her neck. He held it as it dripped onto her breasts. It stuck to her hard nipples, circling them with glistening whiteness.

The woman rolled onto her side. Dust and mud stuck to her face. The semen was smudged in long dirty strands. It mixed with the mud. She lay face down, gasping into the dust and wetness from the water that had been thrown over them all. The soldier grabbed her hair and pulled her up. She was smeared with the mud, his semen and the yellow dust of the earth. She dropped her head in shame. He bent her over his knee and the caning continued.

Eva could stand it no longer. She dropped her hand by her side. Spit ran from her fingers. She tugged at Calliope's lead. Calliope straightened her arms, dipped the small of her back and lifted her beautifully curved buttocks. Eva jerked her forward. The fading sunlight caught the facets of the golden ring in Calliope's clitoris. It reflected between the soft dunes of her cunt, radiating the beauty of her moist crack, illuminating her luscious flesh.

Eva strode out into the square.

Achilles saw her first.

'Ah! The beautiful Eva. And her new pet — the delectable Calliope. I hope your slave is behaving herself, my lady?'

Eva walked over to the chieftains. Calliope crawled on all fours, never letting the leash go slack yet, at the same time, never showing too much resistance to Eva.

'She is, my lord. See how she awaits her mistress's orders. See how she purrs and presses herself against her lady's leg.'

Calliope looked up at Ajax. His blinded eyes stared uselessly ahead. His jaws tightened at the mention of Calliope — the one who had tripped him and sent him headlong into the blinding spears.

Calliope leant against his leg. At first, he tensed. She

pressed harder. He relaxed. She pressed her face against the side of his knee. He felt her warmth and reached down. She poked her tongue out and licked his skin. He touched her head. She pressed up against his hand.

'Yes, my lord Achilles, I tolerate only obedience.'

'Then Praxis will be pleased with you as well.'

'He will, my lord.'

Ajax tensed again. This time at the thought of Praxis. The one who, years before he had himself blinded, but who had returned to take his terrible vengeance by blinding Ajax himself.

Calliope sensed his returning anger. She licked him harder. She let her spit run against him. She let him feel its dribbling heat. She felt him responding to her wet caress.

'And you are here to find slaves for your master?'

'I am.'

'Have you found what you are looking for? Are these women who tease us with their screams to your taste? Will you choose them for Praxis' flock?'

Eva pulled on Calliope's lead. Calliope licked her lips and followed obediently.

Eva walked over to the women. Semen dripped from their wet lips. Water ran from their sweating bodies. Their buttocks glowed with the burning stripes from the caning. Their hair was tousled and stuck together in wet strands. Eva looked at each one in turn. She pinched her thumb and forefinger around the left nipple of the woman who had fallen and was covered in mud. The woman winced then grimaced. Eva squeezed harder. The woman's mouth fell open. Semen ran from it. Eva released her grip and the woman fell back. She stumbled and only just managed to stay on her feet.

'Pathetic!' said Eva in disgust. 'If this is what is on offer in Troy, I am wasting my time.'

She snatched at Calliope's lead and strutted back towards

the seated chieftains.

'You are quick to find fault, lady,' said Ajax.

She shrugged and tossed back her mane of red hair.

'Yes, lady Eva. Finding fault is useless unless there is also a remedy. Do you have the remedy?' added Achilles.

Agamemnon and Menelaus both laughed.

Eva stopped. She would not be mocked, even by the great Greek lords who sat before her. She turned and walked back past the four women. She stood against one of the legs of the great wooden horse. She pushed Calliope away with her foot. Calliope sat back on her knees and scowled.

'I shall be the remedy, my lord. And the example. I will take the cane. Command your soldiers, Achilles. Have them punish this poor slave, Eva. And tell them not to hold back.'

Still holding Calliope's lead, Eva bent forward and rested her arms against the leg of the wooden horse. She dipped her back and lifted her buttocks. Their smooth skin, touched by a hint of moisture, stretched tautly. The dark crack between them opened at its base as the oval of her cunt pressed it out. The crack that ran at its centre, was tight, a darker pink than the flesh that surrounded it. It glistened with moisture — a delectable stream, a drizzle of delight. At its lowest part, her hard clitoris rose from its protective shell, throbbing at its exposure, pulsating with her needs for more.

Eva's long red hair fell over her face. She waited.

A soldier stepped forward with a cane. He laid it against her buttocks. He measured their distance from him. He pressed it down, testing the springiness of her flesh. He tapped the cane several times against her pale skin. He pulled it back and waited.

'Remember, do not hold back!' ordered Achilles.

The cane came down. The air was cut by its loud swish. It bent sharply as it neared its target. It landed squarely across Eva's upturned buttocks. It cracked as it made contact. It reddened her skin instantly. She jerked, but did not pull away.

The soldier took the cane back again. This time he did not wait for an instruction. He brought it down harder. It whipped in a bend then slashed against her skin. She jerked again, as another red line appeared on her fair skin.

She pulled on Calliope's lead. Calliope moved closer to her.

Eva stared down at the ground. The thrashing continued.

When spit ran from her mouth, she licked it back. When she felt the pain urging her to scream out, she bit on her lips and contained it. But every slash of the cane stoked the fire within her. Her heat built. The agony of the beating only fed her desire for more. Each stroke made her want the next. Each licking flame of pain, only ignited a wish for something more severe. She took it all, and still was not satisfied.

When the soldier stood back with the cane, Calliope crawled up behind her mistress. She pushed her head between Eva's legs. She moved her cheeks up and down against the insides of Eva's thighs. She straightened her arms, stretched up and laid her tongue across the hot lines the cane had cut into Eva's buttocks.

Eva rose as she felt the coolness of Eva's moist tongue against her stinging skin. Calliope licked along each line. She dribbled her spit along the raised welts. She saturated them with her own cooling moisture. Eva felt Calliope's salving spit running down the crack of her buttocks. She felt it against the swollen flesh of her cunt. She sensed it dribbling along her open crack. She felt it flowing against her throbbing, hot clitoris.

She pulled tightly on the lead. Calliope held herself against the tension. She let her tongue drift between Eva's buttocks. She found her anus. She tasted it. She probed her tongue at is centre. Eva tightened with expectation.

She opened her buttocks to let it in. Her anus dilated — opened for the tip of Calliope's tongue. It slipped in — probing, investigating — forced in by Calliope's eagerness, sucked in by Eva's desire.

Eva clung onto the huge leg of the wooden horse. Her nails clawed into the timber — scratching at it, transmitting her fevered passion into it. She had to let it run away. She had to drain it. She could not contain it. She breathed hard. She sucked back her dribbling spit. She fought for breath as her heart pounded in her tightened chest. She wanted to feel the flesh of her cunt. She wanted to run her hands down between her thighs and plunge her fingers inside it. Still she held back, savouring Calliope's penetrating tongue and the staring eyes that she knew were upon her.

She pressed back onto Calliope's tongue. She let her probe her rectum with its tip. She let her taste her innards. She let her know her insides. She dug her nails into the leg of the wooden horse.

Suddenly, she pulled away.

Eva stood up, containing her passion, holding it back. She walked to one of the four women who still stood in a line. She took her mouth between her thumb and fingers. The woman's mouth opened. Semen ran from it. Eva pressed her lips against the woman's mouth and drank it from her. She licked inside her mouth and lapped it from inside her cheeks, from the pool that lay cupped in the centre of her tongue. She went to the next two and drank from them as well. She licked it up. She swilled it around her mouth and swallowed it down in heavy eager gulps.

The woman who was smeared with mud, she saved for last. First she licked her mouth clean of any semen. Then she licked the mixture of dust and semen from her body. She lapped her tongue around her nipples and breasts. She ran it around her hips and between her thighs. She probed its tip into her cunt and insinuated it into her anus. She bent down and licked it from her dirty feet. She sucked her toes, each one in turn, encircled tightly at its base by her warm full lips.

When she had finished, she stood before the chieftains.

'Now, have my pet thrashed. All she wants is what I command. You will see how she longs for nothing but obeying her mistress. Thrash her and you will see me satisfied. Then you will have the answer to your own question. You will know if I have the remedy.'

Eva lay back in the massive chair Achilles pushed forward for her. She straightened her legs out and opened them wide. Calliope crawled between them. She squeezed her face between the tops of Eva's thighs and poked out her fleshy tongue. She licked along Eva's crack, still wet, still open, still available. She lifted her buttocks, tightening them together, pulling them in against the flesh of her own cunt. When the cane came down, she only raised herself for more.

Eva let her long red hair fall back on her shoulders. She pulled hard on Calliope's lead. She drew her in as close as she could. She pulled harder. Calliope's face pressed against Eva's wet, open cunt. Eva dragged her into it, yanking the lead urgently when she felt Calliope's nose against her clitoris. She raised her hips and twisted her feet outwards, turning the insides of her thighs so that her cunt was fully available for Calliope's feast. Calliope bit into its flesh. She pinched it hard between her teeth. She bit around Eva's clitoris, clamping her teeth around its base and sucking it at the same time. Her spit bubbled around her mouth. It mixed with Eva's flowing moisture and ran down her chin.

Eva lifted herself. She pressed her hips high. She braced her forearms on the arms of the massive chair. She let her head fall back. She craned her neck backwards, exposing her gulping throat. She looked up into the sky. She stared at the burning sun. Her head filled with its blazing golden rays. She tightened again. She throbbed all over. Her heart beat heavily in her constricted chest. Her temples pounded. Her head spun. She opened her mouth. She held her breath. She fell back — completed, filled, overjoyed.

Calliope licked her for a while. In the end, Ajax pulled her back. She nuzzled up against his leg and purred. He stroked her head. She responded to his attention. Eva did not notice.

The rest of the captured women were whipped or mistreated. Gags were left in their mouths, hoods kept in place over their heads. Many were hung upside down facing outwards over the sides of the great walls. Some had their nipples tied with thongs of leather. Some had their breasts bound tightly with wet leather thongs. Others were dragged away having suffered more than they could bear. They moaned as their heels were lifted off the ground and tied to ropes. Some of them moaned with the pain that had been inflicted on them. Some of them moaned at the thought of the hellish future which lay ahead.

As night fell, soldiers were sent to search the city. Polydorus had evaded capture and Paris and Helen had not been found. Agamemnon would not rest until the aim of the war had been achieved — the capture and return of his brother's wife Helen. Achilles led the search party. They roamed the streets. They prised out those who had hidden in holes and cellars, torturing them for information about the ones they sought. They worked their way through the back alleys, the shops, the places of worship, but they did not find the ones they sought.

Chryseis clung in terror to the bars of her cage beneath the Temple of Apollo. She held her breath as the soldiers searched the rooms above. She heard feet running for safety — other fugitives desperate to avoid capture. She stared out blankly, filled with fear. A figure appeared at the entrance of the dungeon. It wore a cloak. It was a man. He peered into the gloomy darkness looking for a place to hide. She stared back at him. He turned and went.

The soldiers of Achilles returned that night disappointed and angry. Achilles gave them heart, offering them bounty for the capture of the two princes and the truant Helen. They cheered him and swore it would not be long before the fugitives were in their hands.

Chapter 14

Torture on the rack

Chryseis clung to the bars of the cage, afraid to move. She had not eaten. She felt dizzy. She heard a noise. She thought it was a rat. She cocked her head and listened carefully. It was a scratching sound. She cocked her head the other way. The scratching stopped. She saw a shadow at the entrance to the dark dungeon. She thought it was the cloaked man returning. She froze with fear. The shadow darted back. It stopped. It was a woman. The woman's head peered into the cell. Chryseis held her breath. She bit her lips. She felt her cold hands shaking with fear. The head darted back. The shadow disappeared.

Chryseis was shaking as she crept to the doorway. The low ceiling was barely above her back. She shivered. She had not been so aware of the tight confines of the dungeon while in the cage. Now, outside its protection, she realised the low ceiling, the close walls and the tiny entrance, conspired like a heavy weight to press down on her and close her in. She managed to get to the entrance. She looked out. She saw no one. The shadow must have been a trick of the light, a dream, an hallucination.

She crawled back into the safety of the cage. As she entered, she sensed something behind her — a body, someone else. She could not turn — her chest was too tight. She could not breathe. Her mouth dried. A hand touched her shoulder. She went ice cold with fear. The fingernails dug into her skin. Her eyes widened. Her heart pounded. She thought it was going to explode.

'Chryseis,' said a voice. 'Chryseis. It is me, Sappho.'

Chryseis' head spun giddily. Still, she could not move. She must have gone mad. She must be imagining it. It was not possible.

The fingers pressed against her shoulder, urging her to turn.

'Do not be afraid, my darling Chryseis. It is truly me, your dear friend Sappho.'

Chryseis slowly turned. She looked at her friend. Dirtied with mud, stained with semen, her ragged smock filthy and in tatters.

'How? How can this be so?'

'Chryseis, I have been here for days. I heard the Greek army sacking the city. I have been too afraid to move. I have been hiding behind a wooden panel in the main temple. I have found nothing to eat and I was looking for food when saw you here, clinging to the bars of this cage. I thought you were a ghost. I could not believe it.'

'Sappho, my darling Sappho. This is like a dream. I never thought I would see you again. I even thought I heard your voice while I hung, hooded and bound in one of Polydorus' rooms, my dearest Sappho. But I was mistaken. Come. It is safe in here. No one can find us. You must not leave.'

'I will not.'

Sappho dropped down beside the still shivering Chryseis. They lay in each other's arms, feeling each other's warmth, luxuriating in the newfound safety of each other's company.

Sappho felt the pressure of the hard iron bars against her back. She squeezed herself against them. They were cold against her skin. She delighted in the safety of the enclosing cage. She felt a captive of it, a prisoner within its unyielding bars. But it was a prison from which she did not want to escape. She felt a new and welcome sense of safety enclosed within its hard rails.

Slowly, her eyes became used to the darkness. She could see they were in a dungeon, a chamber of torture. Manacles hung from the low ceiling. Chains swung from the walls. A heavy wooden table with a cranking wheel at its end stood between the cage and the low doorway. A pile of leather straps was heaped up by its side. Everything in the dark room lay beneath the low ceiling, barely high enough not to touch when crawling on all fours.

Sappho turned to Chryseis.

Chryseis looked into Sappho's eyes.

'Hold me,' she said. 'I need to feel you close.'

It was so tight inside the bars of the cage that Sappho could hardly move. She pressed her face between Chryseis' breasts. She felt the warmth of Chryseis' silky skin. She felt her shivering body.

'You are cold.'

She let her mouth fall around one of Chryseis' nipples. It was hard and throbbing. She sucked at it. It was delectable — sweet and fragrant, fleshy and firm. She felt Chryseis' chest rising against the pressure of her bite. Sappho increased the force. The flesh of Chryseis' nipple gave way under the sharp edges of her teeth. They dug in deeply. Chryseis gave a quick gasp, a moan of pain, a thrill of surrender.

'Harder,' she said slowly. 'Bite it harder.'

Sappho bit harder. She pressed her tongue against the end of the throbbing nipple. Chryseis gasped, this time louder. She lifted herself against Sappho's bite. Sappho sensed the pleasure of Chryseis' suffering. She enjoyed delivering the pain. She savoured having another surrendering to her will. She relished the tension in Chryseis' body as she braced herself against the penetrating agony.

But Sappho's pleasure was short lived. There was something wrong. Her bite slackened. The bars of the cage seemed to tighten around her. It was as if they were squeezing her body in their shrinking grip, constricting her, wrapping her up in their iron grasp. She did not know what was happening. She pulled back. Chryseis' nipple fell from between her teeth. A wave of distress ran through

Sappho's body. She slid away from Chryseis. The sensation of pressure increased. A dark surge of guilt flowed over her. Tears welled up in her eyes. She could not hold it back.

'Chryseis,' she said falteringly. 'I knew it was you. You were not mistaken when you were hanging, hooded, by your ankles. I was there. I recognised you. I was too afraid to help you. My dearest friend. Chryseis, I have let you down so badly. It is you who must punish me. It is you who must inflict pain on me. Only when you have made me suffer will I know I have been forgiven. Chryseis, forgive me with pain. I have to feel your hand on my skin. I have to feel the smack of your palm on my buttocks. Only when I wince with your angry slaps, will I feel exonerated. Only then will I be absolved of my terrible cowardice. Chryseis, grant me forgiveness with your chastisement.'

Sappho pulled herself away from Chryseis. She crawled slowly out of the cage. She dropped low to the ground. She pressed her face into the dirty mud and dust. She smeared her already dirty body with the filth that lay on the floor of the dungeon.

'See how I defile myself for you, my dearest. I am like the lowest animal grovelling in the filth of the world. I am worthless until you make me beg for your forgiveness.'

Sappho licked at the ground. The dirt was musty. She felt a gush of vomit in her throat. She heaved. She swallowed and held it back. She reached out and laid her hands on the edge of the heavy timber rack. It was a sharp, well-defined edge. She ran her palm forward along its surface. It was smooth and depressed at the centre — worn by the many stretched and tormented bodies of its countless victims. She stretched herself further. Half way along, the bed of the rack was split. The other half joined it closely with only a narrow gap in between. She pulled herself onto it. Her dirty body flattened itself against the smooth, worn timber. A nail near the join caught her tattered smock. She pulled herself against it. The smock ripped down the front. It opened and she felt her breasts cooled by the smooth surface of the rack against them. She reached further and the tear rent the smock to the hem. Her nipples hardened as they scraped across the shiny worn top. She stretched out her hands as far as she could and held the front edge. The front of her shaved slit pressed down against the bed of the rack. She pressed her wrists outwards against two iron clasps. They stood open, ready to be dropped and secured so that any victim of the rack could not get free.

'Please, Chryseis, drop the clamps around my wrists. I want to be fixed to the rack. I want to be made ready for your punishment. Please, I need to feel the tension of captivity. I need to know I cannot escape. I need humiliation.'

Chryseis did not speak. She crawled alongside the rack and knelt by its side. She dropped the heavy clamps over Sappho's wrists. They were stiff and hard to move. They had two holes cut out of them which fitted over two raised bolts. A pinion, secured to each side of the rack on a thin chain, passed through the bolts and held the clamps in place. As Sappho watched, Chryseis pressed the pins in tightly.

Sappho pulled against the securing clamps. She needed to know how firmly she was held. They were hard and unforgiving. Their edges dug into the skin of her wrists. She clenched her fists then released them. She stretched her hands out to their thinnest and tugged them into the iron circles that surrounded them. She could not pull them from the clasps. She was held securely. There was no escape. She swallowed hard.

'And my ankles. Chryseis, my ankles. They need holding as well. I will only suffer if you secure them too.'

Chryseis found some leather thongs. She wrapped them

around each of Sappho's ankles. She passed them through holes in the surface of the rack, yanked them tight, and secured them to rings hanging from bolts beneath the heavy platform.

Sappho pulled against her bonds. She was rewarded by the pain inflicted by their security. The iron clamps at her wrists dug in deeper with each movement. Her skin was sensitised by its contact with the hard edges. Any slight movement that was possible only fed the sensitisation. Her ankles were held fast. She could not move them at all. Her feet felt hot, her legs throbbed. She squirmed with delight. It was exquisite captivity. She felt the front of her crack pull against the split in the surface of the rack. The soft edges of her cunt moistened under the tension. She twisted with a surge of joy. Her buttocks lifted. Her hips moved from side to side.

She realised she was still too free.

'My waist. Please, my darling Chryseis. Secure my waist.'

Sappho tensed herself. She stiffened her arms and legs and pulled against the clamps and leather bindings. She licked out her tongue and ran it along the shiny surface of the rack. The wooden bed against which her face lay was slightly dished. Many faces had pressed in this place before. Many tongues had reached out and dribbled their spit here. Many cries of pain had echoed against its unhearing hardness. She licked again. Yes, she could taste the saltiness of others — their sweat, their spit, their vomit, their pain. She sucked at it, drew it into her mouth, and swallowed deeply.

Chryseis found a long leather belt curled up on the floor. She had to reach beneath the rack to free it. She dropped it across Sappho's waist and pulled it through two holes which were cut in the timber bed. She stretched beneath the rack and secured the leather belt into two rings and pulled them tightly together.

Sappho gasped as the leather belt was pulled down against her waist. Each tightening yank captured her more. Each pull on the leather strap brought her closer to the wonderful subjugating confinement she desired.

Chryseis drew the ends of the strap into a firm knot.

Sappho felt the knot fixing the strap. It sealed her captivity. She stiffened again against the straps on her ankles and the clamps on her wrists. She felt a scorching heat of pleasure running through her whole body. She felt completely enslaved, pinned to the rack, restrained by unbreakable bonds, victim to another, delectably under the control of her punisher. She licked again against the depression in front of her face. Spit ran in bubbles down her tongue. It dribbled into a gluey pool. She drank from it — it was nectar to her overwhelming appetite for punishment.

'I am ready,' she said quietly. 'I am ready.'

Chryseis knelt and smoothed her hand across Sappho's buttocks.

Sappho closed her eyes with delight. She shivered. The palm of Chryseis' hand felt like silk. It slipped across her skin. It felt cool. Sappho felt her buttocks tightening. She felt them rise with the tension, trying in vain to increase the pressure of her skin against Chryseis' hand. She relaxed and let them ease apart. Chryseis' hand slipped into the tight valley between them. Sappho's throat thumped in time with the pounding of her heart. Her head spun. Spit ran from her tongue in a frothing stream.

'More. More.'

Chryseis increased the pressure of her hand.

Sappho wanted to reach up to it. She wanted to lift her buttocks. She wanted to offer them for a beating. She strained against the strap at her waist. The restriction of it, her inability to lift herself at all against its restraining tightness, only increased her ardour. She strained again. It was a delectable frustration — it fed on itself. She was caught in a spiral of wanting drawn from a desire for pleasure and her failure to attain it.

Her need was boiling over. She wanted to cry out to Chryseis to start the punishment. She wanted to call to her to begin the thrashing. But she knew it was too late for that. Chryseis would decide when it should begin. Chryseis would decide how long it would last, how severe it would be, when it would end. Sappho stretched herself as tightly as she could. She breathed heavily. She waited.

Her head buzzed in the silence. She listened to her breathing — it was like the roaring of a storm. Chryseis' hand came away from her buttocks. A coolness passed over them. Sappho tightened more. Her head throbbed. It was going to happen. At last, the circle of disappointment was going to break.

Chryseis' hand smacked down — sudden, hard, stinging. Sappho's breath burst from her. She wanted more straight away. She did not want to savour the biting pain. She wanted more. The hand came down again. It burnt her skin. It was like a branding iron. Sappho felt the flames of pain licking up inside. She tightened her buttocks, imagining she could lift them higher. Still, she wanted more. And more came.

Her buttocks were set alight with the repeated smacks. It was a stinging pain — sharp, penetrating, condensed. It was a pain that penetrated her whole body. No one smack was isolated — they all flowed together. It was a tide of delectable suffering — a surging swell of intense pain. She felt the heat in her cunt. She felt its wetness. She wanted more.

A shadow appeared at the entrance to the dungeon. It was a man. He was covered in a heavy cloak.

Sappho jerked with every smack. She drooled into the

pool of spit beneath her mouth. She pressed her lips into it and sucked at it thirstily.

The man stared at her. Sappho fixed him with her eyes. She held his gaze. Even as she convulsed with the ecstatic agony of the relentless smacking hand, she did not blink or lower her eyes. He reached forward and placed his hand on the hand wheel at the end of the rack. Sappho kept staring deeply into his eyes.

Chryseis' hand came down again and again. One loud smack on Sappho's buttocks, a sudden burst of breath, a penetrating surge of pain, then another, and another.

The man smiled. His hand pulled against the wheel. Sappho heard its iron cog click. She felt a jerk beneath her as the two segments of the rack pulled apart. The clamps at her wrists dug tightly into her skin. Her ankles pulled painfully against the straps that held them. Her chest tightened. Her waist strained. Her heart pounded. The thrashing continued.

Another smack. Again, the flat of Chryseis' hand came down hard. Sappho tightened her buttocks. She tried to absorb the pain. She wanted to be filled by it. She wanted to be it. She looked at the man. He turned the wheel another click. Sappho screamed. Spit frothed from her mouth. Another smack. Another click. Sappho felt the unyielding strain on her body. She felt the stretching tension between her wrists and ankles. She screeched. It was a gurgling cry — a moaning lament of agony. Saliva filled her mouth. She slobbered. She frothed from her lips like a crazed dog.

Another smack. She tightened against it. Her buttocks were on fire. Chryseis' hand was hot now. It burned Sappho. It was a flame. Another click. Another wrenching pain. Another stream of gushing spit. Sappho's wrists were ablaze. She felt like a torch. Another click. Her ankles were encircled by bands of fire. Another smack. She felt the gap in the rack's bed widening, opening up like the jaws of hell itself. She screamed at the top of her voice but the sound was meaningless — a confusion of bubbling spit. It did not alleviate her suffering. She absorbed the pain. There was nowhere for it to go. All she could hear was the click of the rack and the smack of Chryseis' hand. There was nothing else in her world.

Her mind filled with flitting images. It was like watching frantic birds in an aviary. She pictured Chryseis hanging from the ceiling of the room in Polydorus' palace. She saw the hood slipping from her face. She saw her appealing eyes asking for help. She saw tears in her eyes. She watched herself reach forward. She saw herself taking Chryseis' hand and lifting her down. But they could not escape. It was a futile gesture. Instead of escape to safety, she felt the crack of the whip as it was brought down on her back. She felt the savagery of cruel punishment. It was her penalty for showing compassion to Chryseis. But she did not mind the pain of the whip. It was right that she should suffer. It was right that she should feel the pain and save her friend from any more. At last, she felt vindicated. The smacking continued. It blended with the pictures in her mind. Deep within her body, she felt the surging tide of her orgasm. Somewhere, deep inside her, Chryseis' hand had absolved her cowardly betrayal.

Sappho and Chryseis woke to the sound of shouting. The Greeks were above them, in the temple.

The two women crept furtively from their cage, past the rack and out of the dungeon. They held onto each other as they made their way into the centre of the temple. They stared down into the atrium.

They saw the massive marble statue surrounded by the bodies of vanquished Trojans. They saw a small party of Greeks led by Achilles hiding behind the statue of Apollo, pinned down by Paris and some of his faithful guard.

Achilles had been surprised by their attack, but was not prepared to stay cowering at the mercy of the Trojans for long. Suddenly, he ran forward brandishing his sword. His long black hair trailed behind him — it was as though he were part of the wind itself. His mighty shield, fashioned by the god's own armourer Hephaestus, reflected the light of the world as he charged into the open. Achilles stood above everything around him. His brightness was like that of a god. When he looked around, he penetrated everything he saw with his steely gaze. It was as though the universe itself must shield its eyes from his glorious glare.

Sappho and Chryseis held onto each other, unable to take their eyes off the action, unable to resist Achilles' magnificence. Achilles ran into a shower of arrows. He easily parried them with his flashing shield. Sappho and Chryseis saw the handsome Paris load his bow with a poisoned arrow. They watched him take a careful aim. They heard his cry of victory as it penetrated Achilles heel, the only part of his body left vulnerable by his goddess mother. They watched Achilles fall heavily to the ground, his leg disabled, his body already filling with the poison from the cowardly Paris' arrow. They watched the craven Trojan prince run into the darkness — too afraid to stay and see his victim die.

The Greeks gathered around their dead leader. They picked up Achilles' body and took it on their shoulders. Sappho clutched Chryseis in fear. She gulped and gave a barely stifled cry. One of the soldiers wheeled around at the sound. He lunged forward and saw them both, clinging to each other, shaking with fear.

'Bring them! The lady Eva will reward us well for such booty!'

Chapter 15

Eva's revenge

Eva had taken over magnificent rooms in Priam's palace. She wore only a long purple robe which hung from her shoulders and trailed to the ground. It opened at the front and exposed her nakedness as she strutted haughtily along the marble lined corridors.

She sat daily on a bejewelled throne, vetting the slave women who were paraded before her. She kept Calliope on the lead at all times, forcing her to crawl on all fours and drink from a bowl which was placed on the floor before her. When Eva tugged on the lead in different ways, Calliope knew to kneel, or purr or push against Eva's leg. She spent a short time each day training Calliope. She held a thin cane in her free hand and, if necessary, chided Calliope with a sharp clip on her buttocks. Sometimes, if Calliope mistook one of Eva's instructions, Eva brought the cane down hard to remind her pet of how she must respond. In the evenings, when the great fires were lit in the halls of the palace, Calliope curled up at her mistress's feet. Sometimes she rolled on her back and opened her legs, exposing her delectable pink crack, craving attention. The moist slit glistened in the firelight. Sometimes Eva stroked her hand along Calliope's cunt, and Calliope mewed and purred until, filled with pleasure, she raised her hips in a convulsion of ecstasy.

Eva meticulously inspected the women who were brought to her. She prised their mouths open and peered inside. She tapped their teeth with a small silver mallet a slave girl attending kept ready. She stroked their tongues and squeezed them to see how fleshy they were. She pulled at them to see how far they extended. She pinched their nipples and watched carefully to see how they lengthened, how much they hardened. She always sucked them as well, tasting them, feeling their heat, testing their hardness and feeling their throbbing against her tongue. She ran her hands around their breasts. If they were large enough, she cupped her hands beneath them and felt their weight. If they were small, she pressed the flats of her hands against them, pressed them flat and massaged them in circles so that she could feel their ribs. She smoothed her hands along the lines of the women's waists. She felt the curve of their hips and the roundness of their buttocks. She slipped her fingers between the tops of their legs and ran her fingertips along their cracks. She noted how easily the lips of their flesh parted, how moist they were, how readily her fingers slipped inside. She bent and sniffed their slits, sometimes licking them to release their aroma. Those she liked best, she licked deeply. She teased their clitorises with her fingertips. She pressed at the base to see how much they engorged, how much they hardened, how much they throbbed. She bent them over and felt the curve of their taut buttocks. She looked at the oval of their squeezed tight cunts and ran her fingers around them, testing out the softness of the flesh, the tightness of the crack. She licked between their buttocks. She tasted their anuses, probing her tongue inside, forcing the tip of her tongue into the delectable muscular ring. She had them all held and caned. She watched how quickly the red lines appeared on their skin. She sat on her ornate throne, her elbows on her knees, and looked into their fearful faces. She observed how they bit down on their lips, how they dealt with the pain, how they screamed. And she looked down on them as they lay, panting and exhausted, as buckets of water were thrown over them. She watched them gulping and choking and laughed when they heaved or passed out.

Those she accepted were chained and taken back to the beach. There, Praxis incarcerated them in cages stacked out in the burning sun. Those she rejected were thrown outside the walls of the city. There they were used as playthings by beggars and vagrants and others ejected because of disease or deformity.

Eva sat forward, her mouth wide open, as Sappho and Chryseis were pushed down onto their knees at her feet.

'We found these two in the temple, lady. They say they had hidden inside a cage for days. When we checked where they had been, we found a rack. It was smeared with spit and smelled of a woman's flesh.'

Eva rose from the ornate throne. Her purple cloak, pinned at her throat, and opened wide, fell from her shoulders to the ground in heavy swirls. Her beautifully formed body was naked and oiled. The contours of her firm breasts complemented the inward curve of her slender waist. The crack of her cunt was tight. It glistened in the flickering light of the oil lamps ranged along the smooth marble walls. She tugged the lead and Calliope, already on all fours, moved forward with her.

'This is indeed a surprise. For you as well perhaps? Our Trojan priestesses have returned. But this time it is you who are on your knees. It is I who am the lady. Perhaps you have forgotten me? Perhaps you do not remember our last meeting? No?'

Eva stretched her hand down to Sappho.

Sappho looked up at her defiantly.

'I remember you only as a slave of the Greeks. Fit for the company of beggars and vagabonds. The last I saw of you was in their company, crawling in the streets, dirty and despicable. Grovelling in the dirt. An appropriate home for a lady such as you.'

Eva smiled. She took Sappho's chin in her hand. She squeezed her cheeks together.

'What a lady you are. Still too proud for your own good, I think. And your friend as well. Chryseis no less. Your little ally in treachery. The fine priestesses of Apollo. Where is your god now, priestesses of the god of prophecy?'

Sappho spat onto Eva's hand.

Two guards rushed forward and held the heads of their spears at the sides of Sappho's head. She did not move. She spat again. The guards looked to Eva for an order. She smiled. They backed off. She released her grip on Sappho.

She smeared the spit from her hand onto Sappho's short tawny hair.

'You do not have to plead with me for punishment, my little priestess,' she mocked. 'I will punish you anyway. No, you do not have to beg me with your spitting and contempt. It will be my pleasure to humiliate and degrade you. It will be my gift to you. My gift of gratitude for your previous betrayal. Oh, how you will wish you had seen the last of me when you shut me outside the gates of Troy. Your mocking laughter will haunt you as you suffer at the hands of your lady.'

Eva stood over Sappho. She opened her mouth and dribbled her own spit onto Sappho's forehead. It ran down into Sappho's eyes and trickled onto her nose. It ran in a sticky strand down onto her lips. Sappho looked up, still disdainful and filled with contempt. She sucked Eva's spit into her mouth, swallowed it down and smiled.

Eva dropped back in her throne and laughed.

'Your pride is admirable, my little priestess. But it is misplaced. You are forgetting that it is I who am now in the position of power. It is I who will shape your destiny. It is I who will decide on your suffering. And it is I who will decide if it will end.'

Calliope pushed herself against Eva's leg. Eva stroked Calliope's head. Calliope purred.

'It is interesting, my little captives, that you have spent time in a cage. I would not like to take you away from something to which you have become accustomed. Yes, that is where you shall stay while you are with me. I cannot think of anything more comfortable or to your taste.' She turned to the guards. 'Take them to the cages! I will visit them later.'

Sappho and Chryseis were pulled to their feet and dragged away. Sappho, spit dribbling from her lips, kept Eva fixed with a glare until she was finally pulled through the huge doorway of the magnificent room.

The guards stripped away Sappho's torn and grimy smock. They lashed leather thongs around both their wrists and hauled them out of the palace.

Sappho and Chryseis were dragged through the streets. Greek soldiers were still looting houses, women were being dragged from their hiding places, men were being chained and hauled away to the beach. Sappho and Chryseis shrunk back in fear as they were prodded and poked by soldiers and beggars alike. They were stopped when a looting crowd blocked their way near a rich man's house. Some women spat on them and threw clods of mud at them. Sappho felt ashamed and humiliated.

The guards brought them to a courtyard enclosed by a high wall. It had been a transfer station for wild animals, imported from Asia and Africa and sold to the rich nobles of Troy. Most of the animals had escaped, been released or had been stolen. Enslaved women now took their places. They crouched inside the iron barred coops, holding their hands out for food or appealing to their guards for rescue. Many of the cages were stacked one on top of another. Ones near the tops of piles swayed precariously when the women moved inside them. Sappho and Chryseis were pushed into two separate cages sitting in the full glare of the sun in the middle of the courtyard.

Sappho struggled against the guards as they stuffed her inside the cage. She braced her legs against the doorway, itself barely big enough to allow entry. But it was useless.

She was weak and exhausted. She could not resist them. The guards laughed as they prised her legs away. They teased her for acting like a cat. They called her "Calliope" and kicked at her as they bundled her inside.

In the cage, there was no room to move. Sappho's legs were squeezed up so that her knees touched her nipples. Her arms were folded around her shins. Her head was bent at an angle. She had to strain her neck to see what was going on around her.

Some of the women were hooded, some gagged. Some of them were bound by the wrists and by the ankles. Some, like Sappho and Chryseis were bound only by the wrists. When any of them were taken out to be inspected for sale, or thrashed for punishment or amusement, they were chained to a thick timber post near the centre of the hot courtyard.

Sappho crouched in the cage all day. The sun beat down on her. There was no shade. Food was given to some of the women but not all. If any of the women begged for food or complained, they were dragged out of their cages and beaten.

There was always someone chained to the post. Sometimes it was a young girl, pulled from her family house, and now destined for service to a rich Greek lady. Sometimes it was a delicate woman, once noble and used to a life of favour and ease, and now reduced to slavery and servitude. Sometimes it was a beautiful African or Nubian slave, proud and tall, slender and perfectly shaped. These, the guards took particular pleasure in punishing. They chained them carefully so that they could not move their wrists at all. They bound leather thongs around their waists and pulled them tightly to the post. They beat them slowly and methodically with canes, or whips. Sometimes they smacked them with the flats of their hands. They counted how many strikes it took before the women cried out. They laughed as they watched them jerk in response to their punishment. They felt between their legs. They prised their fingers into the cracks of their cunts. They bent down and licked along their beautiful slits. They listened to their cries when they came. They increased the strength of their beating so that the cries grew louder. They let them hang there still screaming long after the punishment had ended. Sometimes they forgot about them and they were left tied to the post all night.

All through the night, the naked Sappho shivered with the cold. She thought of the terrible destruction of Troy. She looked at Chryseis, pinned inside her cage. A wave of sadness and fear swept over her. She wanted to shout out, but she knew the guards would come and punish her if she did. She stared at one of the Nubian women still hanging on the post. The outline of her muscular body was picked out by the flickering torchlight. Her head and her pubic hair had been shaved by her previous masters. She was oiled. Her dark nipples were hard and prominent. She stared over at Sappho.

Sappho pushed her fingers between the tops of her thighs and inserted them into the crack of her moist cunt. With her legs bent up, her flesh was stretched tight. The soft edges clung to her fingers. She could barely move, but she managed to shift her buttocks enough to allow her fingers in deeply. She watched the beautiful Nubian, hanging in chains on the post — naked, humiliated, still jerking with the pain of her lashing. Sappho felt a sudden flow of ecstasy. It was set off by the sight of captivity, of suffering. It welled up inside her — she could do nothing to stop it. She dropped down on her fingers and moaned. She moaned again, and quickly looked around to see if anyone had heard — they had.

A guard ran over and shook the cage. She pulled her fingers from her cunt and shrank down as much as she could. Another guard came over. They pulled her out and dragged her to the post. The beautiful Nubian was released and forced back into her cage. Sappho was chained in her place. A leather strap was wound around her waist to bind her tightly to the pillory.

They took turns, one with a short leather lash with several tails, the other with a leather strap.

The lash cut into her buttocks. She felt the sting from every one of its tattered ends. They curled around the side of her buttocks and lashed her hips. Some of the blows were directed downwards and the leather flails cut across her back or in between her buttocks. She hung onto the chain at her wrists, allowing the full weight of her body to hang heavily on its unforgiving links.

The leather belt was heavier. Its pain jolted her. It was thick and dense. It ran deep inside her. It penetrated her with thick, overwhelming pain. Its edges cut her sharply. Its smooth flat surface conveyed bursts of agony that racked her whole body. He lashed her relentlessly with it. She shuddered every time it landed. She sagged on the chains, not knowing when it would end, only hoping that sometime it would.

Sappho blinked her eyes. She squeezed her eyelids tight, then released them quickly. She opened her eyes as wide as she could. She was afraid of passing out. She saw the beautiful Nubian staring at her from inside her cage. Her legs were pulled up, her knees pressed against her breasts. She had her finger inside the tight crack of her delectable cunt.

Sappho bit her lips. Every blow made her bite down harder. She gasped and cried out. It did not release the pain that was filling her. She screamed. She screeched. She heard her cries of suffering echo around the barely lit courtyard. She knew they were accompanying a growing surge of joy that now was running out of control through her. It throbbed in time with the thrashing belt. It kept pace with the rhythmic movements of the beautiful Nubian's fingers as they slid in and out of her wet, glistening cunt. Every gasping scream, every jolting smack of the belt, every fresh glitter of moisture on the woman's fingers fed the ever building fire of Sappho's delight.

They unchained her and pushed her back into the cage. She fought against them. Now she struggled against release. Now she fought to keep out of the cage, not because she feared its imprisoning bars, but because she wanted more pain tied up to the post.

They forced her in. She clung to the door. Her hot buttocks were cooled by the iron bars. She stared at the Nubian woman and, without touching herself, she tightened in the grip of a sudden, jerking ecstasy. She kept her eyes on the Nubian woman until the last quivering of her pleasure subsided. By the time she closed her eyes, the torches had burned out and everyone was asleep.

The next morning, the guards fed some of the women. They held bowls at the bars and the women struggled to slip their hands through for morsels of food. Neither Sappho nor Chryseis was fed. Sappho watched as the guards filled a bowl with their semen. They brought it to all the cages and offered it to the women. All took it eagerly, lapping at it through the cage bars, or slurping it down when the guards held it at an angle against their imprisoning coops. Sappho watched Chryseis accept the bowl. She watched her lick her tongue out and lap at it thirstily. Sappho saw it sticking to her friend's lips. She watched her throat tighten as she swallowed it down eagerly. They came to Sappho. The bars of her cage were too tightly together and she could not get at the bowl. They opened the door and placed the bowl on the ground. She bent forward on her knees and lapped at it until the bowl was empty.

Eva walked into the courtyard with Calliope on her lead.

'Ah! I see we have animals back again in the cages. They feed very well too. Let me see this one.'

Eva bent down and grabbed Sappho's dark hair, pulling her head back.

'Well, it is an animal indeed. I do not know what sort. But I see it is the sort that drinks semen. It is clearly not a very proud animal. And that will suit my purposes. I want an animal who will be easily humbled. Ah! Your bowl is empty. And you still look so thirsty. I cannot have my animals thirsty. Not when it is so hot, and they have no shade. Push her back in her cage!'

The guards kicked at Sappho and drove her back.

She cowered inside and curled up as they slammed the iron grill shut.

Eva paraded around the cage. Calliope followed her on her lead. Eva handed the loop of Calliope's leash to one of the guards. Calliope strained on the lead as Eva stepped away from her.

Eva bent down and stroked her head.

'Do not be afraid, my little pet. I will not be out of your sight. You wait. I will have your lead back in my hand soon.'

Calliope sat back on her knees. The guard pulled at her lead. Calliope turned and bared her teeth. The guard released the tension.

Eva stalked around Sappho's cage. Her robe opened wide as she strode forward purposefully. Her beautiful naked body was exposed. Her mass of red hair bounced heavily on her shoulders. She pulled some strands away for her face and placed her fingers to her lips in mock thoughtfulness.

'I cannot decide what to do. How can I make sure my little animal does not go thirsty? Of course! I am such a fool!'

Eva stepped up onto the top of Sappho's cage. She placed

her feet apart, one on each side. She threw back her robe so that it hung between her shoulder blades and down her back. Her oiled body glistened in the morning sunlight. Sappho cowered beneath her.

'Here, my little animal. You can drink my own liquid. I will quench your thirst.'

A shower of golden urine issued between Eva's legs. It flowed down copiously as it fell. Its central stream broke into a sprinkling downpour of separate droplets. They flooded over the bars of Sappho's cage, separating into a fragrant drizzle before raining down on Sappho herself.

Sappho crouched beneath the showering flow of Eva's urine. She was unable to move. It soaked her hair and pulled it down in straggly strands. It ran across her forehead. It stung her eyes and ran down her cheeks and nose. She tasted it on her lips — salty, piquant, aromatic. She licked it with the tip of her tongue. It ran off her chin and soaked her breasts. Her nipples hardened. It ran from their ends down her stomach and into the crack of her cunt. It flowed in the fleshy valley between the swollen edges on either side of her crack. It cooled her own heat. It mixed with her own moisture. It glistened as it ran against her anus. It dripped around her buttocks and formed a pool of wetness around them. Sappho sat in it, drenched by Eva's urine, covered in the downpour of her golden rain.

Sappho licked at it again. It quenched her thirst. The savoury bite burned her throat. She gasped but, even as she drew breath, she took it down. She swallowed on it. Her lips parted with the keen anticipation of more. She tipped her head back and opened her mouth. The flow continued. It filled her mouth. She swirled her tongue in the pool it formed there. She waited for it to overflow then swallowed it all. Her thirst was both quenched and increased. She was enlivened and refreshed by the beautiful liquid that filled her. But her thirst was increased by its saltiness. The more she took, the more her need was not satisfied.

Sappho let it all run into her mouth until it stopped. She stared up between Eva's legs as the flow ceased. She kept her mouth open, waiting for more — even a single drop. She could show nothing else but that she was not yet satisfied.

Eva ordered one of the guards to stand above her. Sappho waited, gaping, until the flow began again. She closed her eyes in delight as it filled her gaping mouth. She swallowed it greedily, filling herself until she could hold no more. One by one, more guards took their position on the top of the cage. Sappho drank everything that rained down onto her.

When they had finished with her, she sat in a pool of urine. She added to it with her own. She ran her fingers in it. She felt its warmth. She still craved more.

Each day the same happened. All the women were fed semen and given showers of urine to drink. It seemed never ending. Sometimes Sappho was beaten at the post, sometimes it was Chryseis' turn. They never got a chance to speak to each other.

One day all the women were made to stand in a line to be inspected by a Greek noble. Sappho stood by the beautiful Nubian woman. She pressed her fingers into the woman's crack. The woman did the same for Sappho. When they were discovered, they were both bent over at the pillory and beaten with a cane.

One morning they were all dragged from their cages and chained together in a long line. Guards led the way as they were marched out through the great gates of Troy and onto the plain beyond. They walked all day without rest or water. Some of the women collapsed from exhaustion. They were beaten until they got to their feet and continued. When they reached the beach they were herded into groups and tied up for the night. The next day they were chained in a compound lined with shields. They were all told that there was no chance of escape. That they were slaves to the victorious Greeks and that their lives persisted only at the whim of their triumphant masters.

Sappho dropped her head. She was filled with despair. She could not imagine ever again being happy. The idea of being free, with Chryseis as her friend, now seemed an empty dream.

Chapter 16

Sappho and Chryseis are humiliated

Several days passed. The chained women stood each day, huddled together in the compound. The sun burned down on them. They were offered no shelter. All the time, the strict guards watched them. They looked out for the slightest transgression and punished them severely if one was detected. One day, Chryseis was whipped for looking up towards the rising sun.

Day by day, Sappho carefully worked her way nearer to Chryseis until she was close enough to talk.

'Chryseis, dear Chryseis. I am so happy to be close to you again. I have missed you so much. I thought we would never be together again.'

'Sappho. I never doubted we would be together. And I do not doubt we will again take our rightful place, as ladies of the temple.'

'Do not tease me, Chryseis. I am too upset to think of it.'

'I am not teasing, my darling. It will happen. I promise.'

'Then it will be like my dream.'

Sappho felt a surge of excitement run through her body. 'If only,' she thought. She clung to Chryseis' arm. She felt her cunt moisten as she felt again the touch of Chryseis' smooth skin.

There was a clamour of activity outside the compound. The gates were thrown open.

Eva had returned from Troy. There were no more women to be found in the city. Her mission was accomplished. Now she would show her booty to Praxis. Now she would claim her reward.

'Line them up!' she shouted as, with Calliope on her lead, she strode into the compound. 'Lord Praxis will be here to inspect them at any moment. Make sure they are clean and presentable. I want nothing to go wrong.'

Guards pulled the women into a line. Sappho stayed next to Chryseis although she was forced to let go of her arm.

The guards walked along the line checking the bedraggled and dirty women.

'They need washing, lady.'

'Praxis will be none the wiser!' she joked. 'What he does not see, he will not know. And he does not see anything! Do not waste the water on them.'

The guard was unsettled by her words. He did not think it wise to hold the lord Praxis in such contempt.

'My lady — '

'I have ordered you!' she shouted in a temper.

Calliope pressed herself against Eva's leg and purred.

Praxis entered. Master Wang led him to the line of terrified women.

He sniffed around the face of the first.

'This is a sweet one.'

He dropped his head and pushed his face between the tops of her thighs. They widened under the pressure of his bulky head. He probed his nose into the flesh of her crack. He breathed in deeply.

'Yes, very sweet.'

He took her nipples between his fingers and twisted them until she yelped. As soon as she cried out, he put his ear by her mouth and listened attentively. He twisted her nipples more. He listened as her cries turned to screams. Her spit sprayed onto his ear. He rubbed it off with his finger and licked it hungrily. He walked to the next and did the same. She tried to bear the pain in her nipples, but could not. When she cried out, a spray of spit frothed from her mouth and saturated his ear. He smiled, rewarded, as he licked it from his hand.

He sniffed at Sappho's cunt. He stopped and cocked his head to one side.

'I know this one. I have inhaled her aroma before. It is especially fragrant.'

'You have, my lord. She was a priestess in the temple of Apollo. A remarkable find. She will command a good price. As will her friend — the daughter of Pelador himself, the high priestess of the Temple of Apollo.'

Praxis smiled. He was overjoyed. He had never had so many slaves. He saw before him only a future of riches and good fortune.

'You have surpassed yourself, lady Eva. You will command your every wish. Nothing will be unavailable to you. I am your lord, and yet I am your slave. My pleasure is beholden not only to your beauty, but to the gifts you bear. Now, treat me to the sound of suffering. I want to know how these beautiful maidens respond to punishment. I want to listen to their humiliation.'

Eva signalled the guards. Sappho stood behind Chryseis.

'Bring that one to me!' shouted Praxis, hearing her move. 'The one who hides behind her friend. And hold her friend. She will taste my punishment in a moment.'

They dragged Sappho forward. She struggled against them. It was pointless, she knew that, but it was an unavoidable reaction to her fear. The hopeless effort made her feel even weaker, even more feeble and unable to resist the power they had over her. Her stomach filled with a painful burst of anxiety. She was overwhelmed with her vulnerability, but she fought on regardless.

'She struggles, sire. She is like a tireless beast, fighting against the hounds until the last. She does not realise the battle is lost even before it starts.'

'Yes, you are right. She is an animal who cannot see her own doom. Blindfold her! This little beast will share my blindness. Wang! You shall be her eyes as well as mine. We will both see the punishment of our high priestess in the images you paint for us.'

A wide band of black material was pulled across Sappho's eyes. It was tightened with a yank and knotted firmly behind her head. It precluded all light. Flashing lights filled her eyes as the band pulled against their pounding globes. She shook her head and stumbled in the confusion of dizziness, darkness and the dazzling blaze of stars.

She cocked her head to the side and listened. She heard the scuffling of feet. She heard Chryseis gasp under the pressure of being held tightly. She heard her pleas for release. She heard her heavy breathing.

Praxis gripped Sappho's arm and pulled her close against him. She smelled his aroma — cinnamon and frankincense. Its sharpness stuck in her throat. She swallowed heavily. It made her choke.

'Quiet, little beast!' he ordered. 'Listen!'

Sappho followed his order. She had no option. She reached out blindly, hoping to regain her balance. Praxis snatched her wrists and drew her against his massive chest. She gasped as he held her there. Her heart drummed. Its beating pounded in her ears. The pounding turned to a clatter. Sappho's head spun. The clatter to a heavy rattle. Sappho realised that the chains at Chryseis' wrists were being unlocked and dropped to the ground.

'Bring her to her knees!' shouted Praxis.

His booming voice made Sappho jump. She would have shrunk away but he held her too firmly in his muscular grip. Her helpless straining increased the tension in her body. Fighting against him, trying to oppose his will and yet knowing all the time it was futile, incensed her. She felt the heat of effort in the muscles of her arms and legs but, as well as the fire of exertion, it was also a heat of passion, a blaze of frustrated desire. She licked her lips, slaking them against the ever growing heat, stopping them from bursting into flames.

The chains went silent. There was a pause. Sappho

stopped her struggle. She listened to Praxis' thumping heart. She waited in the dazzling darkness behind the tight pulled blindfold.

'Bring her close,' ordered Praxis. 'Make her kneel before her master.'

Sappho heard them pulling Chryseis forward. She imagined the look on her face — frightened, anxious, unknowing. She imagined the tension in her body as she struggled against her captors. She pictured her nakedness, her skin gleaming with sweat, her dark hair dirtied with soil and dust, her full lips moistened with her own spattering spit. She heard her panting breaths and breathed in time with them. She sensed her terror and was herself filled with it.

Sappho listened intently as they forced Chryseis onto her knees. She heard Chryseis knees scraping against the dry dust of the ground. She smelled the cloud of fine red soil as it was kicked up by the struggle. She saw in her mind the image of Chryseis' face — her mouth wide open, dust settling on her lips, its fine red powder clinging to her sweating cheeks. Sappho pictured Chryseis' nipples — hard and throbbing, smeared with dust and sweat, pinched and painful. In her mind, Sappho saw Chryseis' waist, drawn tight in a delectable inward curve as she was made to sit up straight. She saw the glistening hint of moisture at the front of Chryseis' crack. It beckoned her with its sweetness, tantalised her with its appetising succulence. She wanted Chryseis to open her legs so that she could see more. She wanted her to part her thighs and reveal the fullness of her crack, its swollen edges, its gleaming centre, it soft pinkness. She wanted to lay the flat of her tongue against it. She wanted to draw it slowly along its length. She wanted to suck at its sweetness, taste its aroma, drink in its delights. It held everything she desired. She wanted the promise of it fulfilled.

Sappho felt her lips drying. She licked out her tongue and ran its tip across them. Her mouth was dry. She was parched. She gasped with expectation and fear. The hot air of her breath was like a fire scorching in her mouth.

'Ah!' bellowed Praxis. 'It is feeding time!'

Sappho turned her head to the side. She heard Chryseis trying to speak. She knew they were holding her head. She knew they were squeezing her cheeks between their fingers and thumbs. She recognised the stifled attempts at words, the sound of spit dribbling over her lips, the taut voice of terror and fear.

She heard something clatter against Chryseis' teeth. A bowl maybe. Yes, the edge of a bowl. She heard Chryseis splutter as the contents were tipped against her lips. It was a thick glutinous splutter, a sticky slurp, a slow bubbling gulp. It was semen. She could smell it. It was a bowl full of semen. They were forcing Chryseis to drink a bowl of semen.

'Is it full, Wang?'

'Yes, master. It is full to the brim. So full it slops over the edges.'

'And she must drink it dry. I want to hear her licking it until it is empty. Tell me. Is it at her lips now?'

'Yes, master. They are tipping the bowl back. Its edge is against her lips. Her mouth is open because they are holding her cheeks.'

'Is she taking it willingly?'

'No, master. She is refusing it. They are tipping it more so that she has to drink or she will choke.'

'And now? What now?'

'She cannot stop its flow, sire. It is running into her mouth.'

'And is she drinking it?'

'No, master. It is bubbling over her lips. She will not swallow it.'

Sappho listened to the gurgling sounds as Chryseis refused to drink from the bowl of semen. She saw it in her mind. The men holding Chryseis' cheeks, forcing her mouth open. She saw the bowl, overflowing with its liquor — white, syrupy, slopping, warm. She saw it running around Chryseis' mouth, dribbling down her chin, flowing into her mouth then streaming out. She pictured it running down her neck and onto the tips of her exposed breasts.

Sappho licked at her dry lips again. She imagined the gluey semen from the bowl against them. She licked again, trying to taste the salty tang of the semen, imagining it being poured into her hungry mouth.

'And now. Is she taking it now?'

'No, lord. It is running down her neck. It is glistening as it runs across her breasts. It drips from her nipples, but still she will not drink.'

'What now? What is she doing now?'

'Now, lord, she holds her hands clasped together.'

'Is she praying?'

'Yes, master. She prays to her god, Apollo. She begs for him to come and deliver her. She begs for his intervention. She pleads with him to liberate her.'

Sappho heard the prayer. It was one they had said together — a prayer of invocation, a prayer to conjure up a god. Sappho joined in, she could not resist. She imagined Apollo behind Chryseis. She saw Chryseis bending for her master, offering her buttocks for his pleasure.

Sappho's delight turned to frustration. She could not bear the idea that it was Chryseis and not her. She could not bear having to listen. She must take Chryseis' place. It must be her, Sappho, who should feed from the bowl.

She tore herself from Praxis' grip. Still chanting the prayer, she flung herself forward blindly. She gave no thought to what was before her, to what may threaten her.

She dropped to her knees. She brought her hands together

in supplication. She begged for Apollo to appear.

She felt a hand grasping her cheeks. It squeezed them in and forced her mouth open. She let her jaw drop, she did not resist. She waited.

Her nostrils filled with the delectable scent of semen. She inhaled it deeply. She allowed its aroma to fill her whole body, to incense her, to feed her burning desires. She felt the edge of the bowl against her teeth. She bit onto it. She opened her lips. The bowl tipped. She felt the weight of semen in it slopping towards her mouth. It tipped more. The liquid touched her lips. She let it rest against them in a glutinous pool. She sucked at it. It was enough to make it flow. It ran, like a velvet glue into her mouth. She let it swill inside. She let it fill her. She held it on her tongue and against the insides of her cheeks. She tipped her head back. She closed her mouth and swallowed. She took it all down, in one long slow and gulping swallow. She tasted it all the way down her throat. It was ambrosia — the nectar of the gods themselves. She opened her lips and felt the bowl tipping against them again. She sucked harder this time, more hungrily, more needily.

When she had drunk it all, she licked around the bowl. She lapped up every drop, then drank it down, satisfying her thirst, feeding her ever rising tide of pleasure. She was filled by it. Her thirst was satisfied, but her need was not. Her desires had risen to the surface, she was ablaze with them.

Now she wanted the god that Chryseis had invoked. Now she wanted Apollo himself. Now she wanted their lord, their saviour, the seer of the future, Apollo. She brought her hands together again as semen ran down her chin. She cried out to Apollo. She pleaded with him. She begged him to come to her, to penetrate her, to deliver her. She offered everything that she was — her needs, her hopes, her life itself.

She stopped and listened. She rested her hands on the ground and leant forward. She heard a heavy footfall behind her. It was surely Apollo — she smelled his delightful aroma. She saw him in her mind, glowing with the radiance of his godliness, his robe flowing to the ground, his massive cock, hard and throbbing. She parted her hands and bent forward in supplication before him.

She felt his godly heat — the burning fire of Olympus that was flowing in his veins. She widened her buttocks and opened herself to him. The throbbing tip of his cock touched her anus. It pressed against it. It dilated readily so that his searing cock could enter. She would let it run as deeply as he wanted, into her rectum, into her very bowels. She wanted to feel him filling her completely. She wanted to be stuffed by his bulk, scorched by his heat, rent by his thrusting godly mass.

It entered. She gasped. She fell forward, knocked over by its power, its weight. She lifted her buttocks against it. She dug her elbows into the dusty ground so that she did not fall.

She kept her buttocks high as he thrust her. Spit ran from her mouth and mixed with the dirt of the ground in front of her face. Behind the tight blindfold, she could see only the flashing stars of light. They dazzled her —filled her head. His cock swelled. Its massive end expanded inside her. She felt as if she would burst. She sensed its increased heat. She felt the hardened veins against the lining of her rectum. Its end filled. His hands gripped her hips. He held the burgeoning shaft inside. Her anus tightened onto it. Its searing fluid ran into her in a massive outpouring stream.

She dropped her face into the dusty soil. She choked and gasped for air. Her blindfolded eyes saw only confusion. She sucked at the mud and dust around her mouth. It lined the insides of her cheeks. It dried her tongue. It desiccated her.

She could not bear it as it came out. She gasped, frustrated and disappointed. It left her cool and empty. Hands gripped her hips. They held her buttocks high. Semen dribbled from her anus. She felt it running down the insides of her thighs. She was completely dissipated. She relaxed. She slumped against the hands that supported her hips.

She screamed as the cane came down across her buttocks. She had not expected it. The shock disguised the pain. As the shock passed, the pain increased. It stung her deeply. Her flesh was scorched by its heat. Another slashing cut. No shock this time, just pain. She jerked. She screamed. She gasped. Spit frothed from her gaping mouth. Another cutting slash. She twisted and turned as her body was wrenched by the agonising anguish. The hands held her tightly. Another slash. She felt as if she was on fire. Another burning slice. Her skin ignited with its heat.

Each time the cane came down she was shaken forward, jolted by its cutting force, agonised by its searing heat. She licked at the dust. She scooped it up on her tongue.

The thrashing cane continued to inflict its merciless cuts. Within the flashing blindness of the blindfold, she could not separate them. They blended into one. There was no gap between each stroke. Her body was on fire. Its flames raged out of control. The stars she saw in her mind were the stars in the sky. The heavens were ablaze. She was consumed by it. She felt her muscles tightening. She felt the pressure of pleasure within her. She saw only flashing lights. She felt only the fire inside her. She heard only the thrashing of the relentless cane. She wanted to offer her cunt to it. She lifted herself as much as she could. She felt the cane cutting into the soft exposed flesh. She gave a sudden loud scream. Her pent up ecstasy broke from her. She was released by its final escape.

She dropped forward and lapped at the ground. But she had no strength. It had all been taken from her. Her tongue stopped moving. It hung out between her lips. She fell unconscious.

'I will take them all,' shouted Praxis standing to leave. 'Brand them with my mark!'

As night fell, the women were lined up. A brazier stood in the centre of the compound. Hot irons were poked into its red hot coals.

'Bend them here!' a guard ordered. 'Lift their rumps up high. If they are to bear the brand of Praxis, it must be clearly seen. And where better than the part of their body they will show the most. No female slave in Greece goes a day without turning her rump up for a thrashing.'

He laughed and walked to the brazier. He pulled a heavy glove onto his hand and lifted one of the irons from the fire. A splutter of red sparks flew from its end. They danced on the floor in a frantic sparkling shower.

'Bring the first!'

Chryseis was the first in line. Sappho watched as she walked forward into the light of the searing brazier. Her naked body glowed in its heat, her short dark hair flickered as if it was alight. She stood proudly before the scorching iron.

'Ah! The proud priestess. Bend her over! Let me see her rump taut and ready. Let me see her pink cunt drawn tight between the crack of those shapely buttocks. Bend her over!'

They forced Chryseis onto her knees. They pressed her head forward until her face touched the dusty ground. She opened her mouth and licked it. It was her earth — Trojan earth.

'Lift her buttocks! And hold her tightly. Even she will jolt as the burning brand chars her noble skin.'

Sappho watched Chryseis bend low. She watched her buttocks rise and tighten. She saw the tight pulled oval of her cunt in the cleft they made. She looked at the glistening slit, moist and ready. She felt her own heart pounding, her own throat tightening, her own breath quickening.

She watched the brand getting closer. She winced as it touched Chryseis' taut skin. Chryseis breathed in deeply. She raised her face towards Olympus, fixed her jaw and absorbed the pain.

Sappho knew that she was next. She only hoped she could stand the cauterising pain as well as her friend. She shivered with fear. The thought drew images of pain and suffering into her mind. She dropped her hands between the tops of her thighs. Her crack was moist, its edges swollen and hot. She bent forward and was gripped by a wave of uncontrollable pleasure.

Chapter 17

Sappho and Chryseis plan revenge

A great burial mound was built in the sand dunes behind the beach. Achilles' body was burned and his bones were mixed with those of his friend Patroclus. Agamemnon decreed that Achilles' armour should be offered to the winner of a competition for the best orator. Ajax, long envious of Achilles' heavenly armour, vied against the great speechmaker Odysseus for the prize. Odysseus beguiled the audience with his tales of courage and valour. Some were moved to tears. Votes were cast and Ajax lost. He bowed gracefully to Odysseus as Odysseus claimed his reward from King Menelaus. In his heart, however, he was tortured with a burning turmoil of anger and jealousy.

As Odysseus celebrated his victory, Ajax, resting his hand on the shoulder of the slave who now guided him, wandered into the compound of women. Eva lay back in a massive chair, a wine goblet hanging loosely in her hand. She was overcome by her indulgence and unaware of the world around her. Her tired eyes were tightly closed. Her long red hair was tangled about her face. Her legs were stretched out and open wide. Calliope knelt by her side, alert and watchful of all that was going on.

Ajax stumbled clumsily amongst the women. Some of them giggled at his unseeing awkwardness. Any that did were immediately grabbed by the guards. They tied them by the wrists and ankles, face forward to heavy iron grills propped against the wall. Any that had clothing had it torn from them and they were thrashed cruelly with long thin canes.

Ajax listened to their cries with pleasure. Each swishing stroke drew his attention afresh. Each screech of pain, each numbing jerk of their bodies against the iron grill increased his interest, captured his imagination. When the guards thought the women had been punished enough, they threw down the canes and left their victims hanging against the iron grills. Ajax was led to them. He ran his fingers along the raised lines that criss crossed their buttocks and the backs of their thighs. Some were slumped heavily on their bonds and did not respond to his touch. Others winced as he pressed his fingernails into their agonising cuts. These he dwelled on. He dug his nails hard into their striped skin. He followed the lines of the raised weals that marked out their wounds. He savoured their squirming flinches. He enjoyed their captivity. He relished their hopelessness.

Sappho looked at him. She saw on his face the pleasure aroused by the women's torture and suffering. She saw his taste for pain — its infliction and the product of serving it out. But she saw something beneath this. She also saw the lines of anger etched by years of disappointment and failure. This great warrior seethed with regret. She understood the conflict that arose within him. She knew that regret and a taste for the suffering of others was a powerful combination. It was a combination which weakened Ajax, but one which could work to her own advantage. She realised that behind this chink in Ajax's armour there was a chance for freedom.

She moved closer to Ajax's massive, muscular body. She rubbed herself against him. She did not know what to expect. Perhaps he would brush her aside like an irritating fly? Perhaps his guards would pull her away and punish her for her impertinence? Her heart pounded. Nothing happened. It fed her courage. She knew she must take the risk. If she did not act, nothing would be gained. She ran her hand between his thighs and cupped his weighty testicles in their palms.

Ajax lifted his face and sniffed. He inhaled her scent as if he was a beast and she his hapless prey.

Sappho held her breath. There was no turning back.

'Can you smell my fragrance, lord?' she whispered.

He widened his nostrils and breathed in deeply.

'I can. It is sweet.'

Sappho felt a wave of relief flood through her.

'It is for you, my lord.' She pulled his hand against her cunt. 'See how my flesh moistens at your touch. Breathe in my aroma, sire. It is there because of your magnificence, your stature as a warrior and a chieftain. Here sniff closer. Bring your nostrils against its source. Press them against the crack which is the wellspring of my flavour.'

She pulled her hand behind his head and tipped it forward. His slave pushed her back. She froze, suddenly filled with fresh fear. Ajax pushed the slave away. Sappho bit her lips and continued. She squeezed his testicles. She felt them throbbing. With her other hand, she pressed his finger along the soft crack of her flesh. It opened to his touch. His fingers slipped inside. She widened her thighs and dropped herself against them, allowing them in, warming them with her heat, wetting them with the flow of her fragrant moisture.

Sappho looked over imploringly to Chryseis. Chryseis walked over and knelt between Ajax's mighty thighs. Without saying anything, she bent and took the swollen tip of his cock between her dewy lips. He breathed in with delight.

With her one hand, Sappho clung to his testicles. She felt them pounding in her grip. With her other hand, she pressed his fingers deeper into her soft, wet slit.

'You are so powerful, my lord. I feel it in your body like a fire. I suffer pain just being so close to you, just touching you. And I sense your frustration, your need for revenge — and I am excited by the power of it.'

Chryseis dropped her head fully onto his cock. She drew the shaft deeply inside her mouth.

Ajax lifted his head and inhaled heavily.

'What are you saying? What are you telling me?'

'I am saying that I and my friend can help you. That the two priestesses of Apollo can help you take your revenge on your sworn enemy Praxis. You need wait no longer, sire. We are your angels of Apollo. We are here to serve your need for retribution.'

Chryseis drew his cock in deeper. She gagged and drew back. Spit ran from her lips. She slurped it back, pressed herself down hard again and sucked greedily against the venous shaft that plugged her mouth.

'How is such a thing possible?'

Sappho pushed his fingers even further into her cunt. Her moisture ran across his palm and dribbled onto his wrist.

'Bring the downfall of his lackey, Eva, my lord, and Praxis too will fall.'

Chryseis moved her head up and down his massive cock. Her mouth was as wide as it could go. Her lips were stretched tight. She swallowed hard and the throbbing tip was pulled to the back of her gagging throat.

'And how can slaves perform this miraculous feat?'

Sappho squeezed his testicles hard. She gripped them tightly in her fingers, feeling their pliability under her grasp. She felt his cock throbbing in Chryseis' mouth — hardened into a rigid staff by her warm tongue and the talk of revenge. She felt the surging of his semen — the need for relief from the pleasure he was suffering.

'In matters like this, my lord, slaves are the most powerful. Because our enemies do not suspect us, they do not see the threat that we carry. Those held in contempt are often the most dangerous, my lord.'

'Does that mean I should not trust you either?'

'No, my lord. We ask only one thing. It is our only wish. And it is a wish you can grant with no effort or sacrifice.'

'And that is?'

'Our freedom, lord. Our freedom.'

'And how will this victory you speak of be accomplished?'

'With guile, my lord. With guile. The lady Eva will bring about her own downfall. She will inflict her own suffering. She will bring defeat upon herself. And with her subjugation, your enemy, Praxis, will topple.'

She tightened her hand around his testicles. She felt the pounding throb of his semen as it streamed into the shaft of his cock. She sat heavily on his hand. She watched Chryseis plunge her head down on his cock until her lips were pressed against its base. Sappho tensed her buttocks. She forced her soft flesh against his knuckles. He tensed his body and pressed his huge hand against the back of Chryseis' head. His semen splattered into her throat and filled her with its scorching flow.

Sappho did not let go. She held onto his testicles. She gripped them tightly as they throbbed.

He threw his head back and roared.

'I will have more of a guarantee than your promise, my fine priestesses! You will not have the allegiance of Ajax without some investment of your own.'

Sappho and Chryseis fell back, frightened and shocked by his sudden outburst.

He grabbed both by the hair and lifted them off the ground.

'Can you suffer pain for the cause you propose?'

'My lord,' begged Sappho. 'We have no intention to deceive. You do not need to test us. My lord!'

He dropped Chryseis to the ground. She fell on her side. Her mouth dropped open. Semen dribbled from its corners.

'Ah! But there you are wrong, my little priestess,' he said gleefully, shaking Sappho like a toy. 'Ajax has been tricked before. He is wiser now. He will not be deceived again. Bind their ankles!'

He tossed Sappho to the ground alongside Chryseis.

Guards ran forward. They grabbed Chryseis' and Sappho's ankles and bound them tightly with leather thongs. They lay side by side. Semen still oozed from Chryseis' mouth. It mixed with the dusty ground around them and smeared her face with reddish, gluey mud. The dust stuck to Sappho's wet cunt. It smudged her pink flesh with a daub of reddish sludge. Sappho stared into Chryseis' eyes. She wanted to tell her she was sorry. She wanted to tell her she had hoped for freedom, not for further punishment. She opened her mouth to speak. A guard clapped his hand across it and stifled her effort.

The guards tied two long leashes to the bindings at each of their ankles. They dragged them both in front of Ajax. Sappho choked on the dust that was thrown up in clouds around them.

'We have them bound, lord. Shall we drag them as Achilles dragged the vanquished Hector?'

'Yes, haul them for a while. I will decide their test to the accompaniment of their cries for release. Yes, the music of their pleas for mercy will accompany my thoughts on how they should suffer.'

The other women were pulled hurriedly to the sides of the compound. One fell. Her wrists twisted in her chains. She was pulled roughly out of the way and kicked in the buttocks. She screamed in pain. A guard, angered by her outburst, took a cane and thrashed her roughly. Its swishing edge struck the backs of her thighs and behind her knees as she struggled to get back in line.

'Haul them!' shouted Ajax. 'I want to hear the priestesses cry out to their master. I want to hear them pleading for mercy. I want to hear them begging to be spared.'

Guards took hold of each of the two leashes that trailed from Sappho and Chryseis' ankles. They pulled them tight.

Sappho gasped as they were drawn taut. She was frightened and confused. She was shocked by the suddenness of Ajax's response. She had not expected it. She was filled with guilt and remorse. She looked again at Chryseis. She wanted to reach out to her and tell her that she was sorry for bringing this upon them. She tried to speak, but her words were suppressed by the sudden jolt as the two men yanked the leashes hard and ran forward.

The men laughed as they drew both the women across the ground by the ankles.

Sappho bounced on the dusty ground. Her shoulders scraped against the rough red soil. Her mouth filled with the acrid tasting dirt as it billowed up in clouds around her. Her hands trailed above her head. She tried to grip the ground. She clawed her nails into it, struggling somehow to arrest the giddying motion, to prevent the bruising bounces, but it was impossible. She tightened her jaws. She held her teeth locked together. She hoped she could bear it. She hoped she could survive until it stopped.

They both twisted on the leashes, bouncing onto their fronts then onto their sides and backs. When she was face down, Sappho's nipples, already hard and throbbing with fear, scraped the ground. The pain was intense — penetrating, unstoppable. Her face dug a furrow in the red soil. Her nose filled with it. Her gaping mouth was stuffed by it. She choked and coughed. When she tried to swallow, she could not — her throat was too dry and filled with the desiccating dirt.

The woman who had been caned, kicked out at them as they were pulled past — she blamed them for her own punishment, her own suffering and pain. When they were pulled past her again, she spat at them. The glob of saliva landed on Sappho's face and ran into one of her eyes. Straight away, it became a clogging smear of caked dust. The next time they were pulled around, more of the women spat on them — each one venting their anger at their own captivity and helplessness. More of the gluey froth splattered onto Sappho's face. She licked at it to try and slake her dust-filled mouth. She sucked some of it in. She ran it around the insides of her cheeks and over her dry tongue. She gulped with relief as a trickle of it dribbled into her parched throat.

Sappho's head spun giddily. She did not know which way was up. The sky and the dusty ground spun around her in a flashing madness of blurred images. She heard Chryseis groaning every time she bounced on the earth. She heard her choking as she too tried to lick spit from around her mouth and use it to ease the dryness of her mouth and throat.

With every thump, with every slobbering slurp, Sappho was overcome with a fresh wave of guilt. Her body was racked with pain, but the feeling of guilt filled her more than the agony of her physical suffering.

'What is happening to them?' shouted Ajax. 'What are those sounds I can hear?'

They are being spat on, lord,' said the slave at his side. 'The other slave women are venting their anger on them, they do not know how to lash out, and so they lash out at their own kind. Their spit dribbles on the faces of the two priestesses. They are humiliated and sullied. They are trying to lick it into their dust filled mouths.'

'And is their thirst being satisfied?'

'No, my lord. It is not.'

'Then we must satisfy it. Pull them in front of the other women. The little priestesses must not go thirsty while they are in the care of their master, Ajax.'

Sappho and Chryseis were hauled in front of the line of women. An extra leash was tied to their wrists. Guards pulled this tight and, with the tension still on the leashes at their ankles, the two women were stretched out.

All the women in line spat at them. They covered them with their saliva. Sappho felt it trickling between the tops of her thighs. She felt it running along her tight stretched crack. She felt it dripping from her hard nipples. She tasted it in her mouth as she licked it from her lips and sucked it in. It was delectable. She opened her mouth and let it fill. The bubbling spit gathered in a foaming froth around her tongue. She let it run to the back of her throat. She swallowed on it greedily. She opened her mouth straight away and let it fill again. She felt as if she was bathing in it.

'What now?' asked Ajax. 'Is their thirst satisfied?'

'No, my lord. They are insatiable. I do not know what will satisfy them.'

'Take me to them!'

The slave led Ajax over to Sappho and Chryseis.

They both lay on their backs. They writhed, their mouths dripping with frothing spit, their tongues greedily lapping it up.

Ajax stood over them.

'Bring each of the women to them. Let us see if they can satisfy the thirst of these hungry beasts.'

The first woman was made to stand over Sappho, her legs apart.

Sappho looked up between the woman's thighs. She opened her mouth wide. She let the foam of bubbling spit run down her cheeks. She licked her tongue out. She wanted more.

Sappho watched the stream of urine pouring down on her. She welcomed it into her mouth. She let it fill. She turned her face into it. She let it run up her nose and into her eyes. She swallowed all she could. Its biting, heady taste thrilled her. She consumed it. She was consumed by the delight of it.

The next woman doused her in the same way. Sappho guzzled it down. She sucked from the stream itself, not giving it time to rest in her mouth. She watched the shimmering waterfall. It dazzled her as she stared into it, glistening and twinkling in the bright light of the hot fiery sun.

Ajax listened as each of the women was brought forward. He knelt by Sappho's side as she gulped and swilled down the urine. He held his hand in the flow and watched her reaching after its changing course, desperate not to miss a drop.

The last woman was taken away. Ajax got up and straddled Sappho. She looked up between his legs and waited. She opened her mouth wide and held out her tongue. She braced herself against the bonds at her wrists and ankles. She inhaled deeply, increasing the tension of her body.

The golden cascade flowed down onto her. It splashed heavily in her eyes and stung them. She did not blink or flinch. She gulped it up and swallowed it ravenously. Each time she swallowed, she turned her face into it so that it ran across her cheeks and down her neck. She bathed in it for the few moments it took to take it down. She writhed beneath it, steeped in the ambrosia of his drenching torrent of urine.

As she reached desperately for the last drops, he stood back.

She turned her face to the side and let it rest in the pool of urine that lay around her. She allowed the tip of her tongue fall into it. She still wanted more. She lapped at it. She sucked at it. She was filled with a rising tide of pleasure as she listened to the sounds of her own gurgling efforts to gain satisfaction.

They held her tightly between the leather leashes at her ankles and wrists. The tension inflamed her. She twisted and pushed her face into the pool of urine. It splashed around her. She drank from it. She felt a jerking spasm of ecstasy throbbing in her agonised body.

Ajax bent down to her. His unseeing eyes wandered across her urine soaked skin.

'Now, little priestess, can you tell me how you will bring about the pleasure of your lord, Ajax?'

Sappho lifted her head. She moved her lips. She could hardly speak. Urine ran from her mouth, across her cheeks and into her ears.

'With ... '

She choked. She jerked as another jolt of pleasure ran through her.

'Speak up, my little priestess. That is if you are still offering to help your lord, Ajax.'

Sappho's heart pounded with excitement. She tightened her buttocks together. She felt the wet edges of her cunt squeezed. Another jolt of ecstasy gripped her.

'I am, my lord. I am.'

'Then how will you please me?'

'With guile, my lord. Your revenge is close at hand. With guile, my lord. That is how I will please you. With guile.'

Eva slept heavily in the huge ornate chair. Her arms hung lazily over the sides of its massive clawed arms. She had dropped the wine goblet and let go of Calliope's lead. Her legs were apart and stretched out. Her cunt was exposed, its flesh swollen, its slit soft and moist and glistening in the light of the newly lit torches. She had not roused during the punishing test to which Ajax had subjected Sappho and Chryseis.

Calliope, still on her hands and knees, slunk from the shadow of Eva's chair. She crawled into the open. She had heard everything. She knew what was planned — the conspiracy to overthrow her mistress Eva, the salvation for Sappho and Chryseis, the revenge of Ajax against Praxis. But she did not crawl to her lady's side. She did not rub herself against her drunken patron. She did not wake her from her inebriate slumber. She did not alert her to the threat of treachery, or warn her of the plan for her downfall. No, that was no longer her purpose. Her time of servitude was at an end.

Trailing her lead behind her, Calliope crawled on all fours to Ajax. She rubbed her cheek against his leg.

He dropped his hand onto her head.

'You have heard everything,' he said.

She lowered her head and rubbed her shoulder hard against the side of his knee.

'You know what is planned? You have listened in on our plot to overthrow your lord Praxis.'

Calliope purred. She looked up at Ajax. She stared into his blind eyes. She recalled the trick she had played on him — how her conspiracy with Praxis had led to his terrible fate on the spears. She sneered and bared her teeth. Her time as Eva's pet was drawing to a close. The game was finished. For that is what it had been. Now she would make the final move. Her own conspiracy with Praxis, her game at the expense of Eva, would not, this time, work against Ajax. This time, her secret agreement with Praxis — one which had catered to her own need for the treatment she had so much enjoyed as Eva's pet — would be at the expense of her haughty "mistress". Eva, the captured slave, had been led into the trap like an innocent fawn to a huntsman's arrow. Now it was time to release the bow. Calliope was the hunter and she was ready for the kill. A dribble of spit ran from the corner of her mouth as she anticipated the final chapter of the delectable entertainment.

'You say nothing, mistress,' Ajax said, stroking her head.

'Not against you, my lord,' she replied as she nuzzled up close to him and started purring again. 'Not against you.'

'Then you will be my ally in this?'

Calliope purred her assent.

'Your secret is also mine, my lord.'

CHAPTER 18

Eva's downfall

Eva felt invulnerable. Praxis had showered her with gifts. She walked daily on the beach. She wore her purple robe open at the front. It exposed her naked body — her glowing oiled skin, her rounded breasts, her hard prominent nipples. Her mass of red hair trailed back in the warm wind that blew in from the sea. The glitter of gold at her neck and around her slender wrists reflected from her in dazzling sparkles of light. Slaves fell to their knees as she passed. She was like a god.

She sat alongside Praxis in his huge tent. Torches were placed in stands, braziers burned, colourful curtains hung from the high walls. Naked slave girls, their heads and pubic hair shaved, stood awaiting instructions from their master and mistress. Some held baskets of flowers, some trays of food, some carafes of wine. Three of them had been bent over a bar resting on two heavy supports and were being whipped.

The blind Praxis leant across to Eva

'What is the reason for their punishment, lady?'

'They were too slow when I asked them to bring me wine and sweetmeats. Do you think I am being too lenient?'

He smiled, looking around blindly, listening to the terrified cries of the pain racked girls.

'You are never too lenient, lady.'

Guards came to attention at the entrance as Agamemnon and Ajax entered.

'Who is it, lady?'

'It is King Agamemnon and the lord Ajax.'

Praxis was angered and unnerved by the arrival of his enemy Ajax. He stood and, with a forced grin, masked his displeasure for fear of incurring the wrath of his king.

'Welcome, sire. And you too, my lord Ajax. It is an honour to receive you both.'

Agamemnon slumped on a chair which was hurriedly brought.

Ajax bowed to Praxis

'Praxis, I hope you do not mind me bringing a pair of slaves. I think you must know of them. The lady Eva did not decline my request to take them when I visited her. At least, she did not say anything when I asked her. I am so pleased you found them for me. They are delightful. Ah! Here they are now. The Trojan priestesses, Sappho and Chryseis.'

Praxis' face froze with anger. He could not disguise his annoyance. He had not realised that Eva had allowed Sappho and Chryseis to slip through her fingers.

'And, Praxis, I have forgiven you the theft of my beautiful slave Weena. I bear no grudge. Have her as my gift. I have lost one Trojan beauty, but look, I have gained two! Yes, I am filled with joy and benevolence. They should call me "Ajax the Magnanimous"'

Praxis could not help scowling. He reached back, fumbling to find the arms of his chair.

Calliope pulled on her lead. She pressed against Ajax's leg, moving him up against a complex construction of wood, metal and leather that stood in the centre of the tent. She pressed her cheek against its leather thongs. She remembered the torment of Weena — a torture wrought at Calliope's own hands. Eva yanked her back on the lead.

Calliope looked up at her and tightened her eyes. Eva did not see the contempt and anticipation of release on her face.

'And what is this, my lady?' asked Ajax, as he stretched out his hands and touched the tangle of materials.

'It is called the "shrinking man", my lord. It is a device of captivity. It is the lover's embrace from which there is no escape. It has the power to inflict pain like no other. It is the very perfection of suffering. It is the pinnacle of excruciating pain. To witness its use is like being in the presence of the gods themselves.'

'Is it a device which can also bring pleasure to those who are blind?'

'It is, my lord. The screams the "shrinking man" draws from its victims are a more powerful source of excitement then anything that can be seen. If you request its use, I promise you will be amply rewarded by the tune it brings forth. It will be music such as you have never heard. It will lift you like the lyre of Apollo.'

'You have won me over to its use, my lady. Perhaps the little priestess, Sappho, shall be the first instrument to be played on this amazing apparatus. Yes, my personal guard will bring her.'

Sappho was dragged forward. She drew back at the sight of the terrible "shrinking man". She dug her heels into the soft earth as Ajax's guards pulled on her arms.

The assembly of the wooden frame, laced together with metal fixings was draped with leather straps and thongs. It dripped with water. It looked like a monstrous creature arisen from the depths of a hellish ocean. It was encircled by buckets filled with water. The disc like surfaces of the water reflected the lights from the torches and lamps. It was as if the "shrinking man" was ringed by iridescent moons.

'Your little priestess is fearful now, but she will soon warm to the loving embrace of the "shrinking man". Here little priestess. Do not be afraid to approach your paramour. He will clutch you so close you will never want to be released from his arms.'

Ajax's guards struggled to bring Sappho close. Her heels lost their purchase. She fought against them, spitting and biting and bracing her feet against the heavy timber base.

As the guards offered her up to the device, they looked confused. They seemed unable to carry out their instructions. The apparatus was too complicated. They could not work out which way to place their struggling victim, how to bring the bindings together, how to close them properly around its captive's limbs.

'Sire,' said one. 'It is beyond us.'

Ajax held his hand to his forehead.

'Forgive me, lady. My guards are untutored in such things. And they are right to admit it. I am corrected. I could not allow them to bind one of my slave priestesses into such a contraption for fear of making a mistake. They have made me understand that this apparatus of perfection must be operated perfectly. It seems as though I am to be disappointed.'

'No, my lord,' urged Eva, anxious to please. 'Let my own guards perform the duty. They know well how the mechanism works.'

'I could not lady. You can see, the little priestess is such an animal. I fear they could not restrain her sufficiently well. And she would be injured in the ensuring struggle. Or perhaps bring harm to your "shrinking man". No, lady. That would never do.'

'Then I will instruct your guards myself,' she said with a burst of impatient arrogance. 'And you will have the pleasure of listening to my own commentary. Yes. I will act as the victim so that your guards can learn the technique. Then, when they have mastered it, I will be released and your little priestess will take my place. Yes, it amuses me to do so. Perhaps you will hold my pet, sire.'

Eva handed Ajax Calliope's lead. Calliope pressed herself eagerly against the side of his leg. Ajax smiled.

'First, my lord, you must imagine how the "shrinking man" welcomes his lover. I step into the cage of leather and metal. His drapes are loose at the moment. They have already been soaked so that they are soft and stretched. I can enter with ease. His leather strapping is like silk against my skin. Now, I kneel within him. His shape fits my body perfectly. He welcomes me to kneel on all fours within his carcass. Now, a metal clasp closes around my head. It is tight. It is a constricting band around my forehead. Once in it, I cannot move. Now, your guards must be careful to pull these straps closely across my face. They have done it, but they leave them free of my mouth, for I must give you the commentary. As they pull the leather straps tighter, they close around my body. I feel them tensioning now. The tightness takes my breath away. The straps are broad enough to hold me, thin enough to cut into my skin. There are so many that, as they wrap me up in their clutches, I cannot move at all. My arms are already fixed by them. Now they must wrap each of my fingers, even they will not escape the caress of the "shrinking man".'

Calliope sat up on her knees. Sappho's eyes brightened as the guards slackened their grip on her arms.

'Now, my lord Ajax, I cannot even move my legs. The straps have a hold of me there as well. And each of my toes is bound with delicate wet thongs of leather. Now, they lash more straps around my thighs and knees. They already have my calves and ankles tight. Now they must pull a strap up into my slit. It must be as tight as they can make it. I need to feel it deep between the folds of my crack. They are doing it now. They are pulling it between the flesh. Yes, it is tight. My flesh is wet and the slippery leather slips easily between the mounds on each side. It has made me even wetter with its tension. And it is painful, but I cannot pull away or gain any relief from it. It is truly a delectable tension. And there is more to come. The "shrinking man" has only just begun to work his magic.'

Calliope stood up. She draped her arm around Ajax's shoulder.

'And the gag, my lady Eva? Are you ready for the gag?' she asked.

Ajax smiled.

'Yes, lady Eva. Your mistress asked you a question. Are you ready for the gag? Ah! You look surprised, lady. Has it been so long since you have felt the pain of torture? Had you forgotten that your pet was also your mistress? Did you truly believe that I was your slave? Poor Eva. Deceived so easily. Gag her!'

The guards pulled a large leather ball gag into Eva's mouth. She could not struggle or fight against them. She could not appeal or cry out. Spit ran from her mouth as they stuffed it in. They lashed it tight and bound a leather strap on top of it so that it was held firmly inside and could not be seen. They tightened all the other straps and thongs, pulling them up into their clasps or buckles, locating them into the teethed jaws of their unforgiving clamps.

Praxis sensed the threat of treachery. A wave of fear flooded over him. He jumped to his feet. He was quickly restrained. He held out his hands hopelessly as they chained his wrists and flung him to the ground.

'I hope you have not lost your enthusiasm for the "shrinking man", lady,' mocked Calliope. 'You have only introduced it to us. We need to see what else it can do.'

Eva's eyes flashed in confusion. She could not understand what was happening. She had felt so assured of her place with Praxis. She had been so certain of having overthrown Calliope. Now, the one she had treated as a pet, stood taunting her, and mocking her blind arrogance for entangling herself in her own apparatus of torture. She tried to bite onto the large leather ball in her mouth. The straps across her face and the cage around her head made it impossible even to do that. She tried to move her arms, her fingers, her legs, her toes. It was impossible. She was completely caught in the clutches of the terrible contraption.

She could not move at all. She felt the tightness of the tight drawn strap in her slit. She felt the throbbing of her clitoris against its unrelenting pressure. She tried to relax her thighs, her buttocks, but she was now inseparable from the contraption which held her in its vice like embrace.

'Douse her!' shouted Calliope. 'Slacken the pressure on poor Eva. I cannot bear to see her suffering.'

Eva's eyes flashed for side to side. She heard the buckets being lifted. She heard the sloshing of water. The saw the flicker of light reflected in rainbows around her as it was tossed out. She felt the sudden shock of it as it was thrown heavily all over the "shrinking man" — all over her. It ran down her face and streamed from her chin. She could not move at all as it flowed in rivers over her body. But the wetting brought a fresh pliability to the leather bindings. She felt them slipping against her skin. She managed to move a finger. A wave of relief rushed through her. She pulled against the constricting bonds. They gave under the pressure.

'Now tighten the straps fully!' shouted Calliope.

The straps were pulled again — levered into their clasps, tensioned into their buckles and clamps. Eva could no longer move her finger. The moment of freedom had passed. She knew that there was no escape.

Braziers were brought and set around the "shrinking man" and its victim. Their heat soon began to dry and tighten the tangle of wet leather thongs. Eva felt its increasing compression. Her eyes filled with terror. They were the only part of her body she could command — and they were no longer in her control. Her mind was ablaze with fear. Her head was filled with the terror of it all. She could do nothing to change it. She could not even express it.

The tightening increased. Her skin was pinched by its shrinking straps. Her limbs, already confined by its contracting framework, throbbed and pounded with the increased tension. Her jaws, held wide by the plugging gag, generated pains which ran down her throat and into her bowels. She could not swallow. Her cunt was wet, she could feel that, but its wetness was frustrated by the feeling of numbness across her whole body. She could only move her eyes. But they brought her no hope, no salvation. They flashed around in terror — she was panic-stricken by what was happening. She was overwhelmed by what she knew was in store — and yet she could not guess what that could be.

Eva knelt, held inside the entwining arms of the "shrinking man". The ever tightening bands of leather squeezed her as they continued to shrink in the drying heat of the braziers. She wanted so much to cry out, to scream for release, to beg for her freedom. She thought of how she would do anything to be set free. She would allow herself to be degraded in any way her torturers saw fit. She would serve them, be humiliated by them.

But there was no way of passing her message to them. And she realised they would not care even if they knew. They only wanted her suffering and she could do nothing to deny them. She wanted to shiver, to allow her body to express her fear, but she could not even do that. She wanted to lick her lips, to push out her tongue. Any movement would allow her to know that she had some control over her body. But she could do nothing. She had no control. It had been taken from her. The enfolding caress of the "shrinking man" was all enveloping. Its control over her was total. She was a victim of perfect stillness, a prisoner of absolute bondage.

The bindings continued to shrink, to cut her skin. Her whole body was criss crossed with the marks of its terrible grip. There was no release for Eva. She remained motionless. Her body trapped in arrant silence, a victim of the inescapable grip of the unforgiving "shrinking man".

Calliope knelt beside her.

She ran her hands across the slowly drying leather straps. She felt their tension. She sensed their contraction. She sensed the pain that was passing onto its terrified victim, Eva. She traced her fingers against Eva's skin, taut between the strapping, frozen in its grasp. She rested them against the strap that was pulled up between Eva's crack. She felt the tight pulled swollen mound of flesh on either side. She felt the pounding in Eva's veins. She felt the stillness of her body — taut and clasped in the relentless grip of the eager talons of the "shrinking man".

'Yes, it is your little pet,' she whispered. 'Poor Eva, did you really believe in your silly arrangement with Praxis? Is that possible? Yes, I believe you did. Poor, innocent Eva. I can hardly believe you could be so foolish. Eva. Eva. It was a trick. Eva, it was a trick. I wanted to be your pet so that I could show you that I was truly your mistress. How would you ever know unless you experienced the downfall of your false hope? Oh, you were so proud. You were so arrogant. And I enjoyed it. All the time knowing that soon I would bring you back again to your rightful place. Poor Eva. Nothing to say? Do not worry. There will be time. Yes, you will be going back to Greece as a captive. Do not think you will ever be otherwise. You will carry the brand of Ajax and you will be my lowliest slave. Oh, Eva, I am sad that you will have to suffer so much.'

A sparking branding iron was lifted from one of the braziers. Eva did not move in any way as it was placed first on one of her taut buttocks, then on the next. Her eyes flashed from side to side — frantic expressions of her agony. She was bursting with pain. It ran through her in massive waves. No part of her body was immune to its progress or its ferocity. But she remained still, her flashing eyes the only signal of her agony. Motionless and in complete silence, she was held in a state of perfect pain, embraced in the unforgiving, and still tightening grip, of the terrible "shrinking man".

Praxis cried out for Master Wang, but he was not there. He reached out for a slave to help him, but they had all run away or been stolen by others. He called for Eva and, although she was close by, she could not speak. She had lain all night, shivering and jerking with the shock of her incarceration in the "shrinking man". Her body, was covered in the weals of his embrace. She could not stand up, could not bend. She smelled of urine and had vomited.

Soldiers emptied Praxis' huge tent then overturned a brazier and scattered its flaming coals around the ornate skirting. Praxis was bound by the wrists and, together with Eva, was loaded onto a small hand-pulled cart. The tent burned behind them as the cart was drawn through the sand dunes and along the beach. Finally, they were brought to Ajax's boat and thrown roughly down on the sand.

Praxis was taunted by the soldiers. They prodded him with their spears as he stumbled and fell. He struggled to his feet. He reached out to them blindly, but they avoided him easily. When he dropped to the ground, they taunted him and spat on him. In the end, they chained him and yanked him up against the side of Ajax's beached ship. Praxis hung against the boat, his massive muscles straining to hold his weight, his blind eyes staring emptily out to sea.

Eva was thrown down on her back. Any soldier that wanted, thrust his cock into her splayed wide cunt. They turned her over and held her so that they could drive their cocks onto her anus. Some used the butt ends of spears, to fill her cunt and anus. They poked them into her mouth as they splashed their semen over her. They strapped her to a shield and flayed her with whips. She twisted and writhed, sometimes screaming out, sometimes clenching her jaws in defiant silence. One of them beat her with his leather belt. It raised wide red weals on her back. She was gagged and dragged along the beach by her ankles. They pulled her through the lapping waves and smeared her with gritty sand. In the end, they chained her to Praxis' feet and staked out her ankles wide so that anyone who wanted to enjoy her could. They hung a placard around her neck — "Lady Eva, Mistress of Slaves".

Chapter 19

Sappho and Chryseis — priestesses of Apollo again

Praxis and Eva had lain chained together for three days. Water was sloshed over them each morning and they could lick it up to quench their thirst, but they were given no food.

The Greek army was preparing to return home. The beach was filled with the clamour of armour and bounty being loaded into the ships. For all their suffering, the Greeks had little to show for their sacrifice. Their greatest warrior, Achilles, was dead. The beautiful princess of Sparta, Helen — its most hoped for prize and reason for the war itself — remained unfound. The army of tribes had camped on the beach for eleven years. They had lost many of their comrades. They had missed their wives and their children growing up. When finally they had ransacked the city, they found it without the expected spoils. Paris had disappeared and so had all of Priam's treasure. During the long years of siege, much of the city's wealth had been spirited away. The beach was filled with a yearning to return home. The lightly laden boats road high in the water.

Praxis and Eva watched as the brazen bull was hauled up the side of Ajax's boat. Its massive carcass thudded against the black planking. It swayed precariously on its tangle of hurriedly knotted ropes. The warm onshore breeze whistled through its mouth and nostrils. It bellowed and moaned as it spun giddily in its bonds. Eva remembered her own suffering, hanging by her wrists from the oars of the same boat. She bit onto her lips. She anticipated no salvation, all she could see before her was a life of suffering and pain.

Weena was led up a long gangplank with others. Her petite body, her shaved head and naked crack, glowed silkily in the warm morning sunlight. She looked fresh and beautiful. She stared down at Eva and Praxis. Eva dropped her eyes. Weena took it as deference, smiled and went aboard. But it was not humility that stirred inside Eva, it was boiling anger fed by the need for revenge. The deception which she had been victim to filled her veins with an overwhelming and poisonous hatred.

When his ship was ready for sea, Ajax was brought from his tent.

Calliope hung on his arm and led him down the beach.

'Ah, my new playthings are waiting, lord,' she said gleefully.

Eva stared hard into his unseeing eyes.

Ajax smiled.

'Have them loaded. We must leave this accursed beach. Chain them in the deepest part of the hold. And do not waste water on them. They can drink from the bilges until we reach the welcome shores of our homeland.'

He spat at Praxis. The gluey froth landed in Praxis' blind eyes. It ran in sticky streaks down his cheeks. Praxis licked it up and swallowed it thirstily.

Calliope glanced back at Eva but turned quickly. She threw her head back in disdain. She marched up into the black boat, her naked body covered only by her flowing purple robe. Her hands clung to the arm of her patron and master, the lord Ajax. She stopped at the top and surveyed the clamorous beach.

Eva looked up under her eyes and saw the sparkling flash of light reflected from the faceted gold ring in Calliope's clitoris. A wave of resentment flooded over her. It mixed with a tide of vengeance she knew could only be assuaged by the most terrible retribution. She bit on her lips and forced her fingers into the slit of her cunt. She massaged them up and down, feeding the heat of her anger with the flames of her own passion.

Sappho and Chryseis, naked and covered in dirt, made their way unhindered over the sand dunes and across the great plain of Troy. Ajax had honoured their agreement — they were free. Sappho was overwhelmed by the feeling of liberation. Everything she saw excited her. She felt as though she was in heaven.

They reached the massive walls of the city, now holed and ruined by the victorious Greeks. They stood hand in hand at the yawning entrance which had been the main gate.

Three women hung helplessly on crucifixes. Their arms were stretched out tightly onto the crossbeams where their wrists were secured by tight leather thongs. Their ankles were drawn together and tied tightly against the upright. They had hung there for days and now, hungry and exhausted, slumped heavily on their bonds. Their naked bodies were laced with red lines — the cutting result of relentless beating by the triumphant soldiers who had strung them up.

Sappho stared up at them as she walked with Chryseis between them. One of the women lifted her face. Her head and pubic hair were shaved. She smiled helplessly. Sappho felt compassion of the suffering woman. She looked up between her legs and saw the tight crack of her cunt. Sappho's eyes followed the strained curve of her slender waist and the delicate rise of her hips. Again, she looked at the woman's helpless gaze. The site of her suffering let free a surge of heated excitement that ran through Sappho in a sudden shiver. The more she stared, the more she felt the heat of passion in her own cunt. The more she looked, the more it increased. The more it increased, the more she wanted to satisfy herself.

She held the woman's feet in her hands. The woman moved her toes. Sappho looked up again between her thighs. Her pink slit split her soft cunt precisely at the centre. It was a perfect line of pliable flesh. The mounds on either side — raised up and swollen with their own softness — edged it beautifully. Sappho lifted one of the woman's feet to her mouth. She held her toes against her lips for a moment, savouring their proximity, their closeness. She felt their heat. It combined with her own. The woman's toenails glinted in the sunlight. Sappho licked her tongue out. A drip of spit dropped from its end.

She took the largest toe between her lips. She closed them around it and slipped them past the knuckle to its base. Sappho sucked. The woman tensed in her bonds. Sappho sucked harder. The woman rose against the delightful contact. The movement aroused the stinging left by her beating. She tightened as the delectable blend of pain and delight raced through her. Sappho tasted the woman's skin. She tasted the mud and sweat that clung to it. She drew back and licked it. She took it into her mouth again and sucked it. She washed it away with her probing tongue. She drank the liquor down, stopping only for a moment to swallow it greedily before quickly returning for more.

Chryseis pushed against Sappho. She wrapped her arms around her waist and held her close. She draped her fingers down the front of Sappho's smooth stomach and rested them against the top of Sappho's slit. Sappho sucked harder. She felt the mounting tension in the woman's body. She sensed the pain she felt as it increased. It was transmitted through her toe. All of her pleasure — her delight and her agony — was being distilled through that one place.

Sappho allowed Chryseis' fingers to open her crack. She felt her wetness, silky and moist against Chryseis' fingers. Sappho felt the eager fingers grasp the base of her clitoris.

She forced herself down on them to increase the pressure. The woman tensed again — joy and pain combined. She gave a sudden gasp — an intake of breath. She held it, keeping the moment back, but only just. She could stand it no more. She breathed out with a sudden explosion of air as her ecstasy was released. Sappho felt it all in her mouth — her tongue, the insides of her cheeks, the back of her throat. It filled her. She clung to the woman's toe in her mouth. It seemed to swell and fill her whole body. Her mind was consumed with it. She jerked with delight. It gripped her. It tightened her. She jolted with it. Again and again. She dropped heavily on Chryseis' fingers. She released the toe that plugged her mouth. She screeched with joy.

Sappho grabbed a goblet of wine. It was still full and had been set down beneath the cross as an offering. She shared it with Chryseis. They laughed, grabbed each other and moved on. They were both incensed by their freedom, by the destruction they saw around them, by the suffering, by the filth, by the opportunities for excitement. Their passions were on fire. Everything they saw fanned the flames of their desires.

They ran into the square where the mighty wooden horse still stood. Women had been tied upside down to its massive legs. They held out their hands and begged to be released as Sappho and Chryseis rushed by. Sappho felt her stomach fill with thrills of excitement at ignoring their pleas for help.

They went down an alley. A line of women had been bent over a wall. Their hands and feet were chained to heavy blocks. They were all gagged with a wooden stick pulled across their mouths and secured behind their heads. Sappho and Chryseis stopped and watched as a group of defeated Trojan soldiers thrashed the women one by one. They removed the gag before beating them, and replaced it when they had finished. As they lashed the women's buttocks, sprays of frothing spit formed a colourful halo of mist around their heads.

Sappho and Chryseis ran on. They came across a woman spread eagled on the dusty floor of a grain store. She was tied by the wrists and ankles to four large nails driven deeply into the ground. She cried out as men took turns, forcing their cocks into her cunt, her mouth or her anus. Her face was covered in semen. Sappho could hardly bear to move on without rushing forward and licking the semen from the woman's mouth and eyes. She wanted to lap it up from the woman's cheeks and suck it from her nose. She wanted to be spread out on the dirty floor and violated by the insatiable men.

Sappho shouted out what she wanted, but they both ran away before the startled men realised what was happening.

They passed a group of women drinking semen from a bowl. They ran through a courtyard where women were hanging in cages. They saw women lined up on their knees waiting to be flogged or whipped or doused with semen.

Nowhere was safe. The city was devastated.

They kept running through the ruined streets. Buildings were on fire. Women, sent mad by their loss, searching hopelessly for their menfolk. A girl was being spanked by an older man. He held her over his bent knee and brought his hand down repeatedly on her taut buttocks. A dribble of spit ran from her mouth and dripped onto his foot. Sappho wiped a dribble of spit from the corner of her own mouth as she watched.

She recognised the entrance to Polydorus' palace. The ornate iron gates hung askew, the white marble pillars on each side were blackened by fire.

They went inside.

Filthy beggars drank from the fountains and pools that now flowed with dirty water and blood. Some women covered in lion skins emerged from behind the few still standing statues. They had taken cover like animals during the invasion and were only now finding the courage to show themselves. They stalked slowly on all fours. Their lion skins almost completely covered them, their tails hung loosely and trailed on the ground.

Sappho and Chryseis sat on the edge of one of the pools. A discarded lion skin lay on the ground beside them. They cupped their hands and drank the dirty water thirstily.

A beggar, drinking from one of the pools, himself garbed in a discarded lion skin, suddenly ran up to one of the women. He knelt behind her, lifted her tail and drove his heavy, hard cock into her anus. She yelped, surprised and pained by his penetration. He pushed it deeper. She screeched out loudly. He held onto her hips. He pounded her. She reared back then dropped her face to the ground, lifting her buttocks as high as she could to allow him the deepest possible entry.

Another beggar joined them. He waited until the first one pulled his cock out. He sprang forward and threw him aside. The first bared his teeth and growled. The second stared hard at him. He was more youthful and fit. The first backed down. The second man prowled around the woman. She stayed on her hands and knees. She kept her face close to the ground. He stroked her back. She licked the ground. He lifted her tail. She responded by raising her buttocks even higher. He presented the throbbing tip of his cock against her anus. She allowed her buttocks to open wide. The muscle of her anus dilated. The first man's semen ran from it in a frothy dribble. The second man drove his cock in straight up to the base. The woman yelled out loudly. She screeched as he thrust her repeatedly. She stayed on her knees. She pressed herself back against him as he tightened in a massive orgasm. He took his cock from her burning anus. She fell to her side, gasping for breath, a stream of semen running down into the soft, fleshy folds of her cunt.

Sappho watched breathlessly. The sight heated her body all over. She dropped her legs over the side of the pool and plunged her feet into the dirty water. It was cool. It refreshed her. She leant down and began washing her toes.

Another man prowled around the woman in the lion skin. She lay on her side gasping for air. He lifted her tail and began repeatedly slapping her buttocks. She jerked with shock at every blow.

Sappho ran her hands up her legs. She drew the dirty water across her skin, bathing it, washing some of the smears of mud from it. She breathed in the aroma from the water. It was tangy, heavy, animalistic. She pulled her hand between her legs and splashed water on the insides of her thighs. Some of it splattered against the soft edges of her cunt. It ran between them, cooling her heat, mixing with her own moisture, enlivening her.

She listened to the smacking of the man's hand on the woman's buttocks. The sound inflamed her. The splashing of the water against her flesh, the trickling sound as it ran back into the pool, filled her with a desperate desire for satisfaction. The smacks echoed in her head. She rubbed her wet hand against the crack of her cunt. It was open, available. She ran her finger along it. The flesh was soft and yielding. Her heart pounded in time with the smacking hand. There was another noise. A soft, low mewing. It reminded her of Calliope. Sappho ran her fingers along her crack again. She turned. It was Chryseis.

Chryseis was on all fours. The lion skin was draped over her back. Her face was almost covered by the animal's head. Her long tail trailed out behind her and ended in a tassel of ginger hair. She crept forward towards Sappho. Sappho dropped her hands to her sides. Her legs fell apart. Her cunt was fully exposed. It dripped with water and glistened at its centre with her own silky moisture.

Chryseis crawled forwards between Sappho's thighs. The rough animal hair prickled against Sappho's skin. She shivered with excitement. The slapping sound filled her ears. She watched Chryseis getting closer. She watched the lion's head forcing between her thighs, squeezing between them, driving them apart, opening her cunt, making her available.

The smacking grew into a thunderous roar. She could see the man's hand coming down on the woman's buttocks. She saw the moment of contact — the sudden meeting of the two surfaces of skin. She jumped with every contact. It filled her mind. She was overwhelmed by it.

Sappho reared back as the flat of Chryseis' tongue came against her exposed cunt. Chryseis drew it along the soft flesh. She lapped at it, covering it with her spit, lubricating its already wet flesh. She circled Sappho's clitoris with its tip. She pressed at its base. She massaged its pulsating hardness. She drew out its need.

Sappho's ear pounded. The throbbing of her clitoris, the pounding of her heart, the thunder of smacking in her head. She leant back and slowly slipped into the pool of dirty water. It was shallow. It slopped around her buttocks. Chryseis followed. She kept licking. She licked the dirty water. She licked Sappho's cunt.

Sappho opened her mouth. She wanted to scream. But it was too human. She heard the smacks against the woman's buttocks building to a crescendo. She could not hold back. She let out a terrific roar — a lion's roar. Her whole body was overtaken by a massive explosion of ecstasy. Chryseis forced her tongue in as deeply as she could. Sappho clamped her thighs tightly around Chryseis' head. She squeezed her in against her water-drenched cunt. She threw her head back. She roared again.

Sappho fell back onto her elbows. The dirty water

splashed against her hips. Spit ran in a stream from her mouth. She was overcome. Chryseis lapped softly at Sappho's crack, drinking the moisture, slurping at the water that flowed against it, refreshing herself with Sappho's passion.

Sappho's senses returned. The spanking sound returned. She looked across at the man and woman. The woman was on her hands and knees now. Her buttocks were raised high. The man smacked her ever harder. She held herself against it. Her buttocks were covered in a glowing red smudge. Sappho pulled Chryseis in again. The prickly hairs of the lion's skin set her on fire. She felt another jolting throb of ecstasy surging through her delighted body. She roared again.

At last, there was silence. Chryseis drew back. Sappho stroked her head.

'It is getting dark. We must find somewhere for the night.'

They ran up the raised garden, past the pools and waterfalls, between the obelisks and statues. They came to the small temple at the highest point. Polydorus' statue had been desecrated and knocked over. It lay on its side. Both of its arms had been broken off. Daubs of red paint were smeared across its face.

They stood by the fallen statue and looked towards the setting sun. It hung in the purple sky, swollen and red. Between a yawning gap in the fallen city walls, they saw the Greek ships setting out for home. Their square sails were unfurled from the broad cross spars. Their oars were pushed out from the sides. Sappho heard the distant pounding of the slave masters' drums as the time was beaten out on their taut skins. The two women stood in silence as they watched the oar blades dipping into the water and pulling the victors away.

Sappho heard a noise inside the temple. They went inside to look. A man's form lay huddled in the corner. It was covered in rags. They thought it must be another beggar, a frightened inhabitant seeking safety for the night. Sappho approached. The sight of fear excited her. She straddled the body and pressed her hands between her thighs. A hand stretched out painfully from beneath the filthy covering. She jumped back shocked. A large ruby ring set in a heavy gold ring glinted on the forefinger. Sappho recognised it straight away. It was Polydorus. He was injured and in need of help.

Sappho looked down at him. She felt a great tide of anger flood over her. She remembered how cruel he had been. How he had thrown them out of the temple. How he had taken them into slavery and treated them with unforgiving savagery. She looked again and saw his predicament. She felt a sudden feeling of power. Polydorus, her cruel tormentor, was at her feet, broken and injured. She could do with him as she wished.

His hand reached further. She took it in hers. She looked at his carefully manicured nails — filed smoothly and buffed by the labours of attentive slaves. She looked at her own — dirty and damaged, uncared for and broken. She looked at his ring. A beam of light came in through the broken temple wall. The massive ruby reflected a shower of flashing rays. It spoke of wealth and power, of authority and control. Sappho saw, in its light, a future of pleasure and gain. This man, Polydorus, this one who appealed to her for help, this man who had savagely humiliated her, had lost his brothers and father. He was the inheritor of the power of Troy. It was a broken empire, she knew that, but it was an empire, and it was his. And its wealth was still somewhere hidden in its secret coffers. The height of the Greek boats in the water had testified to that. They had not set out laden with its weight. She had seen that with her own eyes. Yes, Polydorus was the new king and the power of wealth was still at his finger tips.

Sappho drew his hand between the tops of her thighs. She took his extended forefinger and placed it against her moist crack. Its flesh opened at his touch. It slipped between the wet folds, into the warmth within. She rose on it. She gasped. She dropped down.

She pushed herself around the massive ruby ring. It was cool. She felt it inside — his finger reaching and twisting, probing and searching. In her mind, she saw the flashing red beams. She pictured them glittering inside her cunt, filling her with their promise, their power, their wealth. She bit onto her lips. Her body tensed. She held her breath, dropped her head and jolted with a massive, gripping orgasm.

The Roman Slavegirl

Silver Moon — Syra Bond

'Magnus smacked her hard, each time bringing his hand down more firmly. The loud smacks caused Bec to tense her body until it was rigid, but she did not cry out, nor did she squirm or try to avoid the blows. Caristia looked at Bec's taut body and listened to the regular rhythm of Magnus's smacking hand. She leant back against the wall - almost hidden by the shadows - and allowed her hand to drift…'

A beautiful, flaxen haired Saxon girl, captured and enslaved, is bound to cause a stir in Pompeii. And once she arrives at the house of Rufo the slave dealer and comes under the discipline of Magnus, his trainer, Caristia has no choice but to experience every aspect of their brutal world; a world that demands complete submission from her.

Trojan Slaves
Syra Bond

The army of the Greeks is encamped outside the walls of Troy and the legendary war rages all around. So when Sappho and Chrysies, two beautiful Trojan girls are captured by their deadly enemies trying to flee the city, their situation is not a good one.

The question of who will possess and dominate the two slaves becomes the source of friction within the Greek camp and the two hapless captives can only pray that some miracle will help them escape from the cruel and warlike men into whose hands they have fallen.

Africanus is a beautiful North African girl enslaved by Rome from an early age and then given a chance to train at a 'ludus' for a career as a gladiatrix. Her owner's business affairs depend on her success in the arena but immediately she becomes the centre of a web of deceit.

The treacherous slave girl Nydia spies on her. The lady Octavia, wife of her owner is having a torrid affair with the games sponsor and the creditors are closing in on the ludus.

Filled with all the decadence, sex and danger of life in ancient Rome, the first instalment of Africanus' adventures is a headily erotic read in the best traditions of Silver Moon books.

Kerry Smith's job interview turns swiftly into a nightmare as the beautiful youngster is abducted and sold by the sinister Salim.

Enslaved by a man she initially knows only as The Master, she and her friend Amber undergo many frightening rituals to slake the lusts of his guests. But when they escape things get much worse and they find themselves on the island Taransay. There a top secret laboratory is pursuing depraved goals and Kerry and Amber find themselves at risk of becoming helpless slaves' to the depraved lusts of anyone their masters want them to serve.

There are over 100 stunningly erotic novels of domination and submission in the Silver Moon catalogue. You can see the full range, including Club and Illustrated editions by writing to:

Silver Moon Reader Services
Shadowline Publishing Ltd,
No 2 Granary House
Ropery Road,
Gainsborough,
Lincs. DH21 2NS

You will receive a copy of the latest issue of the Readers' Club magazine, with articles, features, reviews, adverts and news plus a full list of our publications and an order form.